D0581866

He knew he ought to take his hands off her—now. But he wanted her. He wanted her with an urgency he couldn't ever remember feeling in his entire life, and that big bed was too damned close...

He forced himself away. 'Damn it, Belle, tell me to stop now. For I swear if we carry on much longer I will not be able to do so.'

'You mean—this is real?' she breathed. 'You actually find me desirable?'

What was she talking about? He gave a harsh, incredulous laugh.

'Adam—we agreed there would be no intimacy!'

There was an edge of panic to her voice that made him freeze. Cupping her face with his hands, he gazed down at her. His blood was pounding, his loins thudding just from her being near, this beautiful woman whose full, tremulous lips he longed to kiss again.

'Belle,' he said quietly. 'You loved your husband very much. I realise that—'

He broke off, feeling her tremble in his arms.

'But it's five years since he died,' he went on, 'and I want to kiss you, Belle. I want to do more than kiss you—I think you want it, too. And if you don't want me to take this further, then say so now. Say, *Adam, I want you to leave.*'

AUTHOR NOTE

For this story I've moved a little later into the Regency period—1819, when the long Napoleonic wars were fading from most people's memories and a new world dominated by invention and industry was bringing changes aplenty to Society's elite.

I wanted to explore how a man of wealth and willpower—Adam Davenant—would cope with the barriers still put up by England's aristocracy against someone like him. The *ton* likes to mutter that he's a jumped-up quarry-owner; it's just Adam's luck that he collides with lovely Belle Marchmain, who's well-born, a widow, and absolutely penniless. Adam offers her an answer to her temporary problems, but soon, thanks to her growing feelings for the ruthless Mr Davenant, she's faced with more dilemmas than ever!

I really enjoyed exploring the clashes between old money and new, and how the rigid rules of class were having to be broken down rather swiftly in the closing years of this decade. I love the way Adam is prepared to knuckle down and help his quarry workers when needs must, and I love the way the defiant, often outrageous Belle gradually has to admit that she's actually found the man of her dreams.

Here is their story.

THE OUTRAGEOUS BELLE MARCHMAIN

Lucy Ashford

First published in Great Britain 2013
by Mills & Boon, an imprint of Harlequin (UK) Limited.
Large Print edition 2013
Harlequin (UK) Limited, Eton House, 18-24 Paradise Road,
Richmond, Surrey TW9 1SR

© Lucy Ashford 2013

ISBN: 978 0 263 23273 8

Harlequin (UK) policy is to use papers that are natural, renewable and recyclable products and made from wood grown in sustainable forests. The logging and manufacturing process conform to the legal environmental regulations of the country of origin.

Printed and bound in Great Britain
by CPI Antony Rowe, Chippenham, Wiltshire

Lucy Ashford, an English Studies lecturer, has always loved literature and history, and from childhood one of her favourite occupations has been to immerse herself in historical romances. She studied English with history at Nottingham University, and the Regency is her favourite period.

Lucy has written several historical novels, and this is her third for Mills & Boon. She lives with her husband in an old stone cottage in the Peak District, near to beautiful Chatsworth House and Haddon Hall, all of which give her a taste of the magic of life in a bygone age. Her garden enjoys spectacular views over the Derbyshire hills, where she loves to roam and let her imagination go to work on her latest story.

You can contact Lucy via her website—www.lucyashford.com

Previous novels from Lucy Ashford:

THE MAJOR AND THE PICKPOCKET
THE RETURN OF LORD CONISTONE
THE CAPTAIN'S COURTESAN

And in M&B:

THE PROBLEM WITH JOSEPHINE
   (part of *Royal Weddings Through the Ages*)

**Did you know that some of these novels
are also available as eBooks?
Visit www.millsandboon.co.uk**

Chapter One

~~~~~~~~~~~~~~~~~~~

Sawle Down, Somerset—March 1819

It was the kind of spring afternoon that touched these green Somerset hills with magic—or so the locals, whose heads were filled with old folk tales, would say. Adam, a hard-headed business-man, had no time for superstitious nonsense, but he found himself doing exactly what an old quarryman would do. He let his long, lean fingers rest on the great slab of honey-coloured stone that had just been hewn from the ground—then he tapped it, once, twice, thrice.

For luck.

May there be three hundred, three thousand times this wealth in the earth below me.

His big roan Goliath was tethered nearby, un-concerned by the noise of the quarry workers and their equipment as they toiled at the excavations in the heat. Adam turned to the man at his side with just the hint of a smile curving his strong mouth.

'So it's going well, Jacob?' he asked softly.

Old Jacob, in his dusty quarryman's garb, clearly couldn't wait to tell him just *how* well. 'Like a dream, Master Adam! Me and the lads, we were resigned to this quarry being worked out for good. Some of them never thought to get a job like this again.' The old quarryman could scarcely conceal his glee. 'But then *you* came last month and told us there was fancy folks in London interested in our stone.'

'More than interested, Jacob. Believe me, builders are clamouring for it.'

'And so they should be!' Jacob gestured towards the fresh-hewn blocks and rapped one with his callused knuckles, just as Adam had done. 'Rings true as porcelain, do you hear, sir? No faults inside her!'

Jacob followed as Adam headed across the uneven ground to speak to a group of bare-chested workers who'd been vigorously plying their pickaxes at the rock face. Clouds of dust rose and clung to their sweating backs, but they put their picks aside and grinned when they saw who was there.

Adam had slung his dark riding coat over one shoulder and moved easily amongst them asking questions, offering words of quiet praise. He was owner of this quarry and much else besides, but the rumour ran that the master had been known to wield a pickaxe himself when the going got tough and had vowed he'd never be too grand to stand shoulder to shoulder with his men.

Jacob Mallin kept close to his side, beaming with pride. 'You promised the lads you'd get this quarry workin' again, sir, and you've kept your word.'

Adam turned to him, the sun glinting on his cropped dark hair and hard cheekbones. 'I always do,' he said softly. 'Tell the men they'll be handsomely paid for their work. If there's anything else you need by way of equipment or supplies, just let my manager Shipley know.'

Jacob nodded approvingly. His men would whisper between themselves, *He's a good 'un, is the master. None works harder than him or treats us better.* Yes, Master Adam had his grandfather's instinct for making money. But he was also a fair man, a man who kept his promises, and the reopening of the old quarry had brought fresh hope to many lives round here.

'Aye, I'll tell the lads,' Jacob promised. 'Will

you be sendin' the stone up to Bristol, sir, when it's ready?'

Adam gazed at the rolling green countryside which surrounded them, then turned back with a new light burning in his dark eyes. 'No. I'm going to build a railway to the Avon canal, and from there this stone—this *new* stone—can be taken by boat to the Thames and to London itself.'

'But it's not your land between here and the Avon canal, Master Adam—leastways, not all of it!'

Adam had moved towards his big roan and was already securing his rolled-up coat to the back of his saddle—far too warm for the garment on a day like this. 'My grandfather never let a simple obstacle like that hold him up. And neither will I,' said Adam in a voice edged with steel.

Jacob shook his grizzled head in wonder as he watched him ride off. 'There's no stopping him,' he murmured, eyes shining with delight. 'No stopping him, that's for sure.'

Goliath was ready to gallop and Adam let him. *There's nothing like the feel of the land under your horse's hooves being yours, my lad. Especially when that land but recently belonged to men who'd cross to the other side of the street rather than acknowledge you.*

Those were the words of his grandfather, who with his work-roughened hands and west country vowels had laboured night and day to remove the shame of the name the upper classes scornfully gave him—Miner Tom. But they'd all come to Miner Tom's funeral, oh, yes. All the gentry of Bath and London had hurried eagerly to the lavish ceremony—because they'd realised by then how much the man they'd despised was damned well worth.

Adam's grandfather had wanted nothing more desperately than for his grandson to be accepted by the society that had spurned him. That wish had come true. But now Adam often thought that he was happiest on days like this, riding Goliath across Somerset's lush green hills and knowing that the chief wealth of those hills, the fine stone beneath them, was his to be harvested.

They'd said the Sawle Down quarry was finished. It had last been profitable fifty years ago; then the expense of extracting the stone had deterred any prospect of new investment. But Adam had anticipated the surge in demand and hence in price for good building materials; he'd made his calculations and investments and proved the doomsayers wrong.

Now his detractors would say there was no way he could get the valuable stone to the canal, that vital water link to the Thames and London. Well, he would prove them wrong again.

Suddenly a distant movement caught his eye. Another rider was enjoying the afternoon sun— and blatantly trespassing on private land. A woman. Eyes narrowed, Adam urged Goliath into a canter towards her.

He swore aloud when he saw her turn her pretty dappled mare's head and set off away from him at a reckless pace. A stupid pace, that was taking her towards the edge of another old quarry.

Adam swung Goliath into a broad circle to head her off. The ground here was treacherous. Yes, the grassy slopes of Sawle Down looked inviting, but—disused quarries aside—decades of quarry debris lurked beneath the sheep-cropped turf, waiting to catch the unwary. And indeed it was only a matter of moments before the dappled mare suddenly stumbled and sent its foolish rider crashing to the ground. Adam was there in moments, swinging himself out of the saddle to kneel beside that prone body.

She was clad in a riding habit of crumpled

crimson velvet. Her abundant black curls fell in loose array; her little crimson hat, set with ridiculously jaunty red feathers, lay nearby. He saw that her face was a perfect oval, with a tip-tilted nose, a rosebud mouth and thick lashes dark against creamy skin.

The faint scent of lavender drifted up to him. Who was she? What the hell was she doing, riding up here on her own? She was a lady of quality, that was clear. Apart from her fine clothes he registered that her complexion was dewy, her figure lissom. Then Adam realised that her eyes were fluttering open. He noted the tremor of fear that surged through her as she saw him towering over her. Adam was suddenly aware that his boots and breeches—his open-necked shirt, too, quite likely—were covered with dust from the quarry.

She was struggling now to stand up. He fought the impulse to offer her his dirty hand. 'Are you hurt?' he said. 'Perhaps I—'

'Stay away from me!'

Adam's lip curled. As he'd thought. Quality. And her age? Twenty-six, twenty-seven, perhaps, and that disdain just had to have been with her from birth. 'You took quite a fall just then, ma'am,' he said. 'I only came over to see if you needed my help.'

She looked so pale, yet there was such determination in that small pointed chin; something rebellious in those startlingly green eyes that were assessing him. Dismissing him, God damn it.

On her feet now, she brushed down her brightly coloured habit, pushed her luxurious curls back from her face and started hobbling after her horse. 'Poppy!' she called. 'Poppy! Here, girl!'

But the mare just whinnied and trotted off to join Goliath, calmly grazing nearby. The woman bit her lip, hesitating, uncertain.

'That's horses for you,' Adam said. 'Your mare's had a fright. It was perhaps a little unwise of you to ride up here. Don't you know there are quarry workings nearby?'

'How can one *ignore* the hateful things?' she shuddered. 'Always so busy. So noisy.'

'Particularly at the moment, yes. But they provide work and wages for many men, and food for their families.'

She stared up at him as if he talked a foreign language, then said, 'Excuse me. You're in my way.'

He did not budge. 'Quarries are no place for sightseers,' he pointed out. 'I'm trying, incidentally, to find out exactly what you're doing up here.'

He saw her tip-tilted nose wrinkle a little at his open-necked shirt and the dust on his boots. The old, familiar bitterness surged in his veins. So. Some lordling's wife, to judge by her mount and her attire, and the wedding band on her finger. She was the kind of woman who would look down on him—until someone enlightened her as to who he was.

He was damned if *he* was going to be the one to tell her.

She darted sideways to pick up her crimson hat then went marching off towards her horse again, clearly wanting no more conversation with a man she'd dismissed as a labourer. Something clenched warningly in Adam's gut as he absorbed the way she carried herself. Noted the way her pert little behind swayed under that luxurious fabric.

He called after her, 'Didn't you come up here with a companion or a groom?'

She swung round, her face still pale. 'I like riding alone. I like *being* alone.' She carried on stubbornly towards her mare, holding her hat with one hand and the red velvet skirt of her habit in the other. He couldn't help but notice small, neatly turned ankles in little leather half-boots.

Her dappled mare had trotted off again, away from her. Goliath watched, interested, and Adam called his big horse over. 'Here! Goliath!'

Goliath came and the little mare did, too; Adam caught the mare's reins and stroked its dappled silken neck. The woman walked back to him reluctantly.

'I'll help you up if you like,' Adam offered. 'Then I suggest you get off this private land before dusk falls. You could break your neck riding home once the light starts fading.'

'Private!' she breathed. 'Why, Mr Davenant has no more right to this land than—' she swept her ungloved hand expressively '—than those *black crows* circling above the trees!'

A sudden cool breeze chilled the perspiration on his back. He said, 'I believe Mr Davenant bought this land a year ago, quite legally.'

She tossed her head. 'Money will buy anything, and anybody. And—legally? Some would think otherwise.'

Hell! This time Adam felt the heat surging through his blood. If she'd been a man he'd have floored her for that!

But she was a woman all right. Her face was

piquant even in defiance, her body all slender curves…

Damn it. This was no time to be distracted. Adam said, 'Are you querying his right to this land?'

She faced him coolly. 'I assume you probably work for him, so I'll limit my words. I've not met Mr Davenant, but I've heard enough to know that he was not born to wealth and it shows.'

Adam hissed out a breath. 'Tell me. As a matter of interest, if you *did* chance to meet Mr Davenant, would you use those words to his face?'

She shrugged her shoulders, but he noticed she'd gone a little paler. 'Why not?' she said. 'He is no friend to my family. What else have I to lose?'

The sun passed behind a cloud; the moorland grasses shivered. 'You've clearly not lost your pride, ma'am,' Adam said at last. 'May I escort you on your way?'

'I know my way very well, I assure you!'

He clenched his teeth and said with icy politeness, 'Then will you—*condescend* to let me help you mount your horse? Or are we going to stand here till the sun goes down?'

She hesitated. 'My thanks.'

His mouth pressed in a thin line, he put his big

hands round her waist and lifted her easily into her saddle. Then he went to check her mare's bridle—and give himself time to cool down.

She was feather-light. She was *icy* with damned arrogance. She'd set his pulse racing with rage—and a flicker of something else even more dangerous.

He looked up at her and patted her dappled mare's neck. 'All set,' he said flatly. 'You'd best be off.'

She nodded her head in curt thanks, then without a backward glance she rode swiftly and competently down the path.

Adam Davenant shrugged on his coat and watched her go, his gaze narrowed.

How her pretty green eyes had glittered with contempt when she spoke his name. *Mr Davenant has no more right to this land than those black crows circling above the trees.*

She hadn't recognised him. But one thing was very clear—she hated Adam Davenant like poison. He'd already guessed who she was. If his guess was correct, she had a brother who was heading for big, big trouble. With *him.*

Chapter Two

London—two months later

Belle Marchmain rather distractedly picked up a length of pink ribbon from the display on the counter, then put it down again in the wrong place. Apprehension shadowed her dark-lashed green eyes as she said at last, 'I'm sincerely hoping this is some foolish jest of yours, Edward.'

Outside in the Strand the May dusk was starting to fall and lamplighters with clanking ladders were hurrying about their business. Normally Belle relished this time of quiet after a busy day. Once her shop's doors were locked she would wander possessively amongst the bright lengths of silk and taffeta, herself resplendent in one of the boldly extravagant costumes that were fast making her one of the most talked-about *modistes* in London.

But just now, her current attire—a striped jacket of black and green over a matching taffeta skirt, with green satin ribbons adorning her luxuriant black curls—seemed ridiculously flippant. Futile, in fact, in the face of approaching disaster.

Belle was twenty-seven years old and had learnt to cope with much in her life. The humiliation in slow, steady steps of her once-proud family. The death of her husband five years ago. But now sheer, blind panic threatened to close in.

It had been no surprise to see her brother, of course, at her glass-paned door, ringing the bell impatiently. She'd known he was in London for two weeks, staying at Grillon's Hotel in Albemarle Street—'catching up on business and old friends,' Edward had told her blithely when he called on her a few days ago.

He'd certainly been spending money. Grillon's was expensive and so were the new clothes he was sporting: new boots, a new silk waistcoat, a new coat of blue superfine and smart yellow pantaloons. And now he perched on the end of her counter, full of casual confidence in his older sister's ability to sort out his latest mess.

'You can help me, can't you, Belle?' he cajoled.

'This little shop of yours is doing mighty well, I hear!'

Just then a young woman with curly brown hair burst in from the back room. '*Madame*, should I tell the girls—excuse me, I had no idea you had company!'

Gabby—Belle's French assistant—bobbed a curtsy to Edward, whose eyes, Belle noted with exasperation, lit up at the sight of her. Belle replied, more curtly than she meant to, 'I'll be with you shortly, Gabby. Yes, send Jenny and Susan home by all means, and thank them for all their hard work today, will you?'

'Of course, *madame*! But there is something else—'

Belle interrupted, 'Tell me later, would you?'

Edward watched Gabby go, then started talking again. 'I just need a *little* more money, Belle.'

'To pay your hotel bill? To pay for yet more new clothes? Edward, I am *not* doing well enough to repay your debts as well as my own.' Belle had sat rather suddenly in one of the dainty gilt chairs her customers used.

'But your business is thriving. You *must* be plump in the pocket!' Edward, who was two years younger than she was, eagerly pulled up a chair to sit opposite her—admiring, she noticed, his own reflection in a nearby mirror. He was slenderly built and with the same shade of green eyes as she, the same raven black hair. But there was a hint of wilfulness, of weakness about his mouth. 'You have clients galore,' he went on, 'you have servants! And dash it, Belle, you're being as ratty as when you came back from Sawle Down that day in March, all of a stew about *something.*'

If Edward had been in any way perceptive, he'd have seen how his sister's cheeks became a little paler. 'I was saying goodbye to the land that was once ours,' she said quietly. 'As for my servants, Edward, as you call them, I have Gabby, two assistants and a manservant—Matt—who works for me a few hours a week. That's all.'

Edward shrugged. 'Yes, but you live the high life, sister mine—you're always being invited to routs and parties. And when you stayed with me and Charlotte you said you were even thinking of setting up another shop in Bath!'

'It came to naught,' she answered rather tightly.

'Hmm.' Bored already, Edward was picking up a little silk fan. 'Nice trinket, this.'

Belle snatched at it and put it down with something of a snap. *'Edward—'* she was gazing directly at her younger brother '—Edward, I think you'd better tell me *everything.*'

So he did. And Belle's heart sank almost as low as she'd known it, while Edward recounted the entire sorry tale. In which everyone in the world was at fault, except, of course, himself.

At twenty-one Edward had inherited the Hathersleigh family's estate near Bath—or what remained of it—and within the year he'd married his sweetheart, Charlotte. By the time of their wedding Belle was living in London. And whenever she saw Edward he was forever telling her how the estate was thriving, and, of course, how clever he was.

Just over a year ago he'd announced to her that he'd sold a large portion of the estate's land to a neighbour—Adam Davenant. Belle had felt apprehension and more. She'd never met the man. He owned, she was aware, estates all over the country and wasn't often in Somerset. But she knew her father had loathed Davenant—called him a money-grubbing upstart.

'Did you *have* to sell to him, Edward?' Belle had asked at the time.

'Yes,' Edward said flatly, 'and Davenant was desperate to buy. You know what all these new-money families are like, Belle. They want as many acres as possible in hopes of making themselves respectable.'

Belle had grieved the loss of the land at Sawle Down, but had hoped that Edward would concentrate on making a success of what remained of their ancestral estate near Bath. Hoped that marriage and family responsibilities might perhaps be the making of him.

Some hope. The amount Davenant offered for the land had, in fact, turned out to be derisory—though he was now set to make a fortune from his purchase, because the sudden surge in price of Bath stone had made the old quarry there workable once more.

He must have known. Must have deliberately set out to swindle them. And now, with the London dusk closing in around her and Edward staring at her with that half-defiant, half-scared look that she knew of old, Belle rubbed her temples with her fingertips as her brother told her anew—rather resentfully, as if it were her fault—that last summer's harvest had been a poor one, thanks to the rain that had ruined his wheat. 'And the taxes, Belle! Last year this blasted government brought in new taxes on barley, on farm horses—anything that grew or moved, basically!'

Then Edward proceeded to remind her that the roof of Hathersleigh Manor had needed replacing entirely. 'Uncle Philip neglected the place so badly,' Edward complained. 'The roof *had* to be fixed, or the thing would have caved in.'

Their father's brother, the dour Philip Hathersleigh, had overseen the estate from their father's death fourteen years ago until Edward reached his majority. Belle didn't feel particularly close to Uncle Philip—even less to his shrewish wife Mildred—but she'd formed the opinion that Philip was a sound, careful man whose advice Edward had rashly spurned, with the result that Uncle Philip and his wife had retreated back to their estate in the north with little love lost.

'Look after the paperwork, young man,' Uncle Philip had said grimly to Edward. 'And get yourself sound legal advice, if you want to stand any chance of holding your inheritance together.'

Edward had blithely ignored Uncle Philip's warnings; her brother's desk, Belle couldn't help but notice on her March visit, was overflowing with neglected files and unread correspondence. And, of course, with bills.

'So the new roof and taxes got you into debt,' she now said steadily. From the back of the shop she could hear the merry voices of her assistants making their departure. Could hear Gabby's laughter and Matt's deep voice as he began to lock up. 'Surely though, Edward,' went on Belle, trying to keep calm, 'the income from the estate could have kept your debts at bay?'

'I did get on top of my debts, Belle. Or at least, I thought I had. You see, back in February—it was just before you came to stay with us, actually—I sold some of the sheep from that land Davenant purchased from me last year.'

'You did—*what*?' breathed Belle. She felt suddenly cold.

Edward shrugged, but his cheeks were pink. 'I sold some of Davenant's stock. He's so rich I thought he wouldn't even notice.'

Belle said, 'You stole from him. Oh, Edward. You stole from that man.'

Edward jumped to his feet and walked around the candlelit shop with his hands thrust defiantly in the pockets of his new coat. 'Stealing? Hardly—his sheep had strayed because he'd not bothered maintaining his fences. And dash it all, Belle, you could say that Davenant was stealing from *me*, you know? He paid me a pitiful amount for that land I sold him and if *that* isn't stealing, I don't know what is! Belle—Belle, are you all right?'

A spring evening, on Sawle Down. A stranger, whose arrogance had made her cheeks burn. *Are you querying his right to this land?* he'd asked cuttingly. And he'd only been one of Davenant's labourers.

Something tightened painfully in her chest, as it did whenever she remembered that hateful day. She dragged herself back to the equally unpalatable present. 'You were telling me you'd stolen some of Mr Davenant's sheep.'

'I wouldn't exactly call it theft! But then Davenant found out about the sheep, curse it, and I got a lawyer's letter…'

Edward told her all this very rapidly, almost indignantly, as Belle sat there in her bright-striped jacket with the green ribbons trailing from her hair.

I have fought. I have fought so hard, to make this new life for myself.

'Davenant himself came to call on me two months ago,' Edward was continuing. 'In Somerset, just after you'd been to visit.'

Belle clenched her hands. 'What's he like?'

'Oh, positively detestable, you can imagine, risen from rags to riches in a generation. "Miner Tom", they called his grandfather—made the family fortunes from tin in Cornwall. As for Davenant—well, he's a big fellow dressed in black, a positive boor—what more can I say? I tell you, Belle, not a pleasant word passed his lips during our conversation. He told me I was nothing less than a sheep-stealer—as if a few sheep should matter to him!'

Belle was finding she could scarcely breathe. She twisted the slender wedding ring on her finger. 'Is this why you've come to London?'

'Well, yes. Davenant demanded another meeting—*demanded*, can you credit it? He said he'd travel to Somerset again to see me if I preferred, but I—actually, I didn't prefer it, not with the baby due, you know?'

Belle *did* know. She knew that Edward's poor wife had already had two miscarriages within the past two years, and she dreaded to think what would happen if Charlotte lost this baby.

'Anyway,' went on Edward, 'we met the other day at my hotel, and Davenant had all the figures with him about his sheep—now, isn't it the sort of thing a normal fellow would leave to his man of business? But, no, I'd swear the creature had gone through all his stock lists with a toothcomb. Dash it, he must make thousands a week from his various interests!' He gesticulated angrily. 'Nevertheless, he told me that my debts regarding those dratted sheep could not be ignored.'

Outside in the Strand a crowd of merrymakers went by on their way to an evening in the clubs of St James's. Belle waited for the noise to fade and asked, 'Has Charlotte any idea of this?'

'No,' he said defiantly, squaring his shoulders. 'Poor Charlotte, not a thing, and I don't want her to. She's delicate, you know?'

And what if I were delicate? Belle bit back the retort, knowing it was ridiculous to expect Edward ever to see her as anything other than his capable, shrewd-headed older sister. But she had to think. This could be disastrous.

Adam Davenant was after Edward, not her. But her shop, her own small savings—would *they* be implicated? Would everything she had worked so hard for since her husband's death be lost?

For a moment sheer panic clawed at her chest. Somehow she fought it down and forced herself to say calmly, 'Is there any possibility that Mr Davenant will let you pay this sum back gradually, month by month?'

'Good God, I doubt it. He's a grasping wretch, Belle!' As Edward distractedly pushed his dark hair back from his forehead, he unintentionally laid bare the old, white scar that puckered the skin there. 'He's told me I've got to bring the money to his house in Mayfair within the week or he'll press charges. Damn it, if I had it, I'd hang

it round the necks of a few sheep and get them
herded up the steps of his fancy house.'

Belle briefly rested her forehead in her hand.

'You'll help me, won't you?' Edward pleaded.
'Charlotte. Our home. The new baby... I can't go
to prison, Belle. I can't...'

Belle had always been aware that the once-
renowned Somerset estate of the Hathersleigh
family had, thanks to the profligacy of succes-
sive generations, dwindled to very little—unlike,
unfortunately, the aspirations of its title-holders.

She'd also had to face up to the fact that her
own prospects were bleak when her husband
died five years ago in one of Wellington's final
campaigns of the war. She'd had to make harsh
choices: either to move in with Edward at Hathersleigh Manor, or to earn her own living. In
fact, imposing herself on Edward never seriously
crossed her mind and the idea of being a govern-
ess or companion horrified her. Certain offers
she'd received from so-called gentlemen repelled
her even more.

Then inspiration had come. She had always
been a talented seamstress and was fascinated
by the women's fashions that ebbed and flowed
like the long Napoleonic wars, so—in the face

of her brother's disapproval—she'd decided to open a dress shop in London.

Her designs were bold and eyecatching. *Outrageous*, some of the *ton*'s older matrons were heard to intone witheringly. Her shop, though small, was well situated in the Strand, and she and Gabby lived in the two rooms above it. Soon she'd begun to attract customers who were tired of soft pastels and wanted something different, but she was by no means making a fortune. She was lucky if her own rent and bills were paid every quarter day. How on earth could she deal with Edward's debts?

Now, as the candles flickered around the bright silks and satins in this little shop, which she felt sick at the thought of losing, she looked at her brother steadily and said, 'There's no point in my even asking the amount of your debt to Mr Davenant, Edward, for I know I won't be able to pay it. But I will go and see him for you.'

'Go and see him?' Her brother was astonished. 'And then what? I'm damned if you'll grovel on my behalf in front of that—that nouveau-riche upstart!'

A flash of anger darkened Belle's eyes. 'I have never grovelled in my life. I will simply explain that you realise you have made a grave error—'

Edward jumped up, about to protest, but something in Belle's steady gaze made him clamp his lips together and sit down again.

'That you've made a grave error,' she repeated, 'and would be grateful if Mr Davenant would accept your word of honour that your debts *will* be paid off steadily over—what? Three years, Edward?'

He looked sullen now, a little boy again. 'Three years! I suppose so. Times are hard, though Davenant's thriving, blast the fellow...'

'I shall go and see him,' said Belle quietly. 'And I'll let you know how I get on.'

He got up to pace to and fro, nodding. 'Very well. And put on some charm, eh? Come to think of it, Belle, a second marriage for you, to some rich fellow—not Davenant, of course, God forbid—could be the answer for both of us. You're really not at all bad-looking, if you'd just make an effort not to frighten the fellows off with those startling clothes and that sharp tongue of yours.'

This time, there was an edge of ice in her voice. 'Let me assure you I have absolutely no intention of getting married again. Ever.'

Her brother shrugged. 'Suit yourself. I'll stay on in town for a week or so at Grillon's, so you can let me know there when it's all sorted with

Davenant, can't you?' He started putting on his hat, checking his reflection in the mirror.

'Edward,' Belle said suddenly. 'You're not going to visit any of the gambling dens, are you?'

He swung round. 'Gambling dens? Never. And thanks for this, Belle. Some day I'll return the favour.'

Breezily Edward let himself out. Belle sat with her hands frozen in her lap, immobile.

Gabby came in rather hesitantly. 'Are you free, *madame*? I wanted to tell you that there was a little trouble earlier.'

Belle's heart sank anew. 'What kind of trouble?'

'Jenny told me about it. It appears that when you and I were measuring Lady Tindall in the back workshop for her new gown, a customer came in and complained about a cuff that was loose on a pelisse she bought last week.'

'What did Jenny do?'

'She mended it there and then, and the customer left—but she was so unpleasant, Jenny said! And she declared she would *not* be using our shop in the future!'

'Well, it sounds as if we're better off without her,' Belle soothed and Gabby went off, looking happier, to tidy the workroom. Originally from Paris, the lively French girl had come to Belle's notice when she'd advertised for an assistant seamstress and Gabby had proved invaluable, good both with the customers and with the two girls Belle also employed.

In addition, it did no harm that Matt was smitten by Gabby—honest, stolid Matt Bellamy, who worked most of the time at his brother's stables just down the road, but was a joiner by trade. Belle had hired him to fit out her shop and he continued to do odd jobs for her. Though Gabby teased Matt outrageously, Belle could see that secretly Matt adored her.

Together against the world, Belle and her staff were a good team. But—*Edward*. Her brother had flushed with anger when she'd mentioned gambling dens, yet Belle couldn't help remembering that when he'd first come into his inheritance the lure of the gaming parlours had pulled him time and time again to London.

Marriage to Charlotte had at least cured her brother of that particular weakness. But trouble was still lurking, clearly. In fact, Belle felt that nothing had been quite right in her life since she'd clashed with the forbidding quarryman on Sawle Down. Just the thought of that encounter sent ripples of unease through her.

Stay away from me! she'd lashed out at him. Why had she been so rude, so hateful to him? Because he was clad so roughly? Because he was employed by Mr Davenant?

She'd never even met Davenant, but one thing was for sure. If he ever learned of the insults she'd uttered about him that day, then she and Edward were finished for good.

Chapter Three

London—four days later

Adam Davenant had issued the invitations to the meeting at his house in Clarges Street only yesterday, but despite the short notice every single person had come and he was under no illusions as to why. Quite a few of them had never visited his Mayfair mansion, and they would all be desperate to get inside and assess his wealth.

Greeting them, he'd cynically noted how their eyes leapt out on stalks as they registered the expensive if discreet furnishings. The number of liveried servants. The superb wine and food on offer. Everything was perfect; it damned well had to be when people were all too keen to rake up your lowly origins.

Though the plentiful wine was perhaps a mistake, Adam decided as the boasting grew louder amongst the rich and ruthless men who'd gathered to feed on the cold repast set out on the vast table in his first-floor dining room. When the boasting began to turn to bickering, Adam knew it was time to start the real business of the day. He rose to his feet at the head of the table and, as was his way, stated his case bluntly.

'In Somerset there's stone to be quarried that's as good for building, gentlemen, as any in the world. With London expanding so rapidly there's a never-ending market, and all of us—whether landholders or business investors—stand to gain. But the issue I wish to discuss today is—transport.'

Adam was dressed impeccably in black with a snow-white, plain cravat and he made an imposing figure. Though not yet thirty, he carried the authority of a man who was accustomed to power.

He carried the authority of money.

All eyes were on him as he turned to point to the large map hung on the wall behind him. 'Gentlemen,' he went on, in the polished voice in which there was no trace of his grandfather's west country vowels. 'What we need is a railway to convey this fine new stone from the Somerset

quarries to the Avon canal and thence by water
to London.'

'There are railways already, Davenant,' someone called out.

'You mean tramways for trucks, pulled by
horses or powered by gravity,' replied Adam.
'I'm talking about a steam railway. All of us with
goods to transport from Bath to London—not
just stone, but farm produce and manufactured
goods, too—would benefit. The carrying times
would be halved and the profits doubled.'

Already several men were nodding and murmuring agreement. But Lord Rupert Jarvis—
who had, Adam noted, been eating and drinking
steadily since he arrived—was sneering openly.
'You mean *your* profits doubled, Davenant. Not
mine.'

The blond-haired Jarvis, as well as possessing
large estates in Somerset, owned a big haulage
business with networks of carriages and teams of
horses all across the south of England. Known to
be a cruel master of both men and beasts, Jarvis
saw the emergence of the railways as the coming of Satan.

Adam countered him with icy calmness.
'There's still room for all forms of transport,
Lord Jarvis. But we cannot ignore the chances

that steam offers. Some of you will already know that the Yorkshire mine owner Charles Brandling has been using steam engines to carry his coal to the ports for years. I'm proposing that each of us become shareholders in this new Somerset railway. And apart from the profit motive, we'll all be aware, I'm sure, that a railway would spare our men and horses much hard labour.'

'Siding with the workers, Davenant? They're damned lucky to have jobs,' said the sleekly dressed, coldly handsome Jarvis crudely. 'If they aren't up to it, tell 'em to get their wives or brats to help out. That's what I do.' He looked challengingly round at the assembled company.

'I'm sure you do,' said Adam. His chiselled face was expressionless, but his grey eyes were hard as granite. A tense silence had fallen.

Jarvis leaned back in his chair. 'Show us your route, Davenant,' he said challengingly. 'Doubtless you've got it all worked out.'

Adam turned and pointed to his map. 'Here's the city of Bath, with the stone quarries to the south and the River Avon flowing close by. And *here*—' he pointed again '—is the canal that links the Avon to the Thames, offering seventy miles of navigable waterway. You'll see that the most practical route for a new railway would be from Monkton Sawle straight to the canal as it runs south, just before it swings east out of Somerset.'

There were murmurs and nods of assent. Then Jarvis, who'd been demolishing another portion of venison pie, cut in, 'I suppose you realise you'll need to cross my land for the last half-mile of your proposed railway?'

'In order to reach the canal at Limpley Stoke, yes, I would need to cross your land,' said Adam. 'Just as I'd need the consent of the other landholders gathered here today who would be affected. It's in all our interests, beyond doubt.'

'Like hell it is,' growled Jarvis, wiping pastry crumbs off his lips. 'And I've listened to enough of this. I'm off, to another more interesting appointment.'

Adam politely indicated the plate on which stood the remainder of the venison pie. 'Certainly. But I would hate you to leave hungry. Shall I ask one of the servants to wrap up the rest of that pie so you can take it with you?'

There was a stunned silence. Then someone chuckled and began to applaud; Jarvis's appetite for a free meal was well known.

Jarvis pushed back his chair angrily. 'Damn

you, Davenant,' he muttered and hurried from the room, letting the door slam behind him.

Some of the others spoke up then. 'I'm with you, Adam,' said Tobias Bartlett firmly.

'And me.' 'Yes, you can count me in on your scheme, Davenant.' More pledges of support echoed round the room.

But there was still the problem of damned Jarvis; the big map made it all too clear that Jarvis's acres of land at Limpley Stoke barred the most direct route between Adam's quarry and the canal. Any other route would add miles to the journey.

'It's not as if Jarvis makes much use of that land anyway,' Adam's friend Bartlett was grumbling. 'And surely he realises he could expect a hefty share of your profits if he negotiated with you?'

'I don't think,' said Adam softly, 'that Jarvis's motive is based on thoughts of profit.'

Siding with the workers, Davenant? Jarvis had sneered.

Well, sometimes Adam wished he and Jarvis could resolve their differences like common workmen—with their fists. Then he would knock Jarvis's block off.

He looked thoughtfully down at his strong hands. As a boy at Eton, Adam had briefly been taunted with Miner Tom's name—until he'd pummelled the sneers from his rash tormentors' faces. On coming into his fortune he'd learnt to fend off his detractors in equally efficient ways. Both in his manners and attire he was unpretentious but faultless, never letting his cool façade slip. Being mighty rich he was happily accepted by most of society, especially by those who had daughters to marry off.

Jarvis, despite his oily good looks and title, was secretly despised by the *ton* for his coarse behaviour. If it wasn't for his damned land, Adam would have been happy to cut him dead—or thump him.

A young housemaid came in just then with more good wine from Adam's cellars. Adam didn't partake—he didn't enjoy fuddling his wits—but went instead to join the group who'd gone to pore again over the map of Somerset.

'If Jarvis won't give way, Adam,' a Somerset neighbour was suggesting, 'you could take the railway down the valley to Midford then head north—see?—to skirt his estates for the last mile. As I said, I would happily sell some land to you in return for some shares in the project.'

Adam was heartened that so many of these men were, like him, all for progress. 'We'll manage without Jarvis somehow,' he said. 'Though if we *do* head north, we'll have to blast some of the higher contours out of the way, here, and here…'

'It'll be worth it,' said another Somerset landowner eagerly. 'Davenant, you mentioned the coal mines in the north-east; I've heard rumours that Stephenson up in Stockton is planning to transport people as well as coal on his railways! Steam is the future, and this scheme of yours gets my backing, if only to take the sneer off Jarvis's face. The way he treats his men and his horses is despicable. Thank God he left early, is all I can say. We can make some progress now, Adam… Adam?'

'Hmm?'

It didn't happen often, but Adam, by the window, was temporarily distracted. In fact, he couldn't take his eyes off a remarkably shabby carriage that had just pulled up at the far end of Clarges Street, from which a woman was getting out; a woman wearing a big straw hat and dressed in a startling ensemble of turquoise and pink as striking on her pert figure as icing on a festive cake. She was probably an expensive courtesan, Adam decided, hired by one of his wealthy neighbours for an afternoon of bed sport. Shrugging, he turned back to his guests—then paused again.

Something about her looked familiar. The way she stepped proudly out of that ridiculous carriage. The slenderness of her waist, outlined by her short pink jacket; the swell of her deliciously trim *derrière* as she stood on tiptoe to say something to her coachman…

She reminded him of that woman on Sawle Down.

The memory made his breathing hitch. She'd insulted him to kingdom come—and he'd stood there and taken it from her! When what he should have done—the thought occurred to him time after time, usually at damnably inconvenient moments like now—was take her in his arms. Hold her close. Drown out those defiant protests of hers with a kiss…

Definitely time to get back to his guests, and his railway.

It *was* Belle, and she was standing on the pavement at the far end of Clarges Street, arguing with Matt. 'This will do, Matt!' she announced firmly after letting herself out. 'I can walk the rest of the way, I assure you.'

Matt Bellamy, up on his seat, frowned down at her. 'Here, Mrs Marchmain? But we're not quite there yet.'

I know, thought Belle tightly. *And no way on earth am I going to risk allowing Mr Davenant or his servants to see me arriving in this rickety old coach.*

She'd tried already to shut the carriage door, but failed; now she tried again. Blast, it was nearly falling off its hinges.

She'd hoped to make an impression arriving outside Mr Davenant's house and had asked Matt to borrow something suitable from his brother's stables. But when Matt had turned up outside her shop at half-past two with this, Belle had been secretly horrified.

And the door still wouldn't shut. She tried again; this time the handle came off in her hand. Somehow she rammed it back. Matt had jumped down now from the driver's seat to hold the horses and was simply gaping at the four-storeyed, cream-stuccoed dwellings that surrounded them.

Belle resisted the same impulse to let her own jaw drop. She'd known, of course, that Davenant dwelt in the most exclusive part of London. But the thought of confronting him in one of these magnificent mansions made her heart quail within her.

It was four days since Edward had called at her shop with his dire news. She'd written twice to

Davenant requesting an appointment and heard precisely nothing, so she'd decided there was no alternative but to confront him in his lair. Sternly quelling her apprehension, she'd dressed appropriately and left her shop in Gabrielle's capable hands.

Of course, *appropriate* wouldn't be the word most people would use for her twill silk gown of turquoise and pink or her snug-fitting pink jacket. *Appropriate* didn't perhaps apply to her large straw hat adorned with turquoise satin ribbons. Oh, dear. When she'd put on the outfit she'd felt full of confidence. But now she was feeling rather sick.

Davenant's grandfather made the family fortunes from tin mining, she remembered Edward saying scornfully. But as she gazed down Clarges Street, she felt her breath catch in her throat because the miner's grandson had done rather well for himself.

Still standing by the rickety coach, she smoothed the sleeves of her jacket, adjusted her straw bonnet and emphasised to Matt a little too brightly, 'This will most definitely do, Matt. Return the vehicle, will you? I shan't be wanting you again.'

Big Matt set his face obstinately. 'Don't seem

right, Mrs Marchmain, leaving you here alone, callin' on an unknown gentleman.'

Belle very much wanted to say crisply to Matt and to anyone else within hearing, 'Believe me, Adam Davenant is no gentleman!' But that would simply make poor Matt even more anxious; so instead she retorted, 'Matt, I'm a twenty-seven-year-old widow and, as you see, I'm at no risk whatsoever in a neighbourhood like this. There is absolutely no need for you to stay. Besides,' she added in a moment of inspiration, 'Gabby will be expecting you. You promised her you'd fix that loose counter in the workshop today, remember?'

As she spoke she was horribly conscious that halfway down Clarges Street a couple of liveried footmen stood on the steps of the biggest house of them all, gossiping in the sun. She'd been aware for some time that the footmen were staring in her direction and felt newly embarrassed by the scruffy equipage and the presence of loyal Matt in his ancient greatcoat and battered hat.

'Won't you want escortin' home afterwards, ma'am?' frowned Matt.

'I shall walk,' Belle announced. 'I shall enjoy the fresh air.'

'But…'

Just then the door handle fell off again; she

kicked it under the carriage. 'Matt!' she hissed. 'Please—just go!'

Matt, his burly visage expressive, heaved himself back on to the driving seat. Belle found herself urging his departure under her breath rather frantically. Then, lifting her head high, she set off down Clarges Street. The footmen watched her as she drew nearer.

She knew it. She knew, before she reached them.

They were outside Adam Davenant's house. They were his footmen. *Oh, drat and botheration.* And they had seen everything; the ancient carriage, Matt, herself kicking the blasted door handle out of sight...

They had sprung to attention, stiff-faced, their arms straight at their sides, but Belle had seen a hint of malicious humour in their eyes.

'Is this Mr Davenant's house?' she asked crisply.

'This is Mr Davenant's residence—ma'am.'

'Then I wish to speak to him, if you please. And before you ask, I have not an appointment, though I have written to him twice informing him that—that it is in his *interests* to see me.'

The footman's lips pursed. 'Mr Davenant happens to have company.'

'Then I will wait.'

The impudent scoundrel almost sniffed. 'Very well, madam. I will take you to await Mr Davenant's convenience.'

'But...' Belle bit her lip. She didn't exactly have a choice, did she? He held the door open; she sailed inside.

Oh, my. This place was incredible. Her entire shop would fit inside this lofty hallway, with its huge chandeliers and sweeping staircase. *Money from mining and quarrying,* she reminded herself steadily. Money from other men's backbreaking toil.

The footman—who she reckoned might stop breathing soon if he lifted his nose any higher in disdain—ushered her along the vast hallway to a room that led off it, pointed her inside, then disappeared, closing the door rather firmly on her as he left.

She was too agitated to notice much, beyond the fact that she could hear the sounds of loud male talk and laughter from upstairs. Would the sneering footman trouble to deliver her message? Would the hateful Mr Davenant even bother to leave his rowdy companions and grant her a few minutes' audience? She paced to and fro. This had to be one of her stupidest ideas ever.

Suddenly she heard a man's bellow of rage from out in the hallway, then the pattering of feet and the sounds of a girl sobbing. Just as she turned towards the door it burst open and a young maid-servant tottered in, clearly in a state of some distress. Tears were rolling down her cheeks.

The maid saw Belle. 'Oh! I beg pardon, miss, I'm sure!' Knuckling the tears from her eyes, the girl was already turning to hurry away, but Belle grabbed her by the shoulder. 'What is it, my dear?'

The girl, in her white cap and apron, was shaking. 'Nothin'. It's nothin', miss...' She hurried out again into the hall, Belle following. But the girl stopped with a low cry when she saw, from the other direction, an extravagantly dressed, fair-haired man prowling towards her with an unpleasant smile on his face. 'Now, what's all this, missy?' he said to the cowering maid. 'I thought we were having a pleasant conversation. Not trying to run from me, are you?'

This time it was Belle who let out a gasp of shock. She knew this smooth-tongued aristocrat whom some would call handsome. Her stomach clenched. Dear God, if this man was a friend of Davenant's, things were even worse than she'd thought.

Belle said to the young maid quickly, 'I will see to this. Go, now.' The maid scurried off, still sobbing. The man lurched closer—clearly he had been drinking, she could smell it. He was staring down at her. 'By God. Mrs Marchmain. Well, isn't this a happy coincidence?'

Belle held her chin high. *Loathsome, loathsome man.* 'Not for me, Lord Jarvis, I assure you.'

At first Jarvis scowled. 'I see your pride is still as damned lofty as ever...' Then he began to laugh—a bitter, ugly sound. His pale blue eyes were assessing her greedily. 'Hold a minute. Now, let me think. Here you are, in Davenant's house— can it be that my money wasn't enough to tempt you, but Davenant's *is*?'

He laid his hand on her shoulder and let it slide to her breast. Belle's stomach heaved as she knocked it away.

'You disgust me, my lord,' she breathed. 'You did when we last met and not a thing has changed—'

'What the deuce is going on?'

The man's voice came from the wide staircase above them. Jarvis jumped away from Belle and looked up angrily at the speaker. 'Davenant. Damn it, I'd no idea you were there...'

Belle looked up, too. And with this second

shock she felt so dizzy that her ribs ached with the need for air. No. Impossible. *Please...*

The newcomer scarcely glanced at her. It was on Jarvis that his iron gaze rested as he came steadily down the stairs; he was tall and broad-shouldered, dressed in the sober perfection of black tailcoat and pristine white neckcloth.

He said to Jarvis, 'I thought you were on your way out a while ago.'

'And so I was,' declared Jarvis furiously. 'Until I was delayed, by an encounter with this woman here.'

'Not true,' breathed Belle.

'Oh, it *is* true. She insulted me, Davenant, damn it!'

Belle thought she'd been prepared for almost anything. But not for the fact that Adam Davenant, her brother's enemy, was the man on Sawle Down into whose ears she'd poured insult after insult.

Desperate hope rose in her breast. *He might not remember me. He might not recognise me...*

Lord Jarvis did though, all too well; Jarvis was still glaring at her, and to him she said as steadily as she could, 'You claim I insulted you, Lord Jarvis. All I did was tell you to stop pursuing that serving girl because you were frightening her out of her wits.' Belle met his glare squarely, though she truly wished the ground would open up and swallow her.

'I'll escort you to the door, Jarvis,' she heard Davenant saying.

The two men were moving away from her along the hall; she saw Jarvis pausing by the open doorway, still muttering angrily to Davenant, jabbing his finger in her direction. Dear God, she could just imagine what foul lies he'd be concocting.

'Good day to you, Jarvis,' Davenant was saying.

Jarvis gave a swift nod. 'Good day to *you*, Davenant. We'll speak soon, I've no doubt.' The footman closed the door after him and Adam Davenant was coming back towards her. The footman hadn't bothered to ask her name; there was a chance, just a chance she might still somehow be able to wriggle out of this...

'Well,' Mr Davenant said softly. 'So we meet again, Mrs Marchmain.'

Her last hope died.

Chapter Four

Adam Davenant was astounded and annoyed. As if Jarvis wasn't enough—the damned man caused trouble wherever he went—*she* was here.

A footman had warned Adam that a rather odd lady had come to call and within moments of first seeing her in the hall it had all fallen into place. She was the woman who'd emerged from that dreadful old carriage.

And who'd stirred memories of that sunlit March afternoon in Somerset.

Stirred more than memories, in fact. She was clad outrageously in a clinging outfit of turquoise and pink with a loud bonnet trailing ribbons everywhere. Her eyes were emerald, her raven-black curls set off the perfect creaminess of her skin, her lips were full and rosy.

And he steadily reminded himself that just a few weeks ago she'd heaped such insults on the name of Adam Davenant that they were etched like acid on his memory. Even more ominously—she knew Jarvis.

'You're very quiet, Mrs Marchmain,' he drawled. 'Surely you aren't trying to conjure up *more* insults to hurl at me? Or have you exhausted yourself being rude to Jarvis?'

Belle swallowed on the dryness in her throat and lifted her chin. 'He was treating that young serving maid *abominably*. You will perhaps remark, Mr Davenant, that I had no right to interfere, but I could not stand by!'

He was watching her with something unreadable in his eyes. 'You do tend to say what you think, don't you?' he said. 'You have a neat way with put-downs. You told me, for instance, that I wasn't born to wealth and it showed.'

Oh, Lord, thought Belle rather faintly. He hadn't forgotten or forgiven a single word. Something shook inside her, seeing him like this, no longer wearing the garb of a rough quarry worker, but dressed as the rich, powerful man he was, here in his mansion. And how well he fitted the part. To say he was handsome wasn't enough. His strong features and formidable stature implied power and dominance. Edward had described him as a boor. No one else in their right mind would.

But she was damned if she would grovel. 'How was I supposed to know who you were? How could I have guessed, when you were—you were—'

'Dressed like a labourer?' he cut in. 'That was because I'd been inspecting my quarry. I judge people by their words and actions, Mrs Marchmain, not their attire; a lesson you might try learning. Now it's my turn for questions, the most obvious being—why exactly are you here?' His voice licked somehow at her senses, soft and dangerous. Dear God, her errand was doomed before it had even begun.

But she had to try. 'I have business with you, Mr Davenant, which concerns my brother. I wrote to you, but you did not deign to reply!'

'I leave begging letters to my secretary, Lowell.'

Begging letters. 'How dare—?'

'Mrs Marchmain,' he interrupted, 'I'm an extremely busy man. And your brother—Hathersleigh—has taken up too much of my time already.'

Heat surged through her veins. 'You could at least give this matter your *attention*!'

'Why? Because you're members of the once-illustrious Hathersleigh family?'

She bit her lip. 'We are not without influence still.'

He sighed heavily. 'Please don't remind me that you have a great-uncle who is a duke, as your brother once did.' She visibly flinched. 'I really don't care,' he went on, 'if you can trace your ancestry all the way back to William the Conqueror. Why should I waste my time on you, when your family is reduced to sheep-stealing?'

Oh, Lord.

She remembered how at Sawle Down the dust had clung to this man's breeches and boots and perspiration had gleamed on his hard cheekbones. Today, he could have claimed to be a duke himself and no one would have doubted it. His clothes were exceedingly plain, yes, but that coat of his had clearly been cut by a master to fit those broad shoulders so perfectly. Sleek buckskins clung to his powerfully muscular thighs and his polished top boots were exquisite. His thick dark hair was cropped short, his pristine neckcloth was quite perfect.

He made no effort to clamour for attention. He didn't need to. And as his slate-grey eyes rested on hers, she felt a sharp jolt of awareness implode quietly yet devastatingly inside her. Awareness of what, precisely? Of his sheer maleness, that was what. It was impossible to look at him without thinking: here was a man of power, with a man's desires, and all that implied.

And he was her family's enemy. *Her* enemy.

She said, her head lifted high, but her pulse rate in tumult, 'I hope you will accept, Mr Davenant, that I spoke in the heat of the moment that afternoon on Sawle Down.'

'It gave you a wonderful opportunity to reveal your true thoughts, though, didn't it?' he observed caustically. 'So please don't lower yourself in my estimation by trying to take back what you said.'

The smouldering look she gave him said, *Don't worry. I won't.*

Inside Adam was rigid with tension. The witch. The insolent little green-eyed witch.

What Jarvis had said to him just before he left was still ringing in his ears.

I don't know why that woman's visiting you, Davenant, but you'd be a fool to believe a word she says. She's a greedy little widow angling for money—some time ago I made the mistake of not offering her enough.

She'd come here to plead with Adam for mercy for her brother, no doubt. And she must realise her mission was already doomed—because Adam knew exactly what she thought of him.

'I'm in the middle of a meeting,' he told her curtly. 'I'll be with you in fifteen minutes.' He was leading the way along a corridor. 'You can wait here, in my library.' One big hand pushed open a panelled door.

She swung round on him, head held high. 'You expect me to wait? *Again?*'

'You are uninvited,' he pointed out. 'Be glad that I see you at all, Mrs Marchmain.' He turned to go, closing the library door on her. She could cool down in there. And so, damn it, could he.

Adam was a highly physical man and his lifestyle usually accommodated a mistress, kept in enviable style in return for companionship in bed and out of it. He'd recently ended just such an arrangement with an elegant widow, Lady Farnsworth—mainly because she was starting to hint a little too often about marriage.

Marriage was one big mistake as far as Adam was concerned. But it was also an error on his part, he now decided grimly, to be without a mistress. It made him think hungry thoughts about a raven-haired termagant dressed in turquoise and pink who quite simply detested him.

* * *

Belle just stood there when he'd gone, sunk before she'd even begun. *I really don't care if you can trace your ancestry all the way back to William the Conqueror*, he'd said. *Why should I waste my time on you, when your family is reduced to sheep-stealing?*

She cringed anew. The ducal connection came through their mother, who'd died shortly after giving birth to Edward when Belle was only two. It was Belle's father who used to point out to his children that their mother's uncle was the Duke of Sutherland, but as far as Belle knew the Duke wasn't even aware of their existence. Either that or he'd heard of their dwindling fortunes and kept well away.

Belle's father had died when Belle was just thirteen, and that was when the estate had to be put in the care of stern Uncle Philip and his wife. Edward, at twenty-one, had come into his inheritance with considerable joy, hence the youthful gambling spree. But Belle had already grasped the reality—that her family was in actuality impoverished.

Since Belle's widowhood her dressmaking business had given her independence; but it did not give her the deference or protection she might once have expected in society. She'd met Lord Jarvis two years ago, when he'd expressed an interest in investing in her shop and invited her to his big London house for a business meeting with his lawyer.

The lawyer never arrived. Lord Jarvis had locked the door to his study and had proceeded to make her an offer which had left her breathless and shaking.

'Let's *really* get down to business, shall we?' he'd smirked, sidling closer. 'How do you fancy a change of profession?'

He was, in effect, bluntly suggesting that she be his mistress. He'd silkily gone on to tell her that if he didn't appeal to her tastes, he had a choice of stalwart grooms from whom she could have her pick. 'As a young widow you must be quite desperate for male companionship. I'll enjoy watching.' He'd smiled. 'I'll pay handsomely, of course. One hundred pounds a month, Mrs Marchmain—I promise you won't be bored.'

She'd struck him hard on the cheek. His smile had vanished at the same time as the red mark appeared on his pale skin.

'So you want more money, do you?' he'd whispered. 'A greedy little slut, are you, Mrs Marchmain?'

'Let me out,' she'd breathed. She'd run to the door and was struggling frantically to open it. 'Damn you, let me out of here!'

He'd unlocked the door with an ugly look on his smooth features. 'Don't even *think* of telling anyone about what's passed between us today,' he'd rasped. 'Or I'll have you damned well ruined.'

Now she walked round this opulent book-lined room in utter agony of spirit. With a huge effort she tried to steady her racing pulse. She had dealt with Jarvis and she would deal with Davenant, though how, God only knew.

It was scarcely four, but outside the sky was growing overcast. On a nearby table some papers were scattered and, if only to distract herself from her dismaying thoughts, she went across to look. There were maps of Somerset, along with some geological sketches—to do with quarries, she guessed. Towards the back of the table was a tray of mineral samples together with a brass model of some kind of engine about a foot high, beautifully crafted.

Even though Adam Davenant's family fortune had been made in mining and quarrying, it was unusual for anyone to display such an obvious interest in the practicalities of money-grubbing.

'Showing his base blood,' Edward and his friends would sneer.

Yet in spite of herself Belle's attention was caught. She remembered how Davenant had defended the quarries to her that day on Sawle Down—*they provide work and wages for many men and food for their families.*

She remembered her inner acknowledgement that he was right. That sudden, instinctive feeling that he was a man of integrity...

A terrible mistake. An illusion.

She turned the model of the engine by its base, finding that the cold precision of it somehow soothed her roiling mind. A steam engine, she guessed; Uncle Philip Marchmain used to tell them both that steam was the future, and that the end of the world of the horse was in sight.

Well, the end of *her* world was in sight if she didn't find some way of extricating herself from this appalling mess.

She put the model down and sank into a chair. What would Davenant say—what would he do— if he knew that almost every night since that fateful encounter she'd been haunted by dreams of him?

When she'd fallen from her horse that afternoon and opened her eyes to see him towering above her—dust-covered, muscular, roughly clad—she'd felt something tight impeding her breathing. He'd offered to help her to her feet and she'd rejected him, so rudely.

But she'd never forgotten the strength of his hands on her waist as he'd lifted her on to her horse. Never forgotten the sense of sheer male power that emanated from his body, the gleam of the sun on his hard cheekbones; the glimpse of his naked chest revealed by that open-necked shirt...

Her pulse thudded at the memory. She was turning the ring on her finger in nervous agitation when suddenly the door opened. Adam Davenant—Lord Jarvis's friend and her enemy—was here again.

She jumped up from the chair as if it burned her. He pushed the door shut, folded his arms and studied her. Belle in turn acknowledged the spectacular lines of his tall, broad-shouldered figure with bitter eyes. *Handsome. So handsome.*

And trying so very hard to be a gentleman, she'd heard people say. But she didn't think anyone would dare to say that to his face. Whatever his origins, this man was formidable. And most women would simply—melt.

'Ah, Mrs Marchmain,' he said. 'Still here, I see.'

'I'm sorry to disappoint you, but, yes, I am.'

He looked at his watch. 'I can spare you ten minutes,' he said.

Outside the afternoon sun had vanished behind dark clouds. She thought she heard the ominous rumble of thunder in the distance—which was apt, since Thor the thunder god, in the person of Mr Adam Davenant, had her in his lair. *Oh, Lord...*

Belle took a deep breath and began. She explained how Edward had been heir to a much-diminished estate but was working so hard to hold his inheritance together. 'And then there were the new taxes on landowners,' she went on, 'and the weather was truly dreadful...'

She saw Davenant's dark eyebrows rise in faint contempt. 'Ah,' he said. 'So these iniquitous taxes and the unkind weather landed solely on your brother's portion of Somerset, did they?'

She coloured hotly. 'I see it pleases you to mock me, Mr Davenant. But I haven't *finished* yet! A year ago, as you well know, Edward sold some of his land to you because of pressing debts. And you paid him a truly pitiful amount for that land...'

Something happened then. The previously impassive features of his chiselled face had become hard as granite.

'I paid him two thousand guineas,' said Davenant.

Her hand flew to her mouth. 'Two *thousand*?'

'Yes.' His narrowed eyes never left her face. 'You see, I guessed that the old quarry there might benefit from reinvestment. I told him this and also offered him some shares. He turned down my offer and told me I was wrong. Nevertheless I paid him the two thousand—far more than he'd have got from anyone else.'

'Because you *knew* you could make that amount many times over from the stone!'

'Have you any idea,' he countered grimly, 'how much it costs to invest in equipment and labour for a re-opened quarry? It will be years before I start to see a profit; certainly no one else would have paid your brother so much. But fool that I was, I felt sorry for the young idiot.'

Outside thunder rumbled again. Davenant went to light the lamp on the table where the model engine was; his movements were lithe, almost graceful for such a powerfully built man…

Stop it. Stop it, you fool.

Two thousand guineas. Belle sank into the

nearest chair. Now Davenant was saying with lethal politeness, 'I take it there's some discrepancy over figures. Am I right?'

Belle thrust aside a long bonnet ribbon that trailed down her cheek. 'I don't know—I might have misunderstood—'

'I doubt it,' he cut in crisply. 'Try asking your brother again. On this occasion you might find that he remembers the truth.' His expression was glacial. 'You could ask him, at the same time, why he stole my livestock.'

Belle was truly floundering now. 'It must appear to you as theft, I know. But that was all a mistake.'

'I suppose he told you that my sheep had strayed on to his lands,' he drawled icily. 'Told you that it was my fault, for not maintaining my fences.'

The hot blush rose to Belle's cheeks. That was *exactly* what Edward had said.

'I maintain my fences very carefully, Mrs Marchmain,' went on Davenant. 'In fact, every detail of my life is conducted with the utmost rigour. Now, I'm a busy man…' he glanced again at his watch '…it's gone four, and I'm sincerely hoping you've come here with some concise suggestions as to how your younger brother intends to pay back the not inconsiderable sum he owes me for selling off my sheep. Which is a criminal act, incidentally.'

Adam Davenant usually kept his emotions on a tight rein, but by now he was deeply angry. Somehow this woman had got under his guard and he shouldn't have let her. Turquoise and pink, for God's sake—he had to blink every time he looked at her! He should have abided by his first instinct and ordered her off his premises.

'Mr Davenant,' she was saying, that pointed chin still tilted defiantly, 'you must realise that it has been extremely difficult for my brother to see our heritage so diminished.'

She wasn't giving up yet, registered Adam. 'Ah,' he answered. 'The precious notion of blue blood and entitlement. Spare me, Mrs March-main. The Hathersleigh estate has been lurching towards ruin for generations, thanks to a fatal mixture of greed, complacency and sheer care-lessness. Have you observed the way in which your brother conducts his business? Have you *seen* the great piles of unsorted paperwork that litter his so-called study?'

'He is busy,' Belle faltered. 'His wife is not well...'

'And so he sends his older sister to make his excuses for him. I repeat, I bought that land at an excessive price from your brother—not out of generosity, nor out of greed, but because I simply had no desire to have a bankrupt neighbour in Somerset. It's not good for appearances.'

Belle gazed at him whitely. This man was surely as cold and hard as the rock his men hewed from the ground. She rose to her feet. 'Exactly how much does my brother owe you for the sheep?'

'I don't see how you can hope to pay me off. You must have even less money to spare than he does.'

'I run a successful dressmaking business!'

'Not successful enough.'

She sat down again. Adam watched the turquoise ribbons, ridiculously flippant, fluttering from her straw bonnet and reflected that her brother was a goddamned weakling. Adam had rashly hoped to help young Hathersleigh by buying that land, but the fellow was a fool, and a liar, too—he'd not even equipped his rather pluckier older sister with the truth.

And the fact that she was still assuming her goddamned *superiority*, and laboured under the misapprehension that he, Adam, was somehow under obligation to show leniency, sent bitterness surging through Adam's blood.

He knew that people like her despised and feared men of Adam's mould, who were a symbol of things to come, of old values passing. She thoroughly deserved humiliation at his hands. Yet even while she glared up at him as if he was the devil incarnate, he felt something simmer, damn it, that was very like lust in his traitorous loins. Felt the longing to take her very firmly in his arms and plunder that sweet, rose-pink mouth with his lips and tongue...

Jarvis had clearly tried to make her his at some point in the past. Jarvis had failed.

Adam could see her hands trembling now. Yet still she faced him with that damned defiance, still she came up with fresh excuses for her sibling.

'My brother does not deserve prison, Mr Davenant.'

'Really?'

'Indeed. You see, he has a wife who is expecting their first baby very soon—'

'He'll have that in common with many of his fellow-prisoners in Newgate gaol, then.'

She tightened her fists. Then: 'You are despicable,' she said quietly. Her voice was steady, yet he noted how her small, high breasts heaved with distress beneath that tightly buttoned little pink jacket. 'Despicable,' she repeated. 'Both in your behaviour to me now, and your deliberately not telling me who you were that afternoon on Sawle Down. Your deception was truly dishonourable.'

Dishonourable? Damn it! *She's a greedy little widow, angling for money.* Adam went in with all guns blazing.

'Your kind talk always of honour and status,' he retorted harshly. 'Would you say your brother was showing *honour*, in sending his sister to me to plead his cause? There are names for that kind of behaviour.'

She recoiled as if he'd struck her. 'It was *my* decision to come here! If you think that Edward intended—'

'I think,' he cut in, 'that your cowardly brother told you about his plight in the hope that your feminine charms would soften my steely peasant heart. If that's an example of blue-blooded behaviour, you can keep it. In my world, we call it pimping.'

'Oh! I think—my brother did not mean—' She was stammering now, and backing away; somehow her dangling sleeve caught the little steam model and it went crashing to the floor.

She let out a cry of dismay and bent to start picking the pieces up.

'Leave it,' he commanded harshly. 'A footman will see to it.'

'*No!*' She was still flurrying around the floor. 'No, I will pick it *all* up and then I am going, you hateful, hateful man! Edward was right to say you are a boor and a tyrant. And—and I will see Edward and I in gaol *together* before I grovel any more to you!'

With that she bobbed down again, to pick up more pieces of the ill-fated model. As she did so she was presenting that very pert, very rounded *derrière* to Adam's narrowed eyes. Hell. He did try to look away. He despised himself for registering even the slightest flicker of interest. But a picture of her unclad appeared rather tantalisingly in his mind, and his body responded accordingly.

Adam had decided long ago that marriage was not for him. He had neither the time nor the inclination to play the games of courtship, flattery and lies that a permanent commitment would involve. God knew he was offered enough suitable brides; they were pushed before him at every opportunity, thanks to his wealth.

But the example of his parents' marriage had put him off for good. Miner Tom's only son, Charles, had been so rich he was able to choose a bride from the aristocracy, but his well-born wife—pushed into the marriage by her parents—had thoroughly despised her low-born husband and after producing two male heirs she'd embarked on a string of affairs.

Adam had spent a good deal of his childhood trying to protect his young brother, Freddy, from their mother's promiscuity and their weak father's rages. Both parents had died years ago, and Adam felt not the slightest desire to emulate their unhappiness; hence his custom of keeping suitable mistresses to satisfy his own male desires.

He treated them generously, but always Adam made the terms quite clear: 'This ends when I say it ends. Afterwards, if we happen across each other in society, we will acknowledge each other civilly. No more and no less.'

Most of his former mistresses knew better than to cause him any trouble; Lady Farnsworth, his latest, had been an exception. Adam had quickly wearied of the elegant widow's clinging possessiveness and her withering contempt for any suspected rivals.

The trouble was, he hadn't yet chosen himself

another woman for his bed. Usually they were either widows or amicably separated from their husbands and the choice was plentiful. But no one had tempted him to make an offer, since...

Since he collided with this little minx, who'd insulted his name to high heaven one March afternoon on Sawle Down.

The realisation struck him like a thunderbolt. *No.* He *couldn't* have held back from singling out a new *chère amie* because he was thinking of Belle Marchmain. It was damned impossible! But...

She'd come here to ask him a very big favour, but her plans—so far—had come crashing round her pretty ears. Now he looked at her again as she furiously picked up the last bits of his model from the floor.

Her straw bonnet had fallen off and her glossy raven curls were tumbling around the slender column of her neck. 'There! That's all of it!' she breathed, putting two more pieces defiantly on the table. Her face had become a little flushed. 'Whatever you call it,' she added rather darkly, her hands on her hips.

Mrs Belle Marchmain looked delectable. Her pink silk jacket had fallen apart, and the brightly patterned gown that fitted so snugly to her bosom and tiny waist almost made him smile.

What would she be like in bed? If she was, as Jarvis suggested, well practised in the erotic arts and open to offers, it might be interesting to find out…

'And—and you can stop *looking* at me like that!'

Her rebuke shocked him out of his reverie and Adam stopped smiling. 'You were asking about the model you almost destroyed,' he said. 'It's a miniature of a Newcomen steam engine. And that's not quite it, Mrs Marchmain. You came to me with a problem. And I think I might have the solution.' He'd propped his lean hips against the sideboard and watched her with cool, assessing eyes.

Belle suddenly felt that the room was too small. Either that or this formidable man was too close. Something tight was squeezing her lungs. 'Let me tell you now that Edward will never sell more of the estate to you and I wouldn't ask him to. It's his heritage!'

'But of course,' answered Adam imperturbably. 'And your brother shouldn't be expected to dirty his hands for a living as so many men—and women—do.' She swallowed. 'I also imagine,' he went on in the same calm voice, 'that most of the rest of his estate is entailed. You want me to drop charges against your brother for stealing my livestock, don't you? Well, I certainly require payment. And as to what that payment shall be, I have the perfect answer. I think you do as well.'

What? Belle paled. 'I—I thought perhaps we could come to some arrangement, for Edward to pay his debts off gradually...'

His lip curled. 'Impossible, I'm afraid. But I still see no reason, Mrs Marchmain, to dismiss the obvious solution.'

So frozen did she look that her lips could clearly scarcely frame the words. 'What exactly are you suggesting, Mr Davenant?'

'Let's be clear. You surely realise you have only one thing you can offer in payment of your brother's debts,' Adam said softly. 'Yourself. Be my mistress.'

Chapter Five

Belle felt, in that instant, as if all the breath had been squeezed from her lungs. Lord Jarvis's insults had made her feel sick. This man made her feel as if the safety of her world had been rocked to its foundations.

Be my mistress.

He was just watching her, leaning back against the sturdy oak sideboard with his arms folded across his broad chest. The candlelight fell on his cropped dark hair, on his sleepy grey eyes, on his hateful, sternly handsome face. And her pulse was skittering with the unsteadiness of a new-born colt.

The way he was looking at her. Assessing her, damn him. She felt his presence in the pit of her stomach and her dry mouth. She couldn't look at him without tingling anew at the sight of his powerful figure: those heavily muscled shoulders, his broad chest tapering down to slim hips and powerful thighs… Oh, just his being *near* her made the air difficult to breathe.

His mistress. How dare this man make such a proposition? How *dare* he? Yet—oh, goodness, she'd been an arrogant idiot to come here. Straight into the lion's den, armed only with her own stupid defiance—and her brother's lies. She bent to rather shakily pick up her fallen bonnet; how ridiculous its gaudiness seemed now.

She remembered how she'd felt when her husband died and the enormity of the debts she'd faced. Remembered how she'd stood her ground against Lord Jarvis—only, dear God, this man was far more dangerous than Jarvis.

When she eventually spoke her words were, to her, miraculously steady. 'To be perfectly honest, Mr Davenant,' she replied, 'I'm not quite sure whether your—*offer* is intended as a deliberate insult or a very poor joke.'

He shrugged. 'It's neither. There happens to be a vacancy.'

'But I thought you already had a mistress…' She clamped her mouth shut. *You stupid fool, Belle.* She shouldn't have shown the slightest interest. Yet she couldn't help but hear, in her shop, the gossip of the *ton*. Couldn't help but know that

Adam Davenant attracted the attentions of the most beautiful women in London.

His dark eyebrows had already arched in amusement. 'So you take an interest in my *affaires*, do you? Then you should be aware that my latest companion and I have recently parted company.'

Belle returned his smile, sweetly. 'She has had a lucky reprieve.'

He laughed. He actually laughed. 'I wish you'd tell her so.' His voice was silky. 'I thought I was making you quite a reasonable offer. I would provide you, of course, with a London house and an income, so I do wish you'd stop acting like some virgin schoolgirl, Mrs Marchmain.'

She let out a sharp breath. 'I'm merely, as a woman of the world, trying to assess what *you* would gain from such an arrangement. You'll understand I find it hard to believe you are suggesting this out of any kind of—of *liking*.'

He shrugged. 'I'm rather bored with women who think I'm the answer to all their prayers.'

'*So* tedious for you, I'm sure!'

He nodded. 'A little, yes.' Belle gritted her teeth. 'I think,' he went on blithely, 'that you, on the other hand, would enter the kind of relationship I'm suggesting with a refreshing honesty. And of course your weakling brother's error regarding the sheep would be forgiven—' He stopped. He suddenly noticed that she was trembling. 'Is something wrong, Mrs Marchmain?'

'You thought I came here to—to bargain with you.'

'And didn't you?'

'Yes! But *not in that way.*'

He was silent a moment. Then he said steadily, 'I see. Not now that you know exactly who I am, you mean. Tell me, does my low birth make me so much worse a prospect than Jarvis?'

She shuddered. 'Jarvis is *despicable.*' She spoke with such absolute disgust that Adam felt a bolt of uncertainty shoot through him.

'I was under the impression that you were holding out for considerably more money from him.'

'Holding out for… Oh, you are a friend of his,' she retorted bitterly, 'so it wouldn't matter what I said. But do you really think I would contemplate a proposal of any kind from Lord Jarvis?'

Adam shrugged. 'Jarvis would offer a solution to your problems. He's not as rich as I am, but he does have a title. And, oh, I believe his family goes back almost as far as yours, although there might not be a duke in the family…'

Belle had stepped shakily away from him. 'You

are hateful,' she whispered. 'Mr Davenant, I will find some way to pay back the money my brother owes, I swear. But you'll understand, I hope, if I tell you that I can no longer bear to spend another moment in your presence.'

He shrugged. *The taint of Miner Tom.* Well—let her face the consequences of her and her brother's damned arrogance.

She was already making for the door when he saw something sparkling under her dark lashes. *Tears.*

'Stop,' he said.

She turned. She was almost broken, he suddenly realised; he saw it in the paleness of her cheeks, the trembling of her fingers as she crammed her straw bonnet over her dark curls.

Something dangerously like pity twisted at his throat.

'Jarvis is not my friend,' he said curtly. 'He was here on a matter of business and, believe me, that was almost more than I could tolerate. What exactly happened between the two of you?'

She lifted her eyes steadfastly to his. 'Two years ago Lord Jarvis invited me to his house on the pretext of investing in my business. He made me an offer that I found...obscene. Though—' *Oh, what was the use?* Belle was shivering. 'You don't believe me, do you? You still think I'm in the market for... That I visited you to... Oh, I've been so *stupid*. I should never have come here.'

Not now she knew who he was. Adam started towards the door. 'Unlike Jarvis,' he said, 'I don't—ever—force myself on unwilling females. You came here of your own accord and you're equally free to leave.'

She started towards the door, then stopped. 'But—'

'As for those sheep,' he went on pitilessly, 'I'll get my secretary to send you a bill so you can pay me for them. You told me your shop was flourishing, didn't you?' He was holding the door open for her.

Belle froze. Her shop—flourishing? *Oh, Lord, this was bad.* What could she do? He'd offered her a solution and she'd discarded it.

Think again, Belle.

She heaved in a great breath. 'Mr Davenant,' she said.

Now, Adam wanted this woman and her insults out of here. But something was happening. Some new desperation in her voice riveted his attention. 'Yes?'

'Mr Davenant—what if I were to consent to becoming your mistress after all?'

What? What in hell…?

Suddenly she'd tugged off her straw bonnet and tossed it to the floor again. He closed the door. That hat would be lucky to survive the day, thought Adam rather dazedly. Then she was sidling across the room to him and lifting her sweet face with its tempting rosebud mouth to his and—

Hell. She'd raised her arms to run her fingertips along his broad shoulders.

'Mrs Marchmain,' he began.

His voice was thick in his throat as her small hands tugged him closer. That delicate scent tickled his nose again—lavender soap, he guessed. He could feel the warmth now, of her tender body; her nearness was turning his blood to fire and making his pulse throb. He reached out his big hands to take hers and hold them away.

'I thought,' he grated at last, 'that you were going to repay me from your business.'

Her voice was husky. 'Perhaps I've had second thoughts.'

She was playing a mighty dangerous game. Adam swore under his breath; Jarvis had warned him she was a conniving minx, damn it, and Adam wasn't one to be toyed with. With a low growl—half of anger, half of lust—Adam pulled her to him and let his lips capture her soft mouth.

And Belle's world spun until she no longer knew if she was on her head or her heels. In this man's arms, she didn't much care either way.

Faced with that open door and his chilly dismissal, it had struck her most forcefully that—like a drowning seafarer—she couldn't afford to be choosy about her rescue options. Pay him back from her shop? Dear Lord, she'd no idea how much a flock of sheep cost; she *did* know that if this man wasn't going to show mercy she and her brother were sunk.

It wasn't as if she was a youthful, shrinking maiden. One by one the frantic thoughts raced through her brain. *Other women do this.* In fact, he assumed that was why she'd come to his hateful abode in the first place. *Other women use men of influence and wealth to get what they want— why shouldn't I?*

The trouble was that he didn't repel her as Jarvis did. Far from it. The instant his firm, demanding mouth started caressing hers, she forgot she was supposed to be in charge. She forgot he was her enemy. All she wanted was more.

The sweetness of his kiss pulsed through her veins. As his strong hands caressed her she could feel the heat of his body against hers; then he coaxed her lips apart and deliberately set about ravishing her mouth with his tongue. She could taste the maleness of him. He was filling her senses, branding her with shocking demands.

She'd meant to fake her response but, dear heaven, this was no pretence. Her hands instinctively curled tighter around his heavily muscled shoulders; somehow she could not get close enough to him. When he grasped her waist and hauled her against him, she felt his rock-hard arousal pressing against her stomach and it stopped her breathing. Stopped her thinking.

Her response was primeval and passionate. She plied her tongue in his mouth, tasting him, shuddering as he thrust his own tongue between her lips in measured response. She yearned to press her aching bosom closer to the hard wall of his chest, then gasped aloud because his hand, warm and strong, was cupping one desperately sensitive breast, his thumb teasing her stiffened nipple through the silk of her gown, rubbing it gently to and fro until she was crying out for more…

Then he drew away.

Belle swayed where she stood. Needing the warmth of his arms around her. Missing the heat of his hard male body.

He said levelly, 'This is an absurd situation, Mrs Marchmain, and both of us know it.'

She gazed up at him, imagining she saw a glint of concern in his dark grey eyes, but if so it was quickly gone. She felt as wretched as she'd ever felt in her life. 'Absurd? But, Mr Davenant,' she said with a forced smile, 'I was merely indicating that I'd had second thoughts about the offer you'd made earlier—'

'I was damned wrong to make that offer,' he broke in harshly. He was making for the door again, straightening his coat. 'Mrs Marchmain, please forget my proposition. You were foolish to come here alone, foolish to make yourself so vulnerable.'

She gazed at him, white-faced. 'But what about my brother, and…?'

'You can tell the young idiot he owes me nothing for my livestock,' Adam rapped out. 'The matter's dealt with. Finished.'

Belle drew back as if he'd hit her with a sledgehammer. 'So you've got your revenge,' she said steadily.

'What?' His hand had been on the door; now he swung round to her, his jaw set, his eyes ominously dark.

She shrugged and lifted her chin. 'I was desperate and you realised it. You've achieved my humiliation—that was what you wanted all the time, wasn't it?'

Adam said through gritted teeth, 'You misunderstand me.'

'On the contrary—' Belle's voice shook now '—I think I understand you only too well.' Not even Jarvis had made her feel as wretched as she did now.

She saw him utter some low expletive under his breath. Then: 'I'll call my carriage for you,' said Adam curtly, turning to the door again.

She looked distraught. 'I would prefer to walk. In fact—I insist on walking!'

He threw her one last, withering look. 'There's a fine line between independence and sheer stupidity. I repeat: I'll summon my carriage.'

As the luxurious coach moved off Belle was aware that the thunderclouds had passed overhead and once more the sun shone brightly in the late afternoon sky. She was still able to move, she was able to breathe. Yet it seemed as if nothing was working any more. It reminded her of how she'd felt when they came five years ago to tell her that her husband had died. The world went on, but for her nothing could be the same.

Belle was crushed and humiliated by what had just occurred, yet it was her fault for breaking all the rules—not just of civilised behaviour, but of survival. Davenant was a cruel man with massive power; she'd insulted him badly in Somerset and he'd not forgotten. Men like him never did.

Today she'd stupidly attacked him again and he'd swiftly resolved upon the most devastating revenge possible. Without pity he'd provoked her into the ultimate degradation of offering herself to him. In response he'd proved to her with lethal finality that it took only one touch of his firm lips for her to melt helplessly in his arms—then he told her he didn't want her after all.

It was done with utter and casual contempt, because all he really wanted was to be rid of her and her brother as swiftly as he could.

But—what would have happened if he *had* accepted her offer? If he'd carried on kissing her, and...

It simply didn't bear thinking about. She looked around at last, recoiling with a shudder from the rich velvet seats, the satin linings of this luxurious carriage. She'd rescued Edward from the threat of prison and her enemy had got his revenge in spectacular fashion. Her whole body still trembled from his wonderful caresses.

And she felt as wretched as she'd ever felt in her whole life.

Arriving back at her shop just before five, Belle slipped in through the back door, hoping to get upstairs and restore herself to some sort of calmness before joining Gabby in the shop.

But Edward was there, pacing the tiny office at the back with the door open. He sprang towards her as soon as he saw her.

'Well? How did it go with Davenant?' he said importantly. 'I have to set off back to Somerset tomorrow, to poor Charlotte, so I need to be sure that it's all sorted.'

Wearily Belle joined him and shut the door on them both. 'How did you know that I'd been to see him?'

'Oh, I called earlier and heard that Matt had borrowed a carriage for you. Did you twist Davenant round your little finger, sister mine?'

Actually, Edward, it was all rather a horrid surprise. I found out that I'd met him before. I let him kiss me. I made an utter and complete idiot of myself.

Belle gazed at her younger brother. What in

the name of goodness would he say, if he learned Davenant had suggested just now that she be his mistress—then changed his mind?

Edward would splutter. He would spout about their family honour and Davenant's lowly background, and, dear God, Belle couldn't face that just now.

'It is indeed all sorted,' she said tonelessly. 'He's agreed to forget about those sheep you stole.'

'I didn't—' he began.

Belle just looked at him and his voice trailed away. But being Edward, he quickly recovered. 'Big of him to say he'd forget it,' grumbled her brother, 'considering those sheep were on land that should by rights be mine!'

She whirled round on him. 'Edward. You put me in an almost impossible position, by telling me he paid you only two hundred guineas for that land, when, in fact, he paid you two thousand. How *could* you?'

He flushed slightly. 'Whatever, Belle, the fellow's no right to give himself airs.'

'That *fellow* could have put you in a debtors' gaol!'

'He said that?' Her brother's voice shook a little. She nodded. 'The vindictive, low-born wretch,' muttered Edward. 'By God, he'd better not go around dragging our good name in the mud.'

'*What* good name, Edward?' she said in utter weariness. 'For heaven's sake, what good name?'

Her brother fiddled uncomfortably with his high starched collar. She thought again of Adam Davenant's severe but fashionable clothes and for some stupid reason a huge ache rose in her throat.

'Well,' Edward went on, brushing a fleck of dust from his breeches, 'I'll leave you to it, then, with your shop, and all your flummery—such fun for you.'

'I work hard, Edward. Very hard.' She spoke tightly.

'Oh, I know. But you enjoy it, don't you? What else would you do with yourself? You've been a widow for five years, so clearly you've no desire for a doting husband and children.'

'Clearly not,' echoed Belle as she escorted her brother to the back door.

Edward turned to her one last time. The light from the doorway threw the old puckered scar on his forehead into sharp relief. 'I'm glad it's all sorted, at any rate,' he said. 'Oh, by the way, you won't tell Charlotte about any of this, will you? I knew I could rely on you, Belle!' He adjusted his coat, put on his new hat and hurried outside. She closed the door and leaned against it.

I must be the biggest fool in London.

Davenant had spoken of Edward in tones of utter contempt and God help her, she understood why. But to tell him exactly why she protected Edward and would always do so would cause her far more pain than merely to let Davenant go on thinking her a fool.

She wasn't a fool. She knew that what had oc-curred today at Davenant's house was a burden she'd bear for the rest of her life. She'd never for-get the coldness in his grey eyes as he'd put her away.

Gabby's voice penetrated her bleak thoughts. '*Madame. Madame*, are you all right?'

Belle scrubbed her eyes quickly with her hand-kerchief. 'Yes, I'm fine, Gabby. Did you want me?'

Gabby glanced along the corridor towards the shop. 'Well…I tried to deal with her at first. But—oh, *madame*, we have another complaint! It's Lady Jenkinson.'

Oh, no. Belle headed quickly for the shop with Gabby to see Lady Jenkinson pacing the floor with a cowed-looking maid in tow. The room was for the moment empty of other customers and it was as well.

'Disgraceful! Disgraceful, I call it!' Lady Jenkinson was declaring.

'Can I be of assistance, my lady?' asked Belle calmly. Gabby hovered anxiously.

'You most certainly can.' Lady Jenkinson swung round on her. 'You can give me my money back and an apology, too! You, girl—' she was addressing her own unfortunate maid '—stop lumping around like a good-for-nothing and show this hussy the result of her work.'

Belle felt every nerve tensing. 'I'm sure there's no need for wild insults, Lady Jenkinson.'

'Aye, and you think not, do you, madam? Well, look at *this*.' The maid was nervously spreading an apricot silk gown out on the counter and Lady Jenkinson started jabbing one fat, ring-smothered finger at it. Belle wished she'd followed her instinct when Lady Jenkinson first visited the shop and politely guided her towards another *modiste*, as far away as possible.

'Is there some kind of fault in the fabric?' Belle asked with forced calm. 'We usually check every length with the utmost care, but of course we can replace the panel...'

'No fault in the fabric, but in the sewing,'

screeched Lady Jenkinson. 'Look!' She was holding up a split seam in the skirt, displaying an opening that ran for a foot or more.

Belle did look at it, frowning. 'I'm so sorry. Of course, we can repair it as a priority, and perhaps in the meantime you would like to accept one of these silk scarves to make up for your trouble? This light peach one will match the gown perfectly, I think...'

'Now, don't you be thinking you can buy me off. I know your kind! My money back, if you please. And all my friends of the *ton*—Lady Jersey not least of them—will hear about this, you mark my words!'

Belle pressed her lips together and went for the key to her cash box. Gabby caught her eye and pulled a face. The money refund wasn't so much of a problem; the worst of it was that the hideous Lady Jenkinson really would take great pleasure in spreading news of her dissatisfaction all around the town.

Yet Lady Jenkinson had been almost obsequiously keen to be dressed by Belle. 'All my friends tell me you are quite the thing, Mrs Marchmain,' she'd gushed. So—why this sudden turn-around?

Gabby opened the door for her ladyship and bobbed her a tight curtsy. Then, as soon as the door was shut again, she turned to Belle and rolled her eyes.

'The cow,' Gabby declared. 'She must have been clumsy and torn it perhaps when she was climbing into her new town *cabriolet*...' Gabby mimicked Lady Jenkinson's mincing accent.

Belle smiled only briefly. 'Gabby, this wasn't an accident. The thread's been cut.'

'Cut?'

'Yes. Look.' Belle turned to where the apricot gown still lay on the counter. 'It's been cut so thoroughly—*here*, and *here*—that whoever did it has even nicked the fabric itself, with a sharp little pair of scissors.'

Gabby gasped. 'You're right. But why? Her ladyship absolutely loved the gown when she first tried it on!'

'Well, she's clearly changed her mind. Or perhaps one of her new friends was rude about the colour or style.'

'Impossible. She was so eager to be a client of yours, *madame*.'

'Things change rather rapidly in the world of fashion,' said Belle quietly.

For the moment, Belle's order books were full—but it would not take much for a business like hers, that depended on society's whim, to change overnight from minor success to a struggle for survival. Yet even that worry paled into insignificance in the face of the blow dealt to her today by Adam Davenant.

The hateful man had provoked her into offering herself to him. Had kissed her senseless—then turned her down. And every fibre of her being was throbbing rawly with the sheer, damned humiliation of it.

It's just your pride, she told herself bitterly. *Just your stupid pride that's hurt.*

In which case, she would get over her humiliation and forget all about that damnable man very quickly—wouldn't she?

Chapter Six

'Mr Davenant,' Adam's lawyer Turnbull pronounced in some amazement the next morning, 'your missing livestock were worth several hundred pounds. My dear sir, this was an act of deliberate theft, no doubting it!'

Adam had visited Turnbull's Aldwych office early, taking steps to erase the fact that he could have had young Edward Hathersleigh sent to prison.

'I've reason to assume it was an error on Hathersleigh's part,' said Adam. 'And I believe some of those sheep had strayed.'

'But your fences are inspected regularly, and your sheep were clearly marked—'

'They'd strayed,' Adam declared flatly. 'End of matter.'

He left Turnbull bemused. 'Never stops,' the lawyer muttered to his clerk. 'That man never stops.'

* * *

And indeed for the next few days Adam continued to be busy from dawn till dusk, meeting bankers and businessmen in a concentrated effort to make the very most of the fine Bath stone from the Sawle Down quarry. Finding a market would be no problem—London was awash with high-class building schemes like the grandiose Regent Street project being drawn up by the Prince and his friend the architect Nash.

But getting the stone to London was crucial and Adam knew everything depended on building his railway to the Avon canal, with its direct links to the Thames and thence to the capital. *Four miles.* That was the distance between the Sawle Down quarry and the canal, if he followed the obvious route past Midford. The first section of land was his and the next belonged to his ally Bartlett; no problem there.

But the last, crucial half-mile that led to the canal near Limpley Stoke crossed Jarvis's land. It was Jarvis's land, too, for at least a mile both up and down the canal. For Adam to take his railway route north meant making excavations that would be expensive as well as dangerous for his workers.

If Adam tried to avoid the barrier Jarvis presented by taking his route south, there'd be the expense not only of extra track laying, but of more land to be bought, from possibly unwilling landowners. Again and again he studied his maps alongside his chief engineer George Shipley, who'd come to London from Somerset for the sole purpose of helping Adam to devise a rail route.

But for the first time in his life Adam found his sharp brain wandering—to thoughts of an utterly provoking female called Belle Marchmain, who had come to him to plead in sheer desperation for her brother.

He felt nothing but contempt for Edward Hathersleigh. Hadn't Adam tried to help the young fool out already, by paying him far more for that land than it was worth? And Hathersleigh repaid him by lying about the price and stealing Adam's livestock! Yet still Hathersleigh went round boasting of his blue blood, convinced that the world owed him as much money as he wanted. Aristocrats like him certainly helped to explain the French Revolution.

And mere money didn't buy happiness; witness Adam's own parents' miserable marriage. Adam's mother had once brutally told him that had it not been for him and his brother, Freddy, she could have escaped the living hell of marriage to their father. A fine encouragement to wedlock and parenthood, that.

'Look at you, Adam,' Freddy would point out, laughing. 'You'll simply have to cave in to the fortune-hunters some day. You're twenty-nine years old, good-looking and filthy rich, but you've no wife yet, let alone an heir to pass it all on to.'

'So?' Adam had answered mildly. 'Thanks to your three strapping young sons, there's no danger whatsoever of our family line running out, Freddy. And it won't be long before you've more brats on the way, I shouldn't be surprised.'

Freddy's pleasant face had coloured with happiness. 'Well actually, Adam, since you've mentioned it, Louisa's into her third month, but we're keeping it quiet for now.'

Adam had patted his brother on the back. 'Delighted for you. Means I can continue to repel the fortune-hunters with a clear conscience.'

Freddy grinned. Freddy was always grinning these days, like a cat who'd got the cream. So damned happy, he and Louisa both, with their rural home in Surrey where their three boys, the oldest only seven, could roam happily around the countryside on their ponies.

That sort of life wasn't for Adam. The responsibility of the family inheritance—the estates, the businesses and all the people they employed—was his. Though he outwardly bore it lightly, it consumed the majority of his time. And—marriage? To some top-lofty daughter of a noble house who would for ever be remembering that she'd married beneath her rank? *Never.*

Once, in the school holidays when Adam was ten, he'd heard his parents arguing after some lavish party they'd given at Hathersleigh Manor.

'My friends feel sorry for me—do you know that?' his mother had bitterly declared. 'To be married to the son of a *miner.* My God, everyone laughs at your manners, at the way you speak—'

Adam was aware of his father replying in a low voice, of his mother speaking more shrilly now. 'Don't walk away when I'm talking to you! Where do you think you're going?'

Then Adam heard his father clearly. 'Anywhere. I'm going anywhere, to sleep in the stables if need be, to get away from you. Go off with one of your lovers, why the hell don't you?'

So much for wedding vows. Always, when some eligible female sidled up to him with marriage on her mind, Adam remembered his mother's shrill voice that night. He'd sworn to avoid commitment, and his usually careful choice of mistresses had so far served him well. But— *damn it*. That woman, Belle.

He'd accused her of coming to sell herself in return for her brother's debts; indeed, after Jarvis's insinuations it was a natural assumption to make. But things had gone disturbingly wrong. Firstly, she didn't seem like a woman for sale. And secondly, to put it quite simply, she'd found a way past Adam's rather formidable self-control.

She was beautiful—that he'd already acknowledged—and so luscious to hold that his loins still tightened at the memory of her soft, slender body crushed in his arms. She'd been delectable and melting as golden honey, and just as sweet to taste. It had taken a huge effort on his part to pull himself away and tell her his offer no longer stood. And she'd looked absolutely stricken.

A muscle clenched in his jaw as he remembered it. Again, any normal woman out to trick him would have archly referred to the fact that his arousal was still very much in evidence, and would have tried to coax him into even more intimate activity. But Belle Marchmain had backed away at his words of rejection as if he'd struck her.

And she'd told him she hated Jarvis. Told him

Jarvis had made an offer that she'd found obscene… Good grief, he'd found himself almost *apologising* for making his own offer to her in the first place!

Had she been right, to accuse him of deliberately punishing her for those insults she'd uttered at Sawle Down? Perhaps. And certainly as far as he was concerned his business with the Hathersleighs was concluded. He was damned if he was going to stoop to pursuing her feckless brother over a flock of sheep.

But—let Mrs Marchmain dwell on that kiss, because she'd revelled in it as much as he, no denying. Meanwhile it was time for Adam to find himself a new mistress and then, perhaps, he'd take her to buy a new gown or two from Mrs Marchmain's shop. Condescension, he'd found, was often the sweetest revenge possible.

A week after his encounter with Belle Marchmain Adam was hard at work by candlelight in the study of his Mayfair house. At ten he heard a knock on the door and his business secretary Bernard Lowell came in, laden with papers.

'Here are the letters you asked me to draft, Mr Davenant. And some bills for you to approve.'

Lowell put the letters on the table; Adam looked at them quickly.

'Thank you, Lowell. It looks as if you've done an excellent job as usual. Anything else?'

'Two documents need signing tonight. And…' Lowell hesitated. 'Have you seen any more of Mrs Marchmain since last week, sir?'

Adam sat back in his chair and gave his secretary all his attention. Lowell was a thin, mild-mannered clerk whose gentle voice and habit of blinking behind his spectacles tended to disguise the fact that he was sharply intelligent and utterly loyal. Lowell didn't ask a question like *that* without good reason.

'You used to know her family, didn't you, Lowell?'

'I grew up in Bath, sir, as you're aware, near to her family home. And I remember her—Miss Hathersleigh, she was then—as a young girl, always tearing around the countryside on a horse too big for her, though she didn't mind how many times she fell off. She's got pluck, that lady. But her husband died, didn't he, in the war?' Lowell shook his head. 'A blow indeed. I hear she's still single, though from what I remember she could have had her pick of the Bath gentlemen. Now, if I could just ask you to sign this final letter, Mr Davenant...'

Adam signed and handed it back. 'Have you any idea why she's not married again?'

'There was no obvious explanation, sir. I believe the proposals came from perfectly eligible gentlemen. It is just possible, I suppose, that she loved her husband and still mourns him...'

'Lowell.'

'Sir?'

'Does Mrs Marchmain *look* as if she's a grieving widow?'

'I have to admit she does not, sir.'

Exactly. Adam leaned back in his chair. 'Do you know her brother at all, Lowell?'

'Master Edward? I know he's a year or two younger than she is. And the young gentleman...' Lowell cleared his throat '...is unfortunately haphazard, I hear, when it comes to matters of money.'

Adam's fingers tightened round his pen. 'Explain, if you please.'

'Edward Hathersleigh has debts at White's, sir.'

'White's!'

'Indeed. His debts are to the club itself. They are substantial, I believe, for anyone, let alone for a man of straitened circumstances.'

Adam's breath caught in his throat. *The fool. The idiotic young fool.*

'He incurred the debts during his recent stay in town,' continued Lowell steadily. 'Because of his family circumstances—he is imminently, I understand, to enter the state of fatherhood—the proprietor of White's has granted him a month to pay those debts. But someone else is planning at this moment to buy them up.'

'Who?'

Lowell hesitated. 'Lord Jarvis, sir.'

Adam heard the big clock ticking out in the hall, but there was no other sound in the whole of this house. At last he said, 'How much does Hathersleigh owe at White's?'

'In the region of five thousand guineas, I believe.'

Slowly Adam leaned back in his chair. 'Lowell,' he said, 'I'd like you to go there now and buy up that debt in my name.'

Lowell blinked just once. 'Buy it up, sir. Yes. Of course.'

Adam might as well have been telling him to pay for the weekly delivery of coal.

When Adam strolled into his club on St James's Street at three o'clock the next afternoon, he saw

Lord Rupert Jarvis studying stock prices in *The Times*. On spotting Adam, he got languidly to his feet.

'So you wanted a meeting,' said Jarvis, a thin smile playing around his lips. 'But I'm not going to change my mind, you know, about letting you have my land for your railway.'

He sat down and Adam also eased himself into a chair. 'Not even you can halt the future, Jarvis. And some day your horses and carriages will seem as antiquated as the ox or the coracle.'

Jarvis poured them both brandy. 'Horses have been with us for centuries, Davenant, and will be with us for centuries more. Your damned new-fangled steam engines will blow themselves to bits within months.'

Adam gazed at him thoughtfully. Rupert Jarvis had once had a wife, but she'd died some years ago—a poor little thing, she'd always looked terrified. Adam said softly, 'I think you've already made your views on my railway perfectly clear, Jarvis. I've come to talk about something else. Your connection to the lady who visited my house on the day of our last encounter. Mrs Belle Marchmain.'

Jarvis looked startled, then smiled. 'Her?' He steepled his fingers. 'Ah, she's selling herself in her own way, flaunting herself round town in her gaudy clothes. What's she on the hunt for but a damned protector? Though she's choosy. She wants someone well born and rich, but she had the sheer arrogance to turn me down, Davenant!'

Just then a waiter brought the meal Jarvis had ordered and Jarvis started to attack his beef steak with greedy relish. 'You eating here, or not?'

Adam said, 'I'm not. But I'd like to know why you were trying to buy up her brother's debts at White's.'

Jarvis's head shot up from his food. 'Heard about that, have you? Yes, young Hathersleigh's got himself into a fine mess—and my thinking is *this*. I buy up Edward Hathersleigh's gambling debts—they've given him a month, I hear, but he hasn't a hope in hell of repaying them—and I then make it plain to him that he owes me *nothing* providing he sends his pretty sister in my direction.'

'But you've already told me you made her an offer and she turned you down.'

Jarvis put down his knife and fork and chuckled. 'This time, thanks to her brother's debts, she'll have no choice. I'm going to bed her whether she likes it or not. Spread stories about her until she's got little option, by the time I've finished with her, other than to sell herself on the street...'

'Before you get too carried away,' Adam interrupted, 'I'm afraid you're just a little too late.'

Jarvis frowned. 'Late? What the devil do you mean? I'm going round to White's later this afternoon—I've an appointment!'

'Then you'd better cancel it. Because *I've* bought up Hathersleigh's gambling debts.'

Jarvis's face turned red, then white. 'Why in hell—?'

Adam shrugged. 'A whim. A fancy.'

'Sell them to me.'

'Can you give me one good reason why I should?'

'Because I'll pay you double the sum.'

'I don't want your money. I want your land, Jarvis.'

Jarvis leaned back in his chair, breathing heavily. 'Give me the woman and you get it.'

Adam was very still.

'Or,' went on Jarvis, 'let's think this through, shall we?' He poured himself more brandy. 'I know that she loathes me. But *you*, now, Davenant. You can twist any woman round your little finger... I've got an idea.' A reptilian smile flickered round his thin lips. '*You* will have to do what I was going to do to that damned woman.'

Jarvis leaned forwards, wagging his finger; Adam realised he was more than a little inebriated. 'You'll have to enlighten me, Lord Jarvis,' Adam drawled.

'I mean exactly what I said. You, Davenant, have got the Marchmain woman and her brother utterly in your power thanks to that debt, haven't you? I also assume you bear neither of them any kindness?'

'About as much as either of them would show to me,' said Adam flatly.

Jarvis nodded. 'Damn it, I *did* want her, badly. Who wouldn't? But it strikes me she could be hellish difficult, that Marchmain woman, and I've got a far better notion. *You* do it, Davenant.' Jarvis swigged back another mouthful of brandy. 'Yes, you bed the woman, then ditch her—and I'll give you all the land you want.'

The club was filling up. A group of men were talking noisily nearby about a new opera singer who'd caught everyone's fancy at Sadler's Wells, but Adam was focused on no one, nothing but Jarvis.

Adam said evenly, 'An interesting proposal.

But I'd like to think you were sober, Lord Jarvis, when you made it.'

Jarvis clenched his fist and thumped it on the table defiantly. 'Never more so, believe me. We'll get it written up. We'll do this *properly*. What do you say? Oh, I'd have enjoyed taking the woman down a peg or two myself, but on thinking about it, it would give me just as much satisfaction to see her with her fancy airs in thrall to *you*, because...'

His voice trailed away. His pale eyes gleamed. Adam could have finished that sentence for him.

Because you're Miner Tom's grandson. And Mrs Belle Marchmain rates herself above the likes of you.

Adam said nothing. Jarvis was speaking again. 'Another idea. On second thoughts, Davenant, perhaps your merely bedding her isn't enough.'

Adam waited, not a muscle of his face betraying any flicker of emotion. Jarvis, on the other hand, was agitated, toying with the brandy bottle, with his half-empty plate. At last he slapped his hand on the table.

'Betrothal!' he exclaimed. 'That's it! I want you to get her to agree to a betrothal with you. Then you'll jilt her publicly, Davenant—accuse her of something obnoxious, rutting with one of your servants, perhaps—so the whole of society will mock her humiliation. And after that—I'll let you have all the land you need for your blasted railway.'

Adam pushed back his chair and stood up. Jarvis became flushed with anger. 'You're not turning me down, damn it?'

'Far from it.' Adam gave him a chilly smile. 'I'm going to find someone to witness our agreement, Lord Jarvis.'

Within a short space of time Adam had written out two copies of that agreement in the club's library, with Jarvis eyeing every word over his shoulder. After that it was a simple matter of finding a mutual acquaintance—the uncurious Sir Gareth Blakeley—to witness their signatures on both documents while the contents were hidden from him; such arrangements were commonplace amidst London's clubs. Jarvis left with his own copy, but after he'd gone Adam stayed there in the seclusion of the library.

It was a game, Adam reminded himself. Yes, this was just another episode in the long game he'd played all his life, with every move finely calculated to win. Adam wanted his railway and Belle Marchmain was always going to be the loser one way or another. And didn't she deserve everything that was coming to her?

She despised him. She'd insulted him to kingdom come. She gave herself such airs, yet she'd swiftly offered to warm his bed in exchange for him forgetting the sheep business.

Well, now he was going to offer her marriage— or betrothal, to be more precise; he only had to remind her of her brother's debts to have her completely in his power. Then, once he'd got her to accept his proposal of marriage, he'd drop her in a matter of weeks.

Humiliate her, Jarvis had specified. Pictures suddenly seared his mind of the defiant widow melting in his arms. Of her soft, rosy lips parting beneath his questing tongue, her body sweetly pliant against his... No doubt about it, Belle Marchmain still puzzled him. She'd struck him as vulnerable. Inexperienced, even.

Or very, very clever. And either way, what did it matter to him? It was a case of weighing up the affairs of that arrogant, conceited young fool Hathersleigh and his proud sister against the success of the massive future he envisaged for the quarry. It wasn't just a matter of pure financial gain either—that railway would create jobs and save lives, no doubt about it.

Adam left at last, with the signed agreement folded away in his pocket. It looked as if the next phase of the game was about to begin.

Chapter Seven

'*Pardieu, madame*, what is wrong with you?' Gabby teased merrily when Belle dropped her scissors for the third time. 'Best let me cut that ottoman silk, at four shillings the yard.'

It was two weeks since Belle's disastrous visit to Davenant's house, and now Belle had something else to worry about. Though the Strand was as full of shoppers as ever, her shop was virtually empty.

Gabby tried to reassure her. 'We are not as busy as we have been, perhaps—but do not forget that we had an extremely large order from Lady Tindall and her two daughters last week.'

They were the exception, thought Belle. Whatever Gabby said, their shop's order book should be much fuller than this. And what really worried her was that there had been another complaint

only yesterday. A customer had come in to say
that her new gown was an appalling fit.

'The tightness around my arms almost made
me faint,' the customer had declared. 'I am going
to tell all my friends *never* to use this shop again.
My money back, if you please!'

Gabby was furious. 'She lies through her teeth.
Look at this beautiful gown—the bodice has
been taken apart and sewn up again—it was
never *comme ça* when it left our shop. You should
have argued with her!'

But Belle's suspicions were growing that this
was a concerted attempt to ruin her business; so
now, as she worked with Gabby on Lady Tindall's ballgown, she said nothing more, but ap-
plied extra care to cutting the precious silk…
and tried to put the sardonic face of the hateful
Mr Davenant firmly from her mind.

Easier said than done. Again and again the
memory of her visit to him racked her. By proposing that she be his mistress then coldly withdrawing his offer, he'd made her feel quite sick
with humiliation.

He despised her, no doubt whatsoever about
that. He would by now have completely forgotten the incident and Belle only wished she could
do the same. But every time a smart carriage

rolled by outside in the Strand, she wondered if he was inside. At night it was worse, for she couldn't stop thinking about him. She couldn't forget his hands, his strong fingers, the way they had touched her. The way his hard lips and his tongue's possession had sent a surge of dark pleasure to every nerve ending.

Davenant's firm mouth on hers had dragged all semblance of sense from her body, implanting instead a sweet languor that flooded her veins. His caressing hands had urged her to surrender to the sensual and deliberately teasing strokes of his tongue and, to her eternal shame, it was he who'd drawn away, not she. Heat surged through her at the memory.

She'd expressed her scorn for his low birth, but he'd had enough of *her*, quite clearly. And why not, when his conquests of society beauties were legendary? When some of England's most aristocratic families were desperate to throw their marriageable daughters in his path?

His casual cancelling of the business of the sheep had underlined his contempt for her. That, as far as Mr Adam Davenant was concerned, was the end of it.

But it was very much *not* the end for Belle.

Somehow she was going to get together the

money to pay him back for those sheep. Last night she'd resolved to tell Edward about her decision—but a letter from Edward had arrived this morning. The writing was haphazard and scratchy; several words had been crossed out.

My dear Belle, Charlotte has given birth to a baby boy. But you will be grieved to hear that the infant is extremely frail; I do not like to think what will happen if poor Charlotte loses this child...

Belle's hands had been shaking by the time she put the letter down. After two miscarriages, Charlotte had at last given birth to a living child—but this one might bring her even more grief than those earlier tragedies. Belle could imagine only too well the all-night vigils, the grave voices of the doctor and nurse, the scents of the sick room.

Great though the differences were between her and her brother, she could scarcely bear to think of the sorrow of that vulnerable little household.

'But I've said at least twenty times, we need another pleat of silk here— Oh, *madame*. Why don't you take a walk in the fresh air, down to the park perhaps?' Gabby gave a little sigh. 'As you were saying, we're not exactly busy— *Dieu!*'

Something out in the street had caught Gabby's

keen eye and she hurried to the bow window. 'There's a carriage pulling up outside. It's being driven by the most wonderful-looking man...'

Belle sprang to the window to join her. *Oh, horrors.*

Gabby's wonderful man was letting himself down from the seat of a plain but expensive curricle, while his groom held the beautiful black horses. *Adam Davenant.*

Her heart was thudding sickly. Why was he here? Had he changed his mind, about those blasted sheep? Mentally she counted up the money she'd got together to pay him back. *Not enough. Not nearly enough.*

Perhaps they could come to some agreement. But wasn't 'an agreement' exactly what he'd suggested—then withdrawn? Oh, drat the man. Shivers ran up and down her spine.

She could see through the window that he was walking—no, striding—towards her shop door. A man with a figure like his didn't just *walk* anywhere. Belle found she was gripping her scissors defensively. 'Will you go out to him, please, Gabby, and find out what he wants?'

Gabby, wide-eyed, nodded and hurried out; seconds later she was back, her face alight with excitement.

'*Madame*, his name is Monsieur Davenant. He says to tell you that he knows you're in, he saw you through the window. He asks would you come out for a drive with him, in the park, because there are some matters you need to discuss.'

For a second Belle's blood froze in her veins. 'Tell Mr Davenant we have nothing to discuss, Gabby. Tell him a drive in the park is not at all convenient.'

Once more Gabby dashed out and in again. '*Madame*, he says he will stand outside on the pavement until it *is* convenient. Till nightfall if need be!'

And he damn well would. Belle bit her lip in frustration as Gabby rattled on, 'Oh, *madame*, I have heard about Monsieur Davenant. The fashionable ladies of the town, they fight to be his mistress—'

Perhaps a temporary, a tactical surrender was her only option. 'Please tell him,' Belle cut in tartly, 'that given the unexpected pleasure of his invitation, I'm sure Mr Davenant will quite understand that I need to get changed into something—*appropriate.*'

Over twenty minutes later Belle came down the stairs and Gabby's eyes opened wide with awe.

'*Madame.* Are you sure?'

Belle looked down at herself, a dangerous light in her eyes. 'This gown is striking, Gabby, don't you think?'

'But you made it for—someone else! For Mrs Sherville, who is not known, *madame*, for her subtlety in her manner of dressing!'

'*Absolutely* not,' agreed Belle. Harriet Sherville was, in fact, a well-known actress and courtesan. 'But the lady in question hasn't paid us for her last two outfits yet, so I've decided I shall wear this one myself.'

In Belle's eyes glittered a steely determination. Gabby opened her mouth to speak, then, thinking better of it, swallowed and hurried to open the door for her.

Belle was clad in a military-style carriage gown of crimson lutestring. Gold-braid frogging, lavish with knots and loops, adorned it from collar to toe. The crimson collar was high, emphasising her clear complexion; the stiffened bodice cupped her bosom tightly—and was slashed to reveal a tempting display of creamy cleavage.

If this gown embarrassed Adam Davenant, then so much the better. As a finishing touch Belle set on her dark curls a crimson silk shako, with one long gold feather trailing to her shoulder.

Gabby looked stunned. *Thank you, Harriet Sherville*, muttered Belle under her breath. And swept out.

Mr Davenant was looking at his watch.

She expected him to take one glance at her and send her back to get changed again. Or to utter some pithy insult and drive off in his fancy curricle.

He did neither. Instead his dark eyebrow arched. 'Almost worth the wait,' he remarked casually.

Belle fastened her gold-satin reticule with something of a snap. 'I thought I might make you think twice another time, Mr Davenant, before issuing your peremptory summons.'

'Then I'm afraid you've failed,' he said. 'You're making me think I should have treated myself to your company earlier.'

Belle stared at him in astonishment. *Drat the man.* She glanced down and caught sight of her own daring cleavage. Touched, unthinking, her red hat with its trailing feather. 'You mean—you approve of what I'm wearing?'

'I like it very much. Though I'd rather you'd not taken so long over it all.'

'Oh, it's a woman's privilege, you know, to be as late as she chooses.'

'Not at the expense of my horses. My groom's

had to unharness them and walk them up and down the Strand for almost half an hour.'

She bit her lip. Damn. She didn't mind making *him* suffer, but his horses were a different matter. She smiled sweetly up at him. 'Then perhaps on *another* occasion you might do me the honour of giving me a little more notice of your intentions.' Her smile vanished. 'My time is valuable, Mr Davenant. I hope you have good reason for this intrusion.'

He leaned closer—unsettlingly closer. Oh, Lord, her cleavage—he'd be able to see right down... 'I do,' he said softly. 'But I would prefer to discuss the matter in the park. We need to talk. Please climb up.'

He was holding out his hand. 'The park? Mr Davenant, you must know what people will think!'

'People will do more than think, if they see us together.' His eyes assessed her briefly. 'They will talk a great deal about us. And—it might be a good idea to look as if we're enjoying one another's company.'

'Enjoy?' She huffed with indignation. 'You are jesting.'

'Then *pretend* to enjoy being at my side. It's in your best interests, I assure you.'

She tossed her head, setting that long golden feather a-quiver. 'Very well. I'm told I'm quite good at acting.'

Ouch, Adam acknowledged. He helped her up—unable to resist relishing the slenderness of her waist—but he did try not to look at her *décolletage*. Then he told his groom to go and buy himself a pint of ale at the Red Lion nearby.

'Very well, guv'nor.' The little groom, who'd privately been admiring Mrs Marchmain's *décolletage* very much and was familiar with his master's methods of telling him his presence wasn't required, touched his hat cheerfully. 'A pint of best, then I'll find me own way back, eh? You enjoy your drive, now!'

Adam set off at a smart pace, but kept one eye on his companion to make sure she wasn't about to leap off, or perhaps stab him with those sewing scissors he'd seen her clutching rather desperately inside her shop.

If she'd hoped to deter him with that outfit, she was failing abysmally. Once you ignored the violent colour—which actually, he liked, he was fed up with insipid pale muslins—the neat military style rather deliciously hugged the alluring contours of her figure. And though she was clearly having second thoughts about the low neckline—she kept tugging the gold-braided edges of the gown together—the garment was really being remarkably stubborn and insisted on parting to display a tantalising glimpse of her smooth, rounded breasts.

She was nervous, he thought suddenly. Nervous, and also quite delectable. He found himself remembering how that pink mouth had tasted sweet and soft beneath his own...

Adam arrested his burgeoning desire rather grimly and concentrated on the traffic.

Time for business.

Belle sat upright at his side, almost shaking with fury and consternation. *Why?* Why had he sought out her company when he'd told her, at his Mayfair house, that they need never see each other again?

But—it was such a lovely day, and Hyde Park looked so beautiful. As Adam swung his carriage into the fashionable cavalcade, several of the gentry, riding fine horses or driving open carriages, nodded and smiled to Adam, though when they noted that he wasn't alone, many a head was twisted again in blatant curiosity.

The women watched Adam, too, with acquisitive glances; Belle herself couldn't resist stealing a look at her handsome companion as he concentrated on tooling his splendid horses, couldn't help but feel her breath catching in her throat. *Oh, my.*

She'd already noticed he was wearing a dark-grey coat that was unostentatious, but so well fitted that there was always a disturbing sense of his powerful male body beneath the elegant finery. His thighs, encased in skintight buckskins, were iron-hard with muscle—her own legs had brushed against them inadvertently as he seated himself and the heat had flared in her veins just at that touch. He held the reins without gloves; she saw that his hands were strong and firm and lightly tanned, with long, well-manicured fingers...

Stop it, Belle, you fool. She pushed the very physical reality of Mr Adam Davenant to the back of her mind to concentrate on the question—why had he talked just now, in a way that sent shivers down her spine, about the need for them to be seen in public together?

At their last meeting this man—whose grandfather began life as a penniless miner!—couldn't have made it plainer that he despised her thoroughly. She felt cold beneath her ridiculous fin-ery. *So what did he want from her now?*

Clearly he intended to keep her waiting. He pulled up to talk briefly to some friends of his who were on horseback. Belle sat very primly, but she was aware that the men were eyeing her with frank appreciation. Wearing this startling red outfit was a huge mistake. She'd hoped to embarrass Davenant, but had simply succeeded in embarrassing herself.

Her second mistake was to have agreed to this *at all.*

'Well, Mr Davenant,' she said with icy polite-ness once his friends had gone, 'it will soon be all round town that I'm enjoying the dubious plea-sure of your company—but I think we were both of us quite clear at our last meeting that this was something neither of us wanted. As to Edward and the unfortunate matter of the sheep—'

'His livestock thievery,' interrupted Davenant obligingly.

Her teeth clenched. 'It was a matter of only a few dozen, I believe!'

'Ah, yes. A hanging offence, merely,' he said politely.

The colour drained from her cheeks. *'Anyway,'* Belle pressed on, tilting her chin, 'I have decided the situation is far from acceptable to me and I'm well on my way to getting the necessary sum to pay you back.'

He turned to gaze at her. First at her cleavage—for long enough to make her cheeks flame—then at her face. Something in those hooded grey eyes made her stomach quail within her. 'Mrs Marchmain, one of the things I most respect about you is your honesty. Don't let me down. I have, in fact, heard that you've rather desperately been trying to raise money in the last day or so.'

'Y-you've heard? But how?'

'A single woman wearing outrageous clothes and trailing round London's banks inevitably stirs up gossip. I must say, I was a little surprised. I thought—in fact, you told me quite forthrightly—that your dressmaking business was doing well.'

'Oh, it *is*,' Belle said blithely. 'We're simply going through a temporary quiet spell.'

'I see. I gather,' he went on calmly, 'that you've had no success in your efforts to borrow money—otherwise you'd by now have thrust the filthy lucre in my face and told me to go to the very devil.'

She gazed at him, stricken. Adam staunched any sneaking pity for the flamboyant little widow dressed in military red and went on, 'I thought I made it quite clear I do not *wish* to be repaid for those damned sheep. Especially as they were stolen by your brother, who, if he had an ounce of your spirit, would be bowing his head in shame for having sent his sister to me to plead for him.'

'He did not *ask* me to—'

'Then why?' he asked sharply. 'Why trouble to defend such a weak, shallow fool?'

She said tightly, 'Do you have to make everything so hateful, Mr Davenant?'

'I like to understand situations and people,' he rapped out. 'I flatter myself that I have some skill. But one thing about you puzzles me mightily, Mrs Marchmain. Your refusal to see your brother for what he is.'

She turned sideways to face him, and bestowed on him a glittering smile. 'La, Mr Davenant,' she simpered in a Somerset accent. 'How wonderful it would be, to find oneself as all-seeing as you!' Her green eyes glittered; her cheeks were now extremely pale. Slowly, deliberately, she took off her bright red shako with its single trailing feather and dropped it over the side of the carriage. 'Oh, dear,' she said sweetly. 'I seem to have lost my hat. Would you retrieve it for me?'

Frowning, he drew his black horses to a halt, looped the reins and jumped down.

The minute he bent to pick up her hat, Belle slid across into the driver's seat to take up the ribbons. 'Hup!' she called. The horses trotted off smartly. She heard his shouts.

She seethed. *Abominable, hateful man to insult her so! Serve him right if she just left him there.* She tooled on a little, expertly holding the reins. Gentlemen she didn't know pulled up their horses and stared at her in open-mouthed admiration; she was hardly missable in Mrs Sherville's outrageous outfit. She nodded and smiled at them. By God, she would make Adam Davenant regret his high-handedness.

She made a skilful manoeuvre and returned to him at last, holding his mettlesome horses in a neat walk. He was just standing there, watching. No hint of a smile touched his finely shaped mouth.

She pulled up and slid sideways into her own seat. Swinging himself aboard, he handed her the shako without a word, took the reins and sent the horses on at a rather smart trot that nearly threw her off.

He said at last, in a decidedly cool voice, 'That wasn't a bad display. But you were holding the left rein a little too tightly—you should have made adjustments for the longer step of the leading wheeler.' He was irate, she could see. There was something about the set of his jaw that made her tremble a little inside.

No. Don't be afraid, Belle. That's the worst thing you can possibly do, you fool, with a man of his kind. At least—don't let him see *that you're afraid.*

She settled her bright red hat back upon her curls and tilted her chin defiantly. 'Were you scared that I might fall off?'

He turned to her, his eyes iron-hard. 'No. But I *was* afraid you might damage my horses.'

She did not reply, but clenched her hands together very tightly. When Adam turned to look at her he saw she was holding her head as high as ever, but—the devil, was that a glint of tears in her eyes?

He cleared his throat and looked straight ahead. 'I have come to offer you a new proposal, Mrs Marchmain.'

Her heart filled with dread.

'I thought we'd been through this,' she said carefully. 'You asked me to be your mistress. But when I agreed you told me you'd changed your mind.'

She kept her voice steady. But the humiliation of that day at his house—the memory of his kiss, to which she'd so raptly surrendered—was still an unhealed wound.

'This is different,' he announced.

'Oh?' She smiled up at him sweetly. 'You'll forgive me if I tell you that *any* kind of proposal from you, Mr Davenant, is unlikely to be received by me with rapture.'

'You'll at least hear me out, I hope. I've been thinking. You've referred often enough to my lowly background.'

She hissed in a sharp breath.

'You, on the contrary,' he pressed on ruthlessly, 'are related to a duke. And I've been told on many occasions that I should make a match into the aristocracy.'

'I hardly see why you're troubling to inform me of your matrimonial plans, Mr Davenant.' *Though I feel heartily sorry for the woman of your choice*, she added with feeling under her breath.

'Don't you?' He turned to her and raised an eyebrow. 'I've been thinking, believe it or not, that the great-niece of a duke might just suit my purpose.'

Belle could hardly speak. 'If this is your idea of a jest...'

'Not at all. Last time, at my house, we talked somewhat unsuccessfully about you paying for your brother's folly by becoming my mistress. This time, Mrs Marchmain—I'm suggesting a betrothal.'

Now the colour really did drain from Belle's cheeks; in fact, her world spun round. 'A betrothal? With *me*? You cannot be serious!'

He shrugged. 'Why not? You're penniless but blue-blooded. I'm a miner's grandson and rich. A good joke, isn't it?' He glanced at her—to check, perhaps, that she wasn't about to jump off his moving carriage and flee his detestable presence.

She'd whirled on him. 'Your joke fails to amuse me. And anyway, what could I possibly offer *you*, Mr Davenant? You talk of my blue blood, but I know how very little that counts with you!'

'You underestimate yourself, Mrs Marchmain. You could, in fact, be very useful to me.'

'How?'

'I'm only talking about a temporary betrothal— a matter of a month or two. You'll be well aware that during the next few weeks the London Season will reach its height, which is a matter of great inconvenience to me, since to be honest I can't stand the insipid heiresses who are thrown in my path day and night.'

'Leave London,' Belle said flatly.

'I can't. I have vital business here, which involves meetings with lawyers, investors and London bankers. I also have to socialise, or appear extremely rude. But I need a respite from the fortune-hunters, and a convenient fiancée would serve the purpose admirably. During that time you would, of course, enjoy the benefits of my protection as well as my money.'

Belle burst out, '*No.* This is ridiculous. To pretend to be betrothed to you—it's *unthinkable!*'

Too late she saw the dangerous spark in his eyes. 'I have choices, but you don't,' he said abruptly. 'Were you aware that your brother gambled?'

He saw the colour drain from her cheeks. 'Yes, but that was long ago...'

'Not long ago at all. During his recent stay in London, he ran up large debts at White's.'

'No. Please, this cannot be true.'

The look, the unguarded look on her face as she turned to him with such dismay in those wide, dark-lashed eyes... Adam felt, not for the first time in this woman's presence, a sense of utter disquiet. 'Your brother,' he proceeded ruthlessly, 'has debts to the tune of five thousand guineas.'

'Five *thousand*...'

'But,' went on Adam remorselessly, 'I have bought them up.'

'You have bought—' *No. Please, no.*

Adam wondered if she would spend the rest of the afternoon echoing his words. But after that she became so still, so frozen that for a few moments he wondered if she would ever speak again.

Belle felt that the park was whirling around her. That she was clinging on to reality only by a thread. She said at last, very quietly, 'I know, Mr Davenant, that you cannot have purchased my brother's debts out of any sense of duty, or liking. I can only assume you have done this to further my family's humiliation.' She cleared her throat. 'No doubt you expect me to promise to pay you back. But I fear that such a sum is beyond me or my brother, for the present at least...'

'I've already explained,' he said without expression, 'how you can pay me back, Mrs March-main.'

'You—you have?'

'Yes. I will consider your brother's debts can-

celled if you do as I asked and agree to a betrothal.'

The colour drained from her face; she looked
suddenly fragile.

They'd entered a quieter area of the park, where
trees sheltered them from the general throng. She
realised he was pulling his horses to a halt. He
gazed down at her, his eyes slate-grey, his mouth
a thin line. 'I will try not to make your new position too detestable for you, Mrs Marchmain,' he
went on. 'But I'd like you to appear in public as
my fiancée, until mid-July when society retreats
to the country. I think you're as aware as I am
that such an arrangement can be easily ended.'

Oh, he would enjoy discarding her. Clever. So
clever.

She said, at last, 'Am I going to be punished for
ever, Mr Davenant, for those comments I made
about you on Sawle Down?'

He shrugged. 'Punishment? Call it that if you
like, but it's your chance to ensure I'll not serve
notice on your brother for his debts. Do you or
do you not accept?'

Oh, God. What choice did she have? She felt
dizzy and sick. She twisted the ring she wore and
drew a deep, deep breath. 'I fear you will find

you have got yourself a bad bargain, Mr Davenant,' she answered quietly.

He was silent a moment. Then: 'I'll take you home, Mrs Marchmain' was all he said.

Chapter Eight

All the way back from Hyde Park to the Strand Adam had been aware of a restless tension simmering inside his powerful body. This woman was, quite frankly, turning his hitherto well-organised life upside down.

It wasn't just that she was strikingly attractive—he'd known that from the start. It wasn't just her outfit, that ridiculous military-red affair devised to put her breasts almost on full display. It was—everything. Her clothes, her dark curls, her figure—all combined in some incredible allure that made every man in the park snap his head round and stare after her with pure lust.

Adam was accustomed to mere beauty. The difference with Mrs Marchmain was that she was defiant—and vulnerable. She was a twenty-seven-year-old widow, a woman who had lost her husband in the cruel war, yet survived on her own with some success. A woman who despised him. But he felt himself aching to hold her, to protect her... *Face it, Adam, you long to get her in your bed and kiss every inch of her.*

Damn. He glanced down at her as the traffic at the corner of Bedford Street came to a standstill and saw how the bodice of that outrageous crimson dress had slipped apart again, showing the delicious upper curve of her breasts. Thanks to the motion of the curricle her slender legs beneath her gown kept unavoidably brushing his; he couldn't help noticing how some loose curls of her raven-black hair had escaped from her damned hat, trailing down the soft nape of her neck just where he'd like to place his lips...

She must realise the effect she had on any normal red-blooded male. Yet her name had never been associated with any man's since her widowhood; his secretary Lowell had told him so. Lowell had even suggested that she had loved her husband.

Adam had scornfully rejected the notion. Hadn't Jarvis said she was out for what she could get? Hadn't Mrs Marchmain herself offered her services to him, in return for those blasted sheep her brother had stolen?

He'd pulled the horses up a short way from her

shop because a delivery dray made it impossible for him to draw up outside. 'Will you be all right if I set you down here?' he asked curtly.

She was clearly endeavouring to pull that gown together again. She said, in a voice that sounded more than a little distraught, 'Mr Davenant, I really think you ought to know that I am completely lacking in what—in what I realise you will require from me.'

'What are you talking about?'

She jerked her head up. 'I mean in the matters of the bedchamber.'

No. Was that another tear shining in the corner of her eye? Was this all part of her act? Adam offered her his pristine handkerchief as the disturbing urge to put his arm round her and simply offer her comfort unfurled again in his gut. *Stop it.* He said, 'I should, I think, have stressed from the very beginning that *you* will dictate the nature and the pace of our relationship, Mrs Marchmain.'

'What?' She was turning, white-faced, to look up at him.

'People will assume, of course,' he went on, his voice perfectly calm, 'that our relationship is an intimate one.'

She dropped his handkerchief.

'But their assumptions will be wrong,' Adam went on imperturbably, 'because you will *not* share my bed. Unless you choose to, of course.'

He wasn't even looking at her now, but was staring straight ahead. Belle felt her stomach pitch. *Oh, God. All this. Why?*

Because she'd insulted him quite lethally—and her brother had offered him the weapon of revenge that Davenant had probably been looking for ever since. She straightened her bonnet and uttered a light laugh. 'La, Mr Davenant, so you're not even going to pretend to be seduced by my charms? I swear, you put me to the blush!'

He turned to her and said, 'In the eyes of the general public, I'll play the perfect suitor, believe me.' He lifted his hand and very, very gently stroked the pad of his blunt forefinger across the smooth velvet of her cheek and down to her full lower lip. Belle hadn't known that a simple touch could be so sensuous.

She jerked her head away to avoid that intimate caress, but all she did was present him with the opportunity to trail his hand across the nape of her neck, his fingers briefly massaging her tender skin there in a way that sent shivers of incredible warmth fluttering through her veins to pool at the very pit of her abdomen.

She pulled away again and tugged her foolish gold-trimmed crimson gown tighter to stop him seeing how her breasts, with their tautening nipples, betrayed her body's treacherous reaction to his sinuous caress.

To this devilish man's touch. To his mere *touch*. And he knew. Dear God, she felt sick with shame. He was watching her calmly like a hunter preparing to strike. Her pulse still raced tumultuously; her ribs ached with the need for air. He said, 'I repeat: I will expect nothing of you that you're not prepared to give, Mrs Marchmain.'

She moistened her dry mouth and answered, 'You may be quite sure I shall never freely offer you anything at all that I value, Mr Davenant. May I go now?'

But he wasn't quite finished with her yet. 'One last thing,' he put in. 'While you are—in name at least—my bride-to-be, I would prefer you not to live at your shop.'

That was straightforward. 'My shop is my life!' Belle cried. 'And I will need it, for when this ridiculous—*arrangement* is at an end!'

'I know that. But as my prospective wife I think you'll agree that for you to live there would not be fitting.'

This, from Miner Tom's grandson. She clenched

her jaw. 'You surely cannot expect me to live with *you*?'

'I haven't asked you to,' he said cuttingly. 'But I have a house in Bruton Street that I think would suit the purpose. I would expect you to reside there and attend social functions with me for the remainder of the Season. After all, we have to make this convincing, don't we?'

He helped her out and she couldn't reply, because she wasn't able to. *Why was he doing this?* She somehow reached her shop, holding her head high as she negotiated the jostling crowds.

But inwardly she was shaking—because she guessed she knew the answer to her unspoken question. Why was he doing this? Because, quite simply, he was out to break her.

Adam drove thoughtfully away, the first part of his mission accomplished. He would announce their betrothal, then as soon as possible end it; Jarvis would be satisfied and Belle Marchmain would be a target for the gossips all over town and beyond.

She deserved nothing less for the insults she'd hurled at him. Meanwhile he'd saved her brother from ruin, hadn't he? So what was wrong? Why did he feel such a lowlife? She was proud and made no secret of despising him for his lowly background. Why, then, had his stomach clenched at the look of sheer desolation in her eyes when he revealed her brother's calamitous folly?

Adam tightened his jaw. Business bargains were tough and there were always losers. Some deserved to be losers. He'd pay her off well at the end of it all.

But revenge should have tasted a damn sight sweeter than this.

Belle could only be thankful that her shop was for once busy for the rest of the day. So although Gabby kept casting pleading looks in her direction that said, *What happened?* Belle was able to keep her at bay. And that evening, shy Matt had asked Gabby if she would go with him to the Vauxhall Pleasure Gardens, which meant Belle was by herself.

She tried to write to her brother, but her pen kept faltering. She simply couldn't understand how Edward could have left London with those awful gaming debts unpaid. Just as she could not understand why Adam Davenant could want to make such an outrageous proposition to her.

Yes, he'd explained he needed a convenient fiancée, but surely he could have thought up a less drastic solution? Found himself a new mistress, for example, or absented himself from the social scene? No earthly need for such a convoluted form of revenge. Unless it wasn't revenge at all... No. *No.* Such a man as he would never actually fall for a penniless, foolishly defiant dressmaker. Never!

She felt her lips, where his fingers had rested. Oh, Lord. She hated him for his arrogance, his cynicism. Yet—his mere touch filled her with dark, forbidden imaginings. She sat very still with her pen in her hand as the shadows lengthened.

In the end she just wrote, *I am so sorry, Edward, about your baby. Please let me know if there is anything I can do.*

Afterwards Belle tried to do some sewing by candlelight up in her sitting room. Anything to distract herself from her dark thoughts. At last she heard the back door opening, and Gabby ran up the stairs and came in.

'Did you enjoy Vauxhall Gardens, Gabby?' Belle knew that lovelorn Matt had hired sculls at Westminster to take the two of them across the river and had also booked a private box that would give them a prime view of the acrobats and the singers. He had even bought himself a new striped waistcoat. Belle fervently hoped Matt had made the most of the opportunity to press his suit and hadn't simply sat speechlessly watching Gabby with adoring eyes.

'Oh, yes!' Gabby eagerly pulled up a chair. 'We had a wonderful time. Matt danced with me and he talked extremely foolishly—oh, *madame*—about love!'

Good for you, Matt. Belle smiled. 'Why do you consider him foolish, Gabby dear?'

'For a grown man to talk of how his heart will be broken if I turn him down—*tenez*, it is absurd. But none of it as foolish as *you, madame*, sewing at this late hour when I hear that all your difficulties are at an end!'

Belle put her sewing down slowly. 'What are you talking about, Gabby?'

Gabby wagged her finger. 'Why, about Mr Davenant! I know, of course, that he took you driving in the park this afternoon. But this evening I met dear Lady Tindall at Vauxhall Gardens, and—well, it's all over town that you and he are betrothed!'

My God, Davenant works quickly, thought Belle rather dazedly. She drew in a deep breath. 'Listen, Gabby.' She tried to sound calm. 'There will be an announcement of a betrothal—' Gabby gave a little squeak of delight '—but it is to be purely a matter of convenience for both him and me, do you understand?'

'But he *must* have fallen in love with you, *madame*,' Gabby persisted. 'I thought, when you were so flustered by his arrival in his carriage this afternoon, that there was something going on— though I didn't even realise you'd met before!'

'We've met twice before.' *And both occasions were absolutely calamitous.*

'Well,' said Gabby firmly, 'it's not as if Monsieur Davenant is lacking female company— I told you before, he is well known indeed for the beautiful women he has escorted round the town. And they still talk, so longingly, of him. *Pardieu, madame*, they go on about his good looks. His fine manners. His generosity. When he bids a final farewell to his mistresses—ah, how they must grieve—he sees that they do not want for *anything*.' Gabby sighed, but then her brown eyes twinkled again with mischief. 'And, of course, there is all the talk of his *virilité*...'

Belle froze. 'What on earth do you mean?'

'I mean his—' Gabby shrugged in a very Gallic way '—his manhood, *madame*. His skill as a lover!'

Belle pretended to yawn. 'Oh, do you know, Gabby, I'm so tired. I think I'll have an early night. I'll just go and check that everywhere is locked up.'

'Madame!' Gabrielle was following her down the stairs. 'Don't you want to hear what they say? He keeps his mistresses at a lovely house in Bruton Street, Mayfair, and—'

Belle stood stock still. 'In Bruton Street? His mistresses?'

'Why, yes, *madame*. Are you all right? This betrothal—isn't it what you desire? If not, then why…?'

Belle struggled to compose herself. 'Dear Gabby, I'm not sure of anything just at the moment. But clearly it's going to be the talk of the town, so let everyone think I'm quite happy with it all, will you?'

'Of course.' Gabby pressed Belle's hand then turned to go to her room. Belle just stood there. *Not sure of anything.* It was true. She was no longer sure of anything at all—except that Adam Davenant despised her.

The next day, after Belle had spent a sleepless night, a note was delivered. It said simply, *The house is ready. I will call for you later this morning at eleven, to show you round. Davenant.*

The house where he kept his mistresses—his bits of muslin, his doxies. Belle wanted to weep with rage and vexation. He'd promised her he wouldn't touch her, but shivers of warning surged through her veins at the thought of being in that formidable man's power. He'd told her he needed her to ward off the husband-hunters—but Belle knew he was doing this to humiliate her. Had most likely bought up her brother's debts for the sole purpose of humiliating her.

Well, it wouldn't last long, he'd promised her that. And—Belle drew in a sharp breath at the sudden idea that smote her—wasn't it just possible that Adam Davenant could be persuaded to end this obnoxious false betrothal sooner rather than later?

Chapter Nine

Mr Davenant called at eleven exactly as he'd promised. Belle had dressed so loudly, so brashly that even loyal Gabby's eyes had widened with doubt.

But Adam Davenant did not bat one sleepy eyelid.

It was as if he was used, every day of his life, to escorting a woman dressed in a Spanish pelisse of raspberry-pink sarsenet trimmed with lime-green satin.

Belle adjusted her pink-kid gloves and beamed up at him. 'La,' she declared in her best Somerset accent, 'I be fair up in the clouds with the idea of being your ladybird, Mr Davenant, I be!'

He blinked. He gave a bow. 'My fiancée, to be precise. My carriage is waiting, Mrs Marchmain' was all he said.

She fluttered her dark eyelashes and put her hands on her hips. 'So you're going to show me round this big, fancy house you told me about? I declare, I cannot wait. But how I do happer on; you must tell me if my conversation is too much for you, Mr D.'

'Happer on?' he echoed, frowning.

'It's what they say in Somerset for someone who is a chatterbox. I can rattle away at quite a rate, you see.'

His jaw set, he held out his arm to lead her to his carriage.

It was a fine, warm day. And this time, she realised, he'd brought his open barouche, with a liveried coachman at the reins; it was even showier than yesterday's vehicle.

He said, as he helped her in, 'I want to make very sure we're noticed together. Clearly you've had the same notion.'

Belle glanced down at her dazzling attire—they would be noticed all right. 'Oh, gracious, Mr D.,' she simpered, 'I do declare, you're making my head spin with your flattery.' She crammed on her tall-crowned pink hat with its festoons of ribbons.

Mr Davenant jumped in after her and told his coachman to drive on.

* * *

The journey shouldn't have taken long, but at the corner of St James's Street and Piccadilly the traffic had come to a standstill because of some altercation between a dray and a hackney-cab driver. Adam's coachman was forced to hold in his fine bays while around them the occupants of other stationary carriages gazed around and grumbled—until they espied Adam with his new companion.

Belle could almost believe that the wretched man had *arranged* this.

A barouche had been forced to a halt just behind them. It contained two men and three fashionably dressed women who, irritated by the delay, were casting around them for a topic to relieve the tedium.

It didn't take long for them to find it.

'Look just there, in that carriage ahead of us,' murmured one of the women. 'That's surely the handsome Mr Davenant, with—who would have guessed it?—with Mrs Marchmain, the little *modiste* from the Strand! Goodness, have you ever *seen* such a very loud gown and bonnet? Quite outrageous, especially as I've heard she was once of good family...'

Belle trembled, a flush of anger spreading up

from her throat to her cheeks. Adam was still looking straight ahead, as though he hadn't heard them.

'Of good family?' the chattering went on behind them. 'Really, my dear?'

'Would you believe, her mother was niece to the Duke of Sutherland?'

'Goodness! So perhaps Davenant hasn't entirely lost his wits in taking her up?'

'Taking her up? That's the least of it. They are to announce a betrothal any day, I hear! The little *modiste* must have quite a few tricks up her sleeve.'

'Or up her skirts,' edged in one of the men, sniggering.

Adam's strong hand was suddenly on Belle's. 'Take no notice whatsoever. Smile up at me and pretend we're having an amicable conversation.'

She shrugged. 'I warn you, Mr Davenant. This is just the start. You are going to find my company embarrassing, I assure you.'

'Embarrassing? Good God, not in the slightest,' he said calmly.

She gave her most glittering smile and tilted her chin. 'Then I shall have to work a little harder, shan't I?'

He bent his head low and murmured enticingly, 'Do your worst, Mrs Marchmain.'

Oh, my. The way he *looked* at her, with his dark head a little on one side and his eyes, slate-grey beneath those dark arched brows, crinkling with amusement. It made her lungs ache with the need for air. If she'd been standing, her legs would have given way.

Ahead the traffic blockage was easing, but they were still some way from the quieter streets of Mayfair. Adam's hand briefly tightened on hers. 'Remember we're supposed to be in love,' he said. Then he leaned forwards, to give new instructions to his coachman.

In love. Belle sank back against the seat and suddenly she was overwhelmed by memories.

When Belle was seventeen Aunt Mildred had agreed to take her to a summer gala night at Bath's Sydney Gardens, and Belle had been so looking forward to the illuminations and the music. But her delight had quickly faded when she became aware that she was dressed quite wrongly for the evening.

All the other girls—some of them her old school friends from the Bath seminary—were clad in delightfully wispy muslin gowns with fluttering white ribbons in their carefully curled hair. Belle wore a dress insisted on by Aunt Mildred, made of dull lavender silk and perhaps ten years out of fashion, with her hair scraped back in a bun.

She'd wanted to sink through the floor as the other girls giggled and stared.

Two weeks later she'd asked Aunt Mildred if she could go again. Her aunt had frowned at the frivolity of two outings within a month, but Uncle Philip had peered at Belle over his spectacles and said, 'Why not? Heaven knows the girl needs preparation for her London come-out next year. She has to marry well—she has no other future.'

That time as they travelled to the Sydney Gardens Belle kept herself well cloaked-up, and only when they were there did she reveal what she'd done to her old silk dress. She'd altered seams to tighten the fit over her slender waist and hips. She'd lowered the neckline and cut off the unfashionably long sleeves to remake them into little puff ones. She'd sewn on some white satin ribbons which brought the lavender gown to life.

That afternoon she'd cajoled a housemaid into arranging her thick dark curls in a pretty cascade, all hidden from Aunt Mildred's inspection until they'd reached their destination and Belle handed her drab bonnet and cloak to a footman.

Aunt Mildred was horrified. Belle was the envy of all the girls there and was surrounded by young men. And that night, she fell in love with Captain Harry Marchmain.

'We're there,' Adam Davenant's deep voice said in her ear.

She jumped. 'So—so soon?'

'Indeed.'

They were outside a tall, elegant house. As they climbed the steps a manservant clad in black was there to greet them almost immediately.

'This is Mrs Marchmain, Lennox,' Adam said to him. 'Mrs Marchmain—my steward.'

'Mr Lennox!' Belle beamed at him. 'My, what a delight to meet you!'

Lennox was well trained; there was not a flicker of surprise in his eyes at her gaudy apparel as he bowed his head.

Then Lennox retreated and Davenant began to show her round himself. Every so often he stopped, his eyebrows raised quizzically. 'I'm waiting for your objections,' he said.

'Heavens above, I'm flummoxed! Give me

time, Mr Davenant,' she answered in a merry Somerset lilt, pointing a jaunty finger at him.

But her heart was beating rather fast. This place was—exquisite. It was light, airy and spacious. Everywhere smelled newly polished; the brass and the woodwork gleamed. There must be servants galore under Lennox's direction; she saw them in the distance occasionally. All employed to maintain the house where Davenant kept his mistresses and where he intended to get his revenge.

A faint headache throbbed at her temples. She was feeling tired and somewhat daunted; a feeling not helped by the fact that Davenant once more looked remote, and forbidding, and utterly *male*.

She swallowed quickly on the sudden dryness in her throat as he turned round while leading her up the stairs and caught her staring at him. 'It's delightful, Mr D.,' Belle declared, looking around. 'Such a *pretty* abode.'

He was watching her carefully, his eyes assessing her. 'I sense a "but" on its way. I sense that *pretty* is not what Mrs Marchmain requires.'

'Lawks, Mr D.,' she announced with a sigh, following him airily into the first-floor drawing room, 'you've certainly hit the nail on the head.'

'I have?'

'Well, of course! These furnishings are hideously insipid, I fear. Pastels and beiges—the word "dowdy" doesn't *begin* to cover it, I'm sure you'll agree. This, this and this—' she swept her hand at various pieces of expensive furniture '—will have to go. I rather favour raspberry pink and lime green this season, you see.' She gestured at her own bold costume.

Not one muscle of his handsome face flickered. He said calmly, 'Raspberry pink and lime green it is.'

'And the overall theme must be Egyptian, of course,' she declared with sudden inspiration. 'I think the Egyptian style so—ennobling, don't you, Mr D.? Ah, the glories of a bygone age! So we will need plenty of black marble and gilding. And sphinxes—yes, I have my mind absolutely set on sphinxes.'

'Do what the deuce you like, Mrs Marchmain. Speak to Lennox and he'll tell the tradesmen to send the bills to me.'

Belle blinked. Then—a little faintly—'No financial limit?'

He shrugged. 'Spend as much of my filthy lucre as you like. Though I must admit I draw the line a little at livestock.'

His turn to take *her* by surprise. 'L-livestock?'

'Caged birds. Lapdogs and the like,' he answered. Just then Lennox appeared to ask if anything was needed and Adam said to him, 'Mrs Marchmain will require some refurbishments to the place, Lennox. You will, perhaps, draw up for her a list of tradespeople to whom she might like to give her instructions.'

'Of course, sir.' Lennox gave Belle a stiff bow, and Belle felt her stomach lurch with despair. He looked so *disapproving...*

'Lawks a mercy, Mr D.,' simpered Belle, 'I have heard that amongst the *ton*, you know, it is the latest thing to have all one's servants dressed in purple.'

Lennox almost choked; Davenant's dark eyebrows shot up. 'Really?'

'Oh, yes! Black is so *boring*. Like having dozens of gramfers crawling around one's house.'

Lennox looked horrified. 'Gramfers?' echoed Adam.

'Woodlice, Adam dearest. La, I thought you knew your Somerset!'

Adam Davenant never batted an eyelid. 'I will consider the matter.' He turned to his steward. 'We'll take tea in the ground-floor salon in ten minutes, Lennox, thank you.'

Lennox looked as if he was about to have an apoplexy as he made his way rather dazedly to the door. Belle mentally apologised to the poor man, then turned brightly back to Adam. 'Well? Are you going to show me the rest of my new residence, Mr D.?'

Really, the house was faultless. She'd been in many fashionable homes, but this was simply exquisite. She followed Davenant around in a state of rather helpless awe, though whenever he turned to her, she would wrinkle her nose in a frown and point, wagging her finger. 'I do declare, Mr D., we need brighter colours here—a touch of orange, I think—and oh, Lady Cattermole has some Egyptian-style onyx tables in *her* parlour and I am so wildly jealous of them, you know.'

'There's a sale of Egyptian antiquities at Christie's tomorrow afternoon,' he said. 'I'll arrange for you to attend.'

Yet again Belle was dumbfounded by this man's tolerance. She was behaving ridiculously. Monstrously. Why on earth was he putting up with her whims?

Rather dismayingly, Belle reminded herself that she knew the answer. He was a powerful,

a clever man. He was waging a ruthless cam-
paign against her, her brother and, she suspected,
the whole of the fashionable world that had once
dared to question his right to occupy his place in
the upper strata of society.

She jutted her chin. Yes, he was using her—but
she would make sure he regretted it.

It was easy, of course, to keep up the image
she'd chosen to project while he was showing her
round the house. In every room Belle flounced
about, excited, silly, preposterous. She was mo-
mentarily floored when he led her into the bedroom—*oh, goodness, the size of that luxurious
bed, with all its cream-silk hangings*—but she
very quickly regained her composure by criticis-
ing the lack of colour in the expensive curtains
at the windows and the dullness of the priceless
Aubusson rug.

It was not quite so easy to maintain her frivo-
lous mask when they retired to the exquisitely
furnished salon. Poor Lennox had brought teapot
and cups and also put coal on the fire; he glanced
at Belle rather nervously on his way out, as if expecting her to demand that he dress himself in
purple livery that very minute.

As the door closed behind Lennox Davenant

sat in one of the satin-upholstered chairs and stretched out his long, booted legs. 'Do you mind pouring?' he asked Belle.

'Not at all.' She just hoped her hands wouldn't shake. 'Oh, my, this is all so exciting.' She pointed at the piano in the corner. 'Just to think—of an evening, as your fiancée, I suppose you will require me to entertain you by playing that piano, or singing, or some such delightful pursuit. I declare I cannot wait!'

'Then I must inform you that no musical duties will be required. You see, I'm tone deaf.'

'In that case, Mr Davenant,' she declared brightly, thrusting his cup of tea at him, 'I could play a hand or two at piquet with you. What fun that will be!'

'It won't,' said Davenant. 'One gambler in the family is enough.'

Oh, no. Trust her to walk straight into that one. Damn the man and his superiority.

'Well,' he went on, 'now that it's just the two of us, Mrs Marchmain, can you tell me why you've been prattling like a drunken parrot for the last hour or so?'

Belle had just lifted her own tea to her lips. She put the cup down, too hastily; it shook in its saucer. 'Why, Mr D.—'

He cut in, 'If you're hoping to make me regret our temporary betrothal, then I assure you, you'll fail. I've explained to you quite clearly that I'm going to make use of your presence here to protect me from the marriage-hunters, so you might as well stop wearing yourself out with your inane chatter. And for God's sake, stop calling me Mr D.'

Belle had gone rather pale.

'And if you're intent on putting me off bedding you,' he went on, 'then let me remind you that I'm not going to touch you unless you beg me to.' *And then I'll think twice about it.*

Belle squared her shoulders. 'You will see me in hell first, Mr Davenant!'

'Oh, for heaven's sake,' he said irritably, 'stop behaving like some third-rate actress.' He took his tea cup. 'My God, anybody would think I was about to subject you to a torture chamber at the very least.'

Belle wasn't thinking of a torture chamber. She was remembering that kiss; unwise, because she was just putting down her own cup and missed the saucer so some of the hot liquid spilled on the table.

Davenant was on his feet. 'I will ring for one of the maids.'

'No. Please,' she said rather desperately. 'They will think me so *stupid...*'

He eyed her sharply. 'Then I'll fetch a cloth myself. Mrs Marchmain, you are perhaps finding all this more difficult than you thought.'

'No,' she said quickly. *Edward's debts. Oh, Lord, Edward's debts.* 'No. Please. After all— we *both* of us know this is only a matter of convenience, don't we? And my brother—he will want, I am *sure*, to find some way in the very near future to pay back his gambling debts to you—'

'Your brother hasn't a hope in hell of paying me back,' Davenant broke in curtly. He made for the door again. 'That cloth. I'll be back in a moment.'

She settled her cup back in its saucer, but her fingers were still trembling.

You'll marry again before too long, people had said. *You must. So very tragic, but you've your life ahead of you...*

No, had been her reply. *No, I'll never marry again. Not ever.*

Now she shivered, alone in the grandeur of that lovely house. Oh, God, she ought to be honest. She ought to say, *Mr Davenant, I thought I could play this game, but I find that I cannot.*

He was coming back in with a cloth in his

hand, which he used to blot the tea neatly from the table. Then he said, 'Mrs Marchmain, unless I'm very much mistaken, you're about to spill more of that tea all over your gown, which would be a great pity.' Smoothly he moved her cup away from her side of the table.

'You mean—you actually like my outfit?' Earlier Lennox had taken her pelisse and bonnet, leaving her clad in a pink-muslin walking dress with long sleeves and copious cherry-coloured flounces.

He ran his eye over her as he returned to his chair and sat down. 'Very much so. But if you're hoping to disguise your charms, you're utterly mistaken. If anything, it enhances them.'

She was looking down at herself in dismay. 'How—what do you mean?'

'The fabric of your gown might be all-concealing, but it's nevertheless rather thin. You were cold, I think—fashed, as you'd say in Somerset—just now.'

Belle's eyes shot down to her breasts. Saw them peaking beneath the fine muslin, the nipples prominent... Oh, Lord. Resisting the urge to fling her arms across them, she sat very straight and said quietly, 'You are hateful to remark upon something so personal.'

'Just trying to help.' He smiled his sleepy smile that did something rather strange to her insides.

Belle said with icy sweetness, 'Perhaps you'd like to choose my wardrobe for me, Mr Davenant?'

'Whatever's happened to your Somerset accent? And choose your wardrobe? Good God, no. You have a reputation as a leader of fashion. Live up to that. Surprise me.'

She said bitterly, 'It's difficult for me to surprise you, since you know far too much about me and my brother already.'

'About your brother, yes. But not you.' His expression was suddenly grave. 'Although I do know that your husband died in the war.'

'He was killed at the Battle of Toulouse five years ago.'

Adam remembered Lowell suggesting that she might still be mourning her husband. *Dressed like that? Surely not.* But he said, 'I'm sorry.'

'It's something many women have had to bear.' She faced him without flinching, though just for a moment she'd looked vulnerable, almost afraid. 'But you did not invite me here to talk about my past.' She gave that forced smile again. 'I suppose I ought to be making light gossip, about the latest play, or some such thing. Or flattering you, Mr Davenant...' Her voice trailed away once more.

'Just give me a respite from the husband-hunters for a few weeks,' he said. 'That's all I ask.'

Her green eyes were glittering again a little dangerously. 'So—*inconvenient*, to be rich and eligible. I don't suppose you've considered a genuine betrothal as a solution, Mr Davenant?'

'Good God, no,' he remarked imperturbably. 'Far too much trouble.'

He saw her bite her lip; saw her eyes darken with emotion. Damn, thought Adam. Normally he had no trouble condemning the frivolity of all forms of sentiment. But just at this moment something that was almost uncertainty clouded his well-ordered thoughts. Up till now he'd found this woman infuriating, surprising and amusing in equal measure. Her Somerset accent was so impish that it had made him want to laugh out loud.

But he'd not missed the flash of pain that shadowed her eyes whenever her husband was mentioned. When she looked as she looked *now*, her vulnerability made him long to take her in his arms and...

Nonsense! All an act. She was tough; she'd had to be, to make a success of her business in a hugely competitive world. Holding her own in an upper-class milieu, clinging to the hereditary arrogance of her upper-class birth and thus avoiding the subservience of some of the other fashionable *modistes*, who only clawed their way up through sycophancy towards the rich.

And she was beautiful enough to make any man's blood race.

Adam got slowly to his feet, reminding himself that he didn't want to find his own emotions tangled up in Belle Marchmain's messy life...*bed the woman, then ditch her—and I'll give you all the land you want.* How Jarvis had grinned as he said it.

Well, Adam wasn't going to bed her, but Jarvis wasn't to know that.

And when the time came to do what he had to do, she'd hate him for it—but didn't she hate him anyway? Why, then, did the nagging thought keep lurking at the back of his mind that he rather *liked* her?

Ridiculous!

He walked over to the walnut bureau in the corner and unlocked a drawer. 'By the way,' he went on imperturbably, 'I've placed a notice of our betrothal in the *Gazette*. It will appear on Friday.

And I believe that on an occasion such as this, a token of esteem is customary.'

He handed her a small, wrapped box and watched her open it. It was a ring he'd bought yesterday from Gray's in Sackville Street, made of sapphires set in gold. It was unostentatious, but exquisite, and he'd expected her—she was, after all, a woman—to be pleased.

She clearly wasn't.

Belle Marchmain just looked at it coldly and said, 'I don't want it.'

As she held it in a hand that trembled a little, something inexplicable tightened in his chest. She looked so vulnerable, so beautiful that, damn it, Adam wanted to take her in his arms and hold her. Kiss those full pink lips, and watch her eyes close in hazy desire. Make love to her until she whispered his name in reciprocated passion...

He said, 'It's simply a gift. I'm sorry if you're offended by it.'

She'd already put the ring back in its box and placed it carefully on the table. 'Presumably your gifts are usually welcomed with cries of gratitude?' she enquired brightly.

'God damn it,' Adam swore. 'But you're an awkward creature, Mrs Marchmain! Most people would not understand your damned reluctance to accept my offer of betrothal, especially as it's a...'

'A small price to pay for keeping my brother out of gaol?'

Adam was silent, watching the pulse that flickered in her throat.

She said at last, in a quiet voice that somehow twisted his gut, 'Mr Davenant. I have fought and fought for my independence. It is, perhaps, the one thing I most value above all. But please— *please* don't pretend that all this, your house, your gifts, are anything other than your attempt to express your contempt for me.'

He said, after a while, 'I have my pride, as you surely know. Do you really think I would want to be associated with a woman for whom I felt contempt?'

She heaved air into her tight lungs and lifted her chin. Adam Davenant certainly couldn't be telling her that he *liked* her. 'La, Mr Davenant,' she retorted crisply, 'you are a strange creature, to be sure! But it's your time and your money that's being wasted.'

'Oh, I don't consider it a waste,' Adam said softly. 'Besides—I cannot resist a challenge.'

'A challenge? Ha!' Her brilliant green eyes were glittering again. 'You seem to have this picture of me as a virtuous paragon. But my five years as a merry widow have been full ones, I assure you! Why, I've had admirers by the dozen...'

'Name one of them.'

'What?'

'Your admirers. Name just one.' He folded his arms across his broad chest.

'Well—well, there are *so many*. Five years, Mr D.!'

'I'm waiting.'

'How could I possibly give you names?' Belle said a little breathlessly. 'That would be entirely shabby of me, would it not?'

'You've forgotten your accent again.'

'What?'

'Your Somerset accent.'

Belle went pale. 'Can I go now?'

He looked at his watch, meticulous over timing as ever. 'Lennox has instructions to provide a coach and driver in half an hour.'

Half an hour—oh, Lord, an eternity. Her eyes fell on the piano in the corner of the room.

'Then I have time for my music!' She put one hand to her breast like an opera singer. 'I cannot *live* without my music—I told you so, didn't I?'

'And I told *you*...'

But she was already sweeping to the piano to

pull out the stool. 'Every day, I absolutely *must* practise, for a *whole hour*, and I have to sing as well...'

'You'll have the house often enough to yourself,' he said swiftly. 'So the piano, surely, can wait.'

'But, Mr D., I have to play whenever the music takes me, and that moment is *now*!'

She began to attack the keyboard in a thundering cacophony of notes. It had been one of Aunt Mildred's ideas that she learn to play the piano, one of Belle's ideas that she *didn't*, and as a girl she'd deliberately driven her ancient music master to despair.

She smiled at Adam sweetly and began to warble, *'Cherry ripe, cherry ripe, Ripe I cry...'*

She sang in the ridiculously affected way she'd heard one of the Misses Pomfrey sing, to much applause, in the Upper Assembly Rooms in Bath. Trilling on the high notes, she gazed at Mr Davenant and simpered at him between verses, while her fingers continued to attack the keys with a quite extraordinary variety of wrong notes. *'Full and fair ones, come and buy!'* she sang to him one last time.

His broad shoulders were shaking. She realised he was laughing.

'Stop,' he was saying. 'In the name of God, *stop...*'

She did. She stood up and all trace of mischief had gone from her expression. Her face was rather pale.

She eased the dryness of her lips with the tip of her tongue. 'I warned you that you would quickly tire of me, did I not, Mr Davenant?'

'Will I?' he breathed. 'Will I, Belle?' He was on his feet now, slowly coming towards her like a predatory animal. Something in his husky drawl made her heart race and her pulse thump. She swung away with a gasp, ever alert to danger— this was nothing less than danger!—but he came steadily nearer, the laughter still dancing in his watchful eyes, and captured her with one big hand around her waist. His fingers imprinted themselves through the skimpy muslin, sending pulsing warmth through every nerve ending.

'You are indeed making a mistake,' he said softly, 'if you think I am not the man to respond to your challenge, Mrs Marchmain.'

Chapter Ten

Oh, Lord. 'That was *not* a challenge!' she fired back in desperation. 'That song was to show you what an absolutely hideous fiancée I will be, Mr Davenant—convenient or not!'

'I'm not convinced,' he replied. His voice was strangely husky. 'I think I shall make you play the piano for me every night, wearing pink and lime green. And I shall definitely—most definitely—ask you to sing for me.'

Belle stared at him. 'I'm beginning to think you're mad,' she said flatly.

'No, I'm simply fascinated. I can't wait to find out what other skills you possess.'

Something was tingling through her veins. A kind of sweet intoxication at the sound of his husky voice.

'You talk of many lovers,' he went on, so close now that she could feel the heat of his big body.

'I wonder—did they touch you like this, Mrs Marchmain?'

He was using his lean finger to stroke the satin-soft skin beneath her earlobe and then, when her eyes flew up to his with utter shock, Adam cupped the back of her head and lowered his own.

His lips brushed gently over hers, slow but sure. Tasting. Exploring. At first she was rigid with fear. She felt the blood race through her veins, thundering to her heart. Then she was melting helplessly beneath that tender caress. Like his first kiss, but more of everything.

This was what she had dreamed a kiss could be like. This was what...

Still tenderly, he held her face with both his hands and tipped it up to allow his own lips fuller access. And she found she was yielding to the tingling, building need; aware, in a dark whirlpool of longing, of the searching pressure of his tongue, before she gave way to the hard thrust of it; harsh, yes, but she welcomed it!

Scarcely aware of what she was doing, she'd reached round him and under his coat, her palms gliding with a will of their own up over the crisp lawn of his white shirt to his shoulders, sensing, beneath her palms, those mighty muscles bunching. The feel of his hard body sent her imagination reeling into a realm well beyond kissing. As if to imprint what this was a precursor to, he'd drawn her so close in his arms that his powerful thigh was pushed between hers; she could feel his arousal, thick and taut, against her stomach and her soft breasts were crushed, their nipples hardening, against the broad wall of his chest. Deep inside her was a throbbing ache, a fluttering sweet pulse, needing something. Needing—*him*.

Dear God, she wasn't supposed to feel like this. She despised this arrogant, low-born man who'd forced her into a calculated, cynical betrothal. But his satin-textured lips were still tasting her, his slightly rough tongue teasing, then withdrawing and slowly teasing again, mingling with hers in dark insinuation as his arms held her close. And she felt a low moan of need escape her.

He continued to explore her with half-kisses and devastating strokes of his tongue until she found herself reaching to run her hands through the thickness of his hair. At the same time his hands were finding and cupping her breasts and the pads of his thumbs were circling each nipple, sending her spiralling in a delicious whirlwind of torment. She writhed against him, lost in his slow deep kiss.

He drew away just a little. She made an involuntary sound of loss and her eyes flew up to meet his heavy-lidded gaze.

'Belle,' he was saying huskily. 'Belle, there's a bed upstairs...'

Her breathing was agitated, the peaks of her breasts hot and hard. She was aching, they were aching, for his touch, for his big, strong hands to cup them again, to rekindle that delicious feeling...

And wasn't that what this man wanted? For her to *beg* him to make love to her, simply so he could reject her and utterly humiliate her? Wasn't that what he'd wanted ever since her words of insult that day on Sawle Down?

A tight pain seized her chest. All her senses felt raw. She breathed, 'I thought you said you would wait for an invitation.'

His grey eyes were hooded. Dangerous. 'By God, Mrs Marchmain,' he said with a gravelly edge to his voice, 'if that wasn't an invitation to bed you, then I don't know what the hell it was.'

She stared up at him in utter dismay. 'Yes. I'm sorry. I didn't mean...'

Adam gazed down at her, the painful throb of his erection not even beginning to ease because with her lips swollen and her sweet breasts pouting beneath that pink muslin flimsiness, she looked more desirable than ever. A widow, a woman of the world; funny, clever and beautiful, yet with a little-girl-lost look that if he wasn't careful might just have the power to melt his hard heart. Except there was no way on earth that he would let it. And anyway, she hated him.

Remember the railway. His bargain with Jarvis had to come first. Using her? Yes, he was using her—just as she was using him, to save that contemptible brother of hers from ruin.

'Let's make things clearer between us next time, shall we?' Even as he spoke Adam was walking towards the door. 'As I said—I'm not going to force myself on you. But on the other hand, I won't be toyed with, do you understand me, Mrs Marchmain?'

She licked her dry lips. 'I understand,' she whispered.

He held himself very still for a moment, then said levelly, 'I think you should move in here as soon as you can. I've already told you it's not acceptable for my fiancée to live above a dress shop.'

Her cheeks whitened; she lifted her chin. 'I see. Yet it's acceptable for her to live in a house usually inhabited by your mistresses?'

Adam registered the scorn she flung into that word with a renewed flash of anger. *Damn her for her upper-class self-righteousness.* 'Oh,' he answered smoothly, 'as you're fond of pointing out, I wasn't bred to live by the rules of polite society. You'll move in, as soon as possible.'

Belle closed her eyes. She was condemned to spend the next few weeks under the protection of a man who despised her. Who could also—he'd just proved it yet again—reduce her to a molten heap of need with just one kiss.

And she could see no way out. Already he was autocratically leading the way into the hall where his steward rather warily stood holding her raspberry-pink and lime-green pelisse.

'My coachman will call for you tomorrow afternoon,' Adam told Belle curtly as he escorted her to the coach waiting in the street. 'As I said earlier, there's an auction of Egyptian-style furniture at Christie's. He will take you there.'

Oh, God. That Egyptian furniture she'd made such a song and dance about. Now, she simply felt an idiot for pretending to like such gaudy ostentation. 'Will you...?' she began.

'Yes, I'll be there waiting for you,' Davenant went on ruthlessly. 'And even if you feel you're not quite ready to move in here yet, people will

observe that we are together, and will guess that
we're preparing this house for your occupation.
What with that and the announcement in the
newspapers, no one can doubt that you and I are
serious about our commitment.'

Deadly serious. Belle swallowed. 'Very well.
But I will dress in my own attire, as usual!'

'By all means. I expect you to make an impact,
Mrs Marchmain. And I trust your taste.'

'You—you *do*?'

'I do.' A hint of gentleness in his voice now.
Misleading, dangerous even, because this man
bore her no kindness.

He was holding open the door to the carriage
for her. At the last moment she turned, the pink
and green ribbons on her tall hat fluttering, and
said in desperation: 'I am not *sure*. I really cannot be sure about all this and you, too, in your
heart of hearts must doubt the wisdom of what
we are entering into...'

His eyes were unreadable. 'In my heart of
hearts? Clearly you haven't listened to enough
gossip about me. You see, it's rumoured that I
simply don't possess a heart, Mrs Marchmain.'

He was already giving her his hand to help
her inside and the beautiful bay horses moved

smoothly off. Despite the warm afternoon sun, Belle found she was shivering.

Adam returned to the parlour, dragging his hand through his cropped dark hair. Damn. Damn it to hell. The room was still imbued with the delicate lavender scent of her clothes and her skin. Her sweet, soft skin...

His body throbbed at the way she had opened to his kiss, at the memory of her low moan as his hands cradled her breasts. He'd known what she was ready for, and so did she. But hell, he'd sworn that he wouldn't touch her unless she begged him to. And hadn't she just done that?

No.

That was the trouble. She'd reacted divinely to his kiss, to his caresses—but as far as she was concerned he was breaking his damned promise. Taking advantage. Hell's teeth, that was the way women *thought*. Even though she must have felt his goddamn arousal burning against her, even while she clutched him close begging for more, it was all his blasted fault.

Adam cursed again. If he wasn't careful, this could go badly wrong. Before this latest, dangerous stage of their relationship, Adam had to admit he'd been enjoying her company far more than he'd have thought possible. He'd found her amusing, original and outrageous. And as for her piano playing—he was grinning just at the memory of it.

Yes, *outrageous* was the word for Mrs Belle Marchmain. But underneath that sparkling veneer he guessed she was as fragile as hell.

He reminded himself that it was her own damned arrogance that had made her vulnerable. *That, and her loyalty to her brother,* a little voice inside him said. Normally Adam let his mistresses down gently; always they were regretful, but he was careful not to upset their pride.

He knew that with Belle Marchmain there could be no gentle parting. No sweet words of regret followed by a handsome payout. He had to humiliate her. That was the price Jarvis had demanded for his land. And Adam needed to get started on his railway before the autumn set in— so this counterfeit betrothal could be for only a few weeks at most.

Grimly Adam suppressed the memory of the taste of her soft pink lips, the feel of her sweet firm breasts that had peaked to his touch, the almost overriding urge he'd experienced to carry her slender body upstairs and make powerful love to her.

Damn it to hell—there must be no more of these kind of riotous thoughts. Pity was a sentiment he definitely couldn't afford, and besides, if she didn't hate him now, she surely would before too long.

Back at her shop Belle swiftly took off her pelisse and bonnet, trying to look calm when inside she felt sick. *To have let him kiss her again...* 'Has everything been all right while I've been out, Gabby?'

Gabby hesitated. 'Oh, *madame*, we have been so quiet that I sent the girls home.'

Belle's stomach pitched. Adam Davenant was forgotten. 'No customers at all?'

'No one, *madame*. But you look so tired, I will make you a cup of tea. And there is a letter for you.'

Belle opened the letter and this time went cold with utter dismay.

It was from her landlord, giving details of the next quarter's rent—and the amount was double what it used to be.

She could not pay it. She simply stood there frozen, while the letter dropped from her hands.

Gabby came back in with the tray of tea things, making an effort to be bright and cheerful. 'And

so, what is it like, the house Monsieur Davenant
has provided for you? Is it very grand? Is it—?'

Belle cut in. 'Gabby, I'm afraid this shop will
have to go.'

Gabby put the tray down rather shakily. 'But—
what about Jenny, and Susan, and Matt?'

'I will find us *something* else,' Belle assured
her quickly. 'A smaller shop, in a less expensive
area. But I doubt if I can keep paying the girls
and Matt.'

Gabby's voice trembled a little. 'Matt and I—
we are going to be married!'

'Oh, Gabby.' Belle hugged her. 'But this won't
stop you, will it? Matt will still have plenty of
work with his brother, surely?'

Gabby was dabbing her eyes. 'His brother says
times are hard also. *Madame*, we all like working here for you so much—' She broke off with
a small sob.

Belle paced the floor. 'I will ensure, then,' she
said almost fiercely, 'that I find somewhere that
makes enough profit for me to employ you all.
Though as I said, it will have to be in a less fashionable district.'

'But if you do that,' Gabby cried, 'we will
surely lose the rich customers we have left! Why
not ask Monsieur Davenant for help?'

Belle shivered. 'He's not a charity, Gabby. In fact, I'm not even sure he particularly *likes* me. He just wants me to fend off the hordes of society beauties he seems to imagine are clamouring for him.'

'But they are!' pointed out Gabby. 'I told you so, remember? He is—'

'Yes,' interrupted Belle, 'I believe you've already told me quite enough about Mr Davenant's—attributes, thank you, Gabby!' She picked up the letter from her landlord and read it again distractedly, then thrust it upon the table.

Gabby sighed. *'Ma chérie,'* she went on tenaciously, putting her hand on Belle's arm, 'Monsieur Davenant is going to a great deal of trouble and expense just to set you up for his convenience. He must have regard for you, and why not? You are so brave, so beautiful.'

He thinks me an utter fool. And no wonder. Belle felt a very strong desire to cry. But she pulled herself up, blew her nose and said, 'I'm going to look at my account books and see how we can cut our losses when we have to close this shop.'

'But—'

'Please don't argue, Gabby. We will have to

search for another shop, you and me, *without* Mr Davenant's help, and there is an end to it.'

When Gabby had gone Belle put her palms to her cheeks, drew a deep breath then walked round rather agitatedly amongst the lengths of silk that gleamed at her cruelly.

She was afraid, because her life was collapsing around her.

She simply couldn't go on with her arrangement with Adam Davenant. What a fool she'd made of herself today—and that was just the *beginning*.

But if she refused to fulfil her part of the bargain, then Davenant might immediately demand that Edward reimburse him for those gambling debts. And as for those dratted sheep…

She felt rather sick. Clearly she'd have to confide in Edward, however distressed he was about his poor baby. There had to be some way out of this, there had to be.

Belle had no other relatives to turn to; Aunt Mildred and Uncle Philip had washed their hands of her nine years ago, when Belle told them she had fallen in love.

After several months of secret if brief assignations in Bath, Harry Marchmain asked Belle to marry him. Harry had been so handsome, so gallant in his army uniform, and Belle had felt so sure of their love that she earnestly told him she would defy not just her family but the world for him. But though Harry was of good family he had no money apart from his army pay. 'It's a totally unsuitable liaison,' Uncle Philip had told Belle sharply.

Together Belle and Harry arranged to be seen passionately kissing in a deserted conservatory at a ball in the Upper Assembly Rooms one night—and the ensuing gossip that spread like wildfire changed everything, just as Belle and Harry had intended. When, a few days later, Harry came once more to ask for her hand in marriage, Uncle Philip had no choice but to stonily agree.

Belle had thought it would never happen again. Thought that she would never let her life be turned upside down by any man. But dear heaven, the feel of Adam Davenant's hands, the taste of him, still coursed through her veins and tightened her tingling breasts. And between her thighs a tender pulse throbbed sweetly, achingly.

She remembered Gabby's awed words with a fresh thud of anguish. 'Monsieur Davenant is well known indeed for the beautiful women he has escorted around the town. And of course there is all the talk of his *virilité...*'

She was as big a fool as any of his conquests, because he'd melted her with just a kiss. Sheer dread had her in its grip again. Her business faced ruin. She would have to start up a new shop in far less elegant, far less profitable surroundings—and surely Adam Davenant would no longer want her as his fiancée. So—oh, Lord, what would happen then to Edward's debts?

She would find out tomorrow, when she told Davenant of this latest blow. And then, next morning, another letter arrived from Edward.

'So you see,' Belle said brightly to Adam Davenant, 'I have decided to close my shop in the Strand and set up a new one. Of course this means a *complete* rethink of my plans and I must end our betrothal, but I will, instead, arrange to repay my brother's debts to you in instalments. And you will save a fortune, Mr D., in not having to spend money on my vastly expensive refurbishments of that big house of yours in Bruton Street. La! The thought of you paying out for all those Egyptian antiquities I was set on acquiring—what a lucky escape you have had, to be *sure*!'

They were at the back of the auction room the next day. The place teemed with the fashionable crowds who'd been eagerly assessing the Egyptian items on display and were now intently watching the auctioneer as he climbed his rostrum.

But Mr Davenant had eyes only for her. And those eyes were hard as flint. 'I've told you,' he said through gritted teeth. 'Do *not* call me Mr D. Where are you opening this new shop?'

'Well, at first I thought of Bath…'

'Bath is full of old maids and dowds,' he said dismissively.

'I haven't *finished* yet. And then I thought of Soho,' she said airily, smoothing down her walking dress of pink-and-white striped percale, over which she'd thrown an emerald cashmere shawl.

'*Soho?*' said Davenant dangerously.

'Yes, I shall rent a stall in the Soho Bazaar, it will be such fun—oh, look at these lions' heads, Mr D., aren't they quaint?'

He ignored her attempt at distraction. 'To set yourself up in the Soho Bazaar,' he pronounced, 'is little better than crying your wares from a stall in Cheapside, and you must know it. Which of your fashionable clients do you think would be moon-dipped enough to follow you there?'

She tilted her head, setting the feathers on her emerald bonnet a-bobbing. 'Oh, women will *always* want gowns, you know. And...' Her voice trailed away suddenly.

'You might as well tell me what's gone wrong,' said Davenant.

'It's the rent,' she said in little more than a whisper. 'The landlord has doubled my rent and I cannot afford it.'

He was silent a moment. 'I thought business was flourishing.'

'It was, until recently!' she uttered. 'But then there were problems. Complaints.'

'I see. And how the deuce, Mrs Marchmain, do you intend to pay off your brother's debts and thus rid yourself of my obnoxious presence— from a *market stall*?'

Belle fought for words as well as for breath. 'Oh, you are so *arrogant*. I will work night and day; I will not stop until I've...'

Suddenly she realised she was being drowned out by the piercing voice of the auctioneer. 'Nineteen guineas, ladies and gentlemen—any advance? Twenty guineas now, and a bargain. Twenty-one! Twenty-two!'

Belle waved her catalogue in frustration. 'I

will *borrow* the money, Mr Davenant,' she cried, 'rather than be bound to you a single day longer...'

'Sold!' cried the auctioneer in triumph. 'Sold for twenty-five guineas to the lady in the green hat with feathers standing at the back of the room.'

Oh, no.

'You've just bought yourself a pair of gilded sphinxes,' Davenant told her flatly. 'You were about to tell me how you're going to pay off your brother's debts. And don't forget that the auctioneer will also need paying—*today.*'

She could have wept. She gazed at him, utterly stricken.

Davenant went on, 'Have you even *told* your brother what's been happening? If he had any decency at all, he would be dealing with all this himself instead of skulking in Somerset. What the hell is he thinking of?'

'His baby died,' she whispered. 'I got a letter from him this morning. The baby was born two weeks ago. It was very ill, and now it's died. And his wife has been told that for the sake of her health, she must not bear another child...'

She tried to swallow down the huge lump of grief that was blocking her throat. This morning as she'd read that letter Belle had felt quite numb with sorrow for the little life lost and for Edward and Charlotte's agony. Her brother, whatever his faults, adored Charlotte and had shared her desperate longing for children.

The auctioneer's voice started to rise again as bidding began for the next item.

'Let's go outside,' Davenant said abruptly, 'before you end up with a six-foot-high marble elephant. I'm sorry about your brother's child. But I am determined our original plan will go ahead.'

'No! I cannot *possibly* accept your charity.'

Adam Davenant clenched his teeth.

Just then a porter came hurrying up. 'Two gilded sphinxes—was they for you, sir?'

Davenant handed him his card after scribbling on it. 'Deliver them to this address in Bruton Street and send me the bill.' Then he guided Belle into the empty hallway beyond the noisy auction room. 'Mrs Marchmain, I've already told you how you can pay me back—by appearing in public with me as my fiancée. And I've a new idea. Yes, you will reimburse me, but we will do it properly, in a businesslike way. I'll invest in your shop. And it won't be in some damned rookery in Soho, but in Piccadilly.'

Now, where the hell had that idea come from? Simple, really; he couldn't let her break off their betrothal. He had to keep his bargain with Jarvis. But damn it, that piece of land for his railway was getting more expensive by the minute.

Belle's hand had flown to her throat. 'Piccadilly! But—'

'I happen to know,' he pressed on relentlessly, 'of a jeweller's shop close to Hatchard's that's becoming vacant shortly. You'll like it—big glass windows for your displays, a workshop at the back for your staff. I'll tell my secretary Lowell to acquire the lease.'

Just like that. 'I will not put myself further in your debt!'

'My intention is that you *won't*,' he said abruptly. 'I will be extremely disappointed, in fact, if I don't make a healthy profit. I'll expect you to become all the rage.'

'But our betrothal is only temporary—'

'This need have nothing to do with our betrothal. This, Mrs Marchmain, is business.'

The porter was trundling past them with the two sphinxes on his wheeled trolley; Davenant gazed at them and said, 'Do you know, I've rarely seen anything quite so hideous in my life. By the way—I assume you'll agree now to move into the Bruton Street house?'

He saw her hesitate. Damn it, she was still desperately trying to wriggle her way out of this. *How she must detest him.*

'You'll do so as soon as possible if you've any sense,' he said. 'After all, the gossip about you and me will do no end of good for your shop.'

A few days before the expiry date of her old lease, Matt and his brother moved all Belle's stock to her new Piccadilly premises. Bernard Lowell had approved the legal work, the shop sign had been painted and hung, and Belle had elegant cards printed and sent to all her clients.

Secretly she was awed by the shop's prestigious situation, its airy rooms. Adam told her to order the furniture she needed, and so she did—no gaudy ornateness, but counters of polished walnut and floor-to-ceiling shelves in pale oak, fitted by Matt to display her valuable rolls of fabric.

Adam's contributions—though he claimed to know nothing about the dressmaking trade—were invaluable. It was he who suggested that she continue with her eye-catching designs, but make them available also in softer colours to appeal to women of less adventurous tastes. He displayed, in fact, a remarkable knowledge of fabrics and styles, and Belle tried to stop herself sharply reflecting that he'd probably visited rather a lot of *modistes* with all his previous mistresses.

There was accommodation above the shop— a small but pleasant bedchamber and sitting room—and when Gabby and Matt told Belle their marriage date was set, Belle offered the rooms to them.

'How convenient,' Adam had approved when she told him. 'Your staff living on the premises means you have security as well as commitment. Well done, Mrs Marchmain.'

'You think I planned it?' Belle flashed. 'You are so cynical! Sometimes love just *happens*!'

'So I'm told.' He shrugged.

On the opening day she was at the shop at dawn. Matt, Gabby and her two assistants Jenny and Susan were there, too; Matt as usual was the odd-job man and furniture mover while Gabby and Belle put finishing touches to the striking fabric displays they'd set up for passers-by to view through the plate-glass windows.

The shop was to open to selected clients at midday. Invitations had been sent out and the champagne was ready. As the minutes ticked by there was one last delivery—dozens of beautiful flowers in shades of cream, ivory and palest yellow. Belle opened the accompanying note with slightly unsteady fingers. *I wish you luck today. You deserve it. A.D.*

Something caught in Belle's throat as she gave her staff their final instructions. 'As from now,' she told them, 'Gabby will be in charge of this wonderful new shop. But I will still come *every day*, and believe me, your welfare and this business will always be uppermost in my mind.'

Gabby's eyes twinkled. 'We can manage here without you, you know, *madame*. I'll keep you very well informed. All you need to do is call in two or three times a week, perhaps meet our most important clients.'

'Two or three times a week?' Belle was scandalised. 'I assure you, I will do a good deal more than that. I'll be here every morning!'

'Every morning?' Gabby said softly, merrily. 'And what will Monsieur Davenant think of that, for goodness' sake?'

Belle coloured slightly. 'My plans have his full approval, since he is well aware I have a business to run.'

'But when he makes you his wife, which surely he will…'

Again Belle felt a sharp lump in her throat. 'Gabby. Please say nothing to anyone else, but I do know that I may well need this shop to come back to. It's my refuge, it's my life. Look after it for me.'

'Of course,' said Gabby softly. 'Oh, *madame*, do not cry. And Mr Davenant—I hear things, so does Matt, and Mr Davenant is said to be a good man, honest and fair.'

Except to those who have mortally insulted him, thought Belle rather desperately. Oh, if only she'd never met him at Sawle Down. If only... Regret was pointless; she had to deal with her life as it was now. Taking a deep breath, Belle went to open the doors to her new shop.

Chapter Eleven

There followed a hectic time in which Belle reached the startling conclusion that—if she pushed aside the precise reasons for her present situation—she was actually enjoying herself.

She'd moved into Adam's house in Bruton Street. The London Season was in full swing, her new shop thrived, and Adam's businesslike advice was invaluable. As for the house, Belle continued to add an outrageous piece of furniture here and a gaudy Egyptian antiquity there. The gilded sphinxes were a damned nuisance—she knocked her shins or caught her gown on them at least once a day. But even so she would find herself wandering around thinking, *This is beautiful.*

Her bedchamber was perhaps the loveliest room, light and airy with pale lemon wall-hangings. Even a huge old Egyptian-style chair she'd insisted on installing in one corner—made of heavily carved black wood with an overarching canopy—failed to mar its beauty.

She saw Adam most days, sometimes in meetings about her new shop together with his secretary Lowell; more often in the evenings, when he would escort her to some of London's most fashionable venues such as the theatre or the ballet. After taking her back to Bruton Street well before midnight, he would leave for his own house in Clarges Street nearby, doing nothing more than nod his dark head in polite farewell.

Some sense of rebellion in Belle—or fear, perhaps, at the obligation under which she found herself—made her seek again and again to shatter Davenant's calm demeanour with her bright clothes or with some outrageous remark. But it was like charging against a brick wall. Or bumping into one of the hideous sphinxes and sarcophagi that littered the corridors of her new house.

He was imperturbable. Indifferent, most likely, thought Belle with a strange little stab. She would be his fiancée for a while—oh, many were the congratulations she was offered on her engagement, and even more frequent the sly glances of envy—but in private he couldn't have made it plainer that this was simply a business arrangement. She would give him respite from the mar-

riage mart till the Season ended in July, then that
would be the end of their betrothal. She would
eventually pay back Edward's debts to him
through her profits, but doubtless that would be
all sorted through Lowell.

Yes, a business arrangement.

Belle tried everything to annoy him. She wore
a purple pelisse sewn with silver frogging to the
theatre and a bonnet adorned with purple-dyed
feathers. She flirted and joked outrageously
with his men friends, interlacing her conversation every now and then with Somerset dialect,
hanging on to his strong arm and calling him
her Mr D., but he coped with all her public ec-
centricities with amused ease.

There was just one evening when she thought
she caught some flicker of emotion in his hooded
grey eyes. They were at the opera; Belle had insisted on being taken there, largely because he'd
told her he loathed it. Indeed so secretly did she,
and once in their private box her own heart sank
at the tedious hours which lay ahead.

But then she began to realise that the story was
about doomed love. The music, even though she
didn't understand the Italian words, was actually
incredibly beautiful. And as the heroine sang her

dying farewell to the hero Belle felt a huge lump in her throat.

Don't be a fool. It's sentimental humbug.

It made her want to cry. Oh, Lord, she *was* crying…

'Are you all right, Mrs Marchmain?' Adam at her side asked quietly.

She hid her handkerchief and smiled up brightly from behind her purple fan. 'Oh, indeed, Mr D., I swear it is *so* diverting!'

He gritted his teeth, but didn't remind her not to call him Mr D. They were due to join his friends for a supper party after the performance, but he said instead, 'You look tired. I'll take you home. You've been at your shop almost all day today, haven't you?'

Belle was silent a moment, still struggling with her emotions. Then she said, 'Does that spy of yours, Lennox, tell you everything?'

'Yes,' he answered imperturbably. 'Do you really have to be there so often?'

She flicked her fan. 'But of course,' she said gaily. 'Only think of your investment, Mr D.!'

And I need to be independent, she vowed. *I have to be. I cannot rely on any man, let alone you.*

She'd quickly realised that she now had considerable status in the eyes of the *ton* because she'd been picked out by one of London's most eligible bachelors. But there were disadvantages. Again and again she argued with Adam over the number of staff at the Bruton Street house. 'There are maids and footmen everywhere and I do not need them.'

'You need the maid I hired, don't you?'

'Simmons? Well, yes, I suppose…'

'Do you object to her?'

'No,' said Belle. 'No, I don't.' She was, in fact, used to dressing herself, but she had to admit that Simmons was invaluable in looking after her new and extensive wardrobe.

But it irked her that at Davenant's insistence she couldn't go anywhere by herself and had to either travel in the coach he'd provided, or, if she chose to walk, be accompanied by one of his grooms.

Davenant would always answer her protests with, 'I have a certain position to uphold in society, Mrs Marchmain. And so do you.'

In other words he was as formal, as correct as ever. But that look in his eyes at the opera, when he'd asked her if she was all right, had fractured something in her carefully maintained defences. And every night when he left her alone in that big house, some part of her ached for him to stay. Not just to stay, but to kiss her again, with those firm warm lips that had set her pulse racing and her insides clenching with forbidden heat...

No. That would make things simply impossible. That would be the ruination of their civilised companionship, which Belle was coming to value more than was remotely wise. *Why* was he going to all this trouble and expense? At first she'd feared he wanted to exact revenge for her insults; now she assumed he was eager for her shop to do well because he'd invested money in it and was expecting some return in order to cancel out Edward's massive debt. But to spend so much time with her...

Could it be possible that he was actually starting to care for her?

No. Belle found the blood pounding hotly in her veins. That was the last thing on earth she wanted. She absolutely *detested* Adam Davenant—didn't she?

Adam, meanwhile, had matters of his own to attend to. One night he invited Lord Jarvis to dine with him at his house in Clarges Street and when the main courses had been removed and the servants gone, Adam poured Jarvis more wine and said calmly, 'You'll acknowledge, I hope, that I'm fulfilling my side of our bargain.'

Jarvis's pale eyes gleamed. 'I thought we'd arrive at the business of the widow sooner or later. I assume you're eager to be getting on with that railway of yours?'

'My engineer, George Shipley, has advised me that the excavations ought to be well on their way by August.'

Jarvis drank half his glass of the rather fine burgundy in one go. Then he said, 'You're being presumptuous, Davenant.'

'Am I?'

'Yes.' Jarvis helped himself to more wine, then sat back in his chair and watched Davenant narrowly. 'You've got to break with her. Humiliate her. Remember?' He suddenly leaned closer. 'She should be counting the days—and nights— to your wedding. She should be beside herself with joy. But people are saying that the pair of you look more like friends than lovers—dear God, man, given your reputation with women, she should be swooning at your every touch!'

Adam looked at him steadily. 'She's a mature widow, Jarvis, not a lovesick girl. We're seen almost every night around the town together and are officially betrothed. But you know that I've absolutely no intention of meeting her at the altar. Isn't that enough for you? I take it you don't expect a ringside view of our more intimate moments?'

'Now, *there*'s an idea,' said Jarvis. 'What's she like in bed, I wonder? Does she squeal, Davenant, when you take her? Is she docile, or does she beg you for more, like—'

Adam put one fist on the table, though he kept his voice calm. 'I don't remember it being part of our agreement that you have leave to insult her. I repeat—when are you going to give my engineers access to the land you promised me?'

Jarvis scowled. 'As soon as I'm sure Mrs Marchmain is head over heels in love with you and is convinced you'll marry her very soon. But devil take it, you've not even introduced her to your family yet!'

'Good God, man, I've little enough family, as you know.'

'You have a brother in Surrey. Has he even met your so-called fiancée?'

Adam laughed. 'That's hardly your business.'

'But this agreement's my business,' said Jarvis softly. 'I want to see her humiliated, if you want that damned land. As for the shop you've set up for her in Piccadilly—I take it that's just a temporary affair also? That you'll pull out from your investment as soon as you break off this sham betrothal and so leave her ruined?'

Adam said nothing. Jarvis frowned down at his glass suddenly. 'Damn it, Davenant, have you nothing stronger than this burgundy? You used to have some fine brandy—or is that reserved for your friends?'

Adam stretched his long limbs and rose to fetch the brandy and two glasses from the sideboard. He started pouring. Said, in a deceptively soft voice, 'You hate Mrs Marchmain, don't you, Jarvis? Did you by any chance contrive to destroy her shop in the Strand as revenge for her rejection of you two years ago?'

Jarvis's hand froze over his glass. 'I don't know what you're talking about.'

'I think you're lying. Someone arranged a succession of complaints, then instructed her landlord to double the rent.' Adam gazed at Jarvis with steely eyes. 'I think it was you.'

Jarvis laughed. 'Dear God, I wouldn't dirty my hands with such a lowly matter. Just remember, Davenant—I want to see her broken if you're to get your land, understand?' He drank down his brandy and stood, straightening his coat. 'Time on that note for me to go.'

Adam had risen also, towering over him. 'I think you *did* try to ruin her business, Jarvis. Be careful. I don't remember anything in our agreement about you being allowed to harm Mrs Marchmain in any way whatsoever. Do you understand?'

Jarvis let out a hiss of surprise. 'Are you threatening me? My, my—a mistake, that, showing your hand too early. Maybe you *are* starting to get a little too fond of her.'

'I've no intention of continuing my relationship with her beyond the terms of our agreement,' said Adam curtly. 'And don't forget we've each got a copy of the details, signed and witnessed.'

'Maybe so. But there's no way I'm letting you have access to the land you need until you've given me a little more proof of your commitment—and until the town is full of the news that you've broken with her. *Ruined* her.'

'You're a bastard, Jarvis.'

'So are you,' said Jarvis calmly. His hand was already on the door. 'And wouldn't the lovely Mrs Marchmain be interested to be told of what we agreed? Because that's what will happen if you try to wriggle out of this in any way at all. Understand?'

Adam saw him out. Off his property. Damn it. *Damn it.*

The next evening Adam escorted Belle as usual back to Bruton Street after a night at the theatre. But—and this *wasn't* usual—he followed her into the house.

She was untying her bonnet, a delicious little affair of sage green and claret that matched her figure-hugging pelisse. Her eyes, Adam noted, were still sparkling with laughter from the comedy they'd both enjoyed. Her lips were full and rosy, and as she took off her bonnet some soft coils of black hair fell enticingly to her shoulders.

Tonight she'd turned to him in the interval and put her small, warm hand impulsively on his. She'd said, 'Oh, I'm enjoying this so much— thank you, Adam, for bringing me!'

'My pleasure,' Adam had said. And that was the trouble. It was. He found her intriguing, amusing and damnably arousing.

He liked her. He wanted her—no use denying it. His weeks of celibacy, and her nearness, were wreaking havoc with his self-control. At this moment, his body was throbbing with need, and he wanted to lead her upstairs and make love to her until they were both giddy with sensual delight...

'Such a lovely evening,' she was saying with innocent pleasure as he followed her into the parlour. 'I'm becoming quite an expert on the playwrights. The merits of Mr Sheridan, as opposed to those of Mr Goldsmith—I did enjoy our literary discussion with all your friends.'

She turned to him with such a sweet smile that Adam sucked in a betraying breath at the way her soft cheek tempted him to press his lips there. At the way the faint, delectable scent of lavender drifted from her body...

He forced himself to smile back lightly. 'I'm sure they enjoyed talking to you. But I fear their attentions weren't entirely on the finer points of the discussion.'

'What do you—?'

'They were enjoying being close to you, Belle,' he said, going to pour her a glass of ratafia from the tray of drinks Lennox had left and using the moment to fight down his uncomfortable erection before she spotted it. 'At this rate—' he turned back to her '—you'll have half of London's male population at your feet. Perhaps as your fiancé

I should show my mettle and drive off some of the more persistent of them.'

She gasped, her smooth brow furrowing. '*Oh.* I really hadn't thought—I mean, especially as we are only pretending...'

Pretending! Good God, she clearly *hadn't* noticed. He clenched his teeth. 'I know you can fend them off,' he said. 'But you should be aware of their interest.'

She blinked. 'Is this why you've come inside with me tonight? To warn me that I'm not behaving correctly?'

'Partly,' he said, 'though with my lowly origins I'm hardly a suitable person to lecture you on the manners expected of the *ton*.' He handed her the glass. 'But chiefly it's to tell you I've got a proposition for you.' He put his hand on the mantelpiece and turned to face her directly.

Belle's stomach unaccountably pitched.

It was a long time since the matter of his so-called lowly origins had even crossed her mind. And something about him tonight—was it the way he'd brushed his hair in a slightly different style? The way his plain but perfect cravat set off the sculpted features of his strong face? Something, somehow, made her feel quite shaky whenever she looked at him. Made her wish...

Oh, Lord. *That this was for real.* And now just being in the same room as him had started to make her feel a kind of aching longing that bewildered and frightened her. She *knew* he felt nothing for her. That he was merely extracting payment for her insane insults.

But it was as if every time she saw him her yearning body was disconnected from her brain. Every time he said goodnight and left her—so politely, so damned politely—she would totter away to her bed with her pulse thumping and her mind a whirling morass of emotions. Of desire— yes, pure, trembling desire—for him to take her in his arms.

Damn Edward and his debts. Because otherwise she could have pretended that this man was falling in love with her.

Tonight she was wearing a sage-green silk dress that demanded a tight corset. But the corset, which ended just below her nipples, had been chafing her breasts all evening, making them so sensitive she'd wanted to scream. Wanted, even more, to feel his cool hands on them or, dear God, his lips, drawing those burning peaks into his mouth...

'Are you listening to me, Belle?'

'Yes. Yes, of course. I'm sorry.' She fixed him

with a bright smile, but her heart lurched. His lean cheek was already shadowed with evening stubble; his mobile mouth looked more tempting than ever as it twisted in a slight, wry smile.

'You looked miles away,' he remarked. 'I was saying, I need to ask a favour of you.' He was pouring himself brandy, only a small glass. His father had often sought refuge from his wife's vitriolic tongue in alcohol; Adam had no desire to follow him down that path.

'My brother,' Adam went on, 'has come to stay in his London house for a few days with his family; it's his son's eighth birthday, and they're going to visit Astley's Amphitheatre as a treat. Would you come with me and join in the celebrations?'

'You have a nephew?'

'Three, in fact. The birthday boy is the oldest; his name is Joshua.' Adam sipped his frugal brandy. 'He and the two younger boys are delightful little rogues and my brother and his wife are quite charming. You'd enjoy it, I'm sure.'

She twisted her wedding ring, giving herself time to think. She needed to remind herself that everything Adam did was for business, not pleasure; but why he should require *this* of her she couldn't fathom. 'Have you told your brother—

Freddy, isn't it?—about the particular nature of our betrothal?' she ventured at last.

'That it's temporary, you mean? I scarcely think it's relevant to him, do you?'

Belle was silent a moment then said, 'Don't you mind deceiving your brother?'

'Freddy knows me well enough,' he answered. 'Please come. I'd enjoy your company.' Then he smiled. 'Any ideas for a birthday present for an eight-year-old boy?'

They talked a little more, while he finished his brandy. She followed him to the door, where he took her hand in his and let his firm lips just brush her fingers. Then he was gone and she sat down again.

Freddy knows me well enough. Belle felt as if he'd just flattened her. He might as well have said, *Freddy knows I pick and discard women as I please.*

And yet, just the touch of his lips on the sensitive back of her hand had sent such a torrent of raw hunger for this man thudding through her veins that she felt real despair.

Adam set off home, opting to walk so the night air would clear his head and dampen down the rather dangerous racing of his pulse that started up whenever he was too close to Mrs Belle Marchmain. Whenever he as much as touched her hand, for God's sake.

He'd spoken to Freddy earlier today, about Belle.

'Another of your beauteous *chère-amies*, Adam?' Freddy had queried.

'No—my fiancée, in fact.'

'Fiancée!' They'd been dining at Adam's club and Freddy almost spilled his wine in surprise. 'Good God, Adam, you vowed you'd never let yourself be leg-shackled. In fact, you've told me repeatedly that our parents' sad marriage was enough to put you off for life. You're not actually serious about this Belle, are you?'

Silence fell. At last Adam said softly, 'If you're wondering whether she's fit company for Louisa and the boys—'

'No. Dash it, Adam, it wasn't that!'

'I think you'll be pleasantly surprised,' finished Adam.

And that was that. Freddy had looked amazed. No doubt there were a hundred questions he'd wished to ask, but he'd enough sense not to bother. And if honest, kind Freddy knew exactly why Adam was so insistent Belle be introduced to them all, Freddy would think his brother the biggest villain in London.

Well, as Adam walked steadily through the night-time streets of Mayfair with the silver moon shining overhead, he felt he probably *was* the biggest villain in London. Even worse than Jarvis. No one in their right mind trusted Lord Jarvis.

But Belle Marchmain, he feared, was beginning to trust *him*.

Chapter Twelve

It was a bright summer's afternoon when Adam called to take Belle over the river to Astley's Amphitheatre. Outwardly Belle was ready for him, with her light smile and defiant air. But as ever these days, just one look at him had her thoughts tumbling into complete disarray.

She'd watched him from the window as he climbed down from his chaise with long-limbed ease, dressed with devastating simplicity in his caped driving coat and shining top boots. Belle met him at the open door; he bowed over her hand then assessed her swiftly.

He frowned a little.

She stiffened, her heart missing a beat; Lord, how sensitive she was to his every gesture, every look. 'La, Mr D., you look as if you'd swallowed a spider. Is something wrong?' she queried with a jaunty smile.

Amusement gleamed in his dark eyes. 'Since you ask, yes. Your clothes disappoint me a little.'

'Disappoint you?' she gasped.

A muscle quivered at the corner of his jaw. 'Indeed. They're almost—conventional.'

She glanced down quickly at her dove-grey pelisse. 'But I thought—since we're meeting your family—I decided you would be embarrassed if I dressed in my usual foolish way...'

'*Not* foolish,' he said quietly. 'Please don't change yourself, Belle. For me, or anyone.'

Dear God. If she didn't have more sense she'd be head over heels in love with this man. But she *did* know better, so she plastered on her bright smile, stilled her shaking heart and hurried inside, to come out very soon in a cherry-pink walking dress with navy ruffles and a wide-brimmed straw hat trimmed with pink-silk ribbons galore. 'Better?' She tilted her head jauntily and waved a cherry-coloured fan.

Adam grinned. 'Oh, *much* better. Shall we depart?'

He held out his arm so she could rest her fingers daintily on it and led her to his carriage.

After driving the chaise over Westminster Bridge, Adam left the vehicle in the tender care

of his coachman Joseph and led her towards
the vast amphitheatre that was Astley's. Such a
throng had gathered for the popular attraction
that she wondered they'd be able to find anyone at all, but soon there were gleeful shouts of
'Uncle Adam! It's Uncle Adam!' and two little
boys were running towards them.

A moment later a cheerful-looking man—
Adam's younger brother, it *had* to be—was striding eagerly forwards to grip Adam by the hand.

'Out of the way, you hooligans!' Freddy commanded. 'Is that the way, brats, to greet your
esteemed uncle?' The grin on his pleasant face
completely counteracted the severity of his words.
He had the same thick dark hair as Adam, the
same chiselled jaw, but was just a little less tall
and looked as though he spent most of his time
smiling. 'Adam, good to see you. And—' his gaze
had fastened on Belle '—Mrs Marchmain? Your
servant, ma'am!' His eyes were widening considerably. 'Come away, brats, and give the lady
some space.'

The oldest boy—he must be Joshua—was gazing up at her, frowning. 'Papa, is she one of Uncle
Adam's *petticoats* that you and Mama were talking about at breakfast when I came in?'

'Oh, Lord. Joshua, you little imp, that's quite

enough!' Freddy turned to Adam and Belle in rueful consternation. 'So sorry, so very sorry. Joshua, no more London treats for you, if you don't remember your manners!'

Joshua, the birthday boy, looked crestfallen. 'Please,' said Belle quickly. 'I don't mind at all—I know my appearance is a little *unexpected...*'

She heard her voice trailing away. *This is awful. I'm not going to be able to cope with this. I should have refused to come...*

'I like her,' said the smaller boy, Tom, stoutly. 'I like her pink dress and her ribbons. I don't see why Mama and Papa were so worried 'bout her coming with us today.'

'Good grief,' exclaimed Freddy, 'my apologies *again*, Mrs Marchmain, you can see that parental discipline is totally lacking here. I've told Louisa many times, we should have tutors and footmen with us on outings like this to instil some kind of order on our brood—but she just won't have it! Oh, here comes Louisa now, thank goodness, with our youngest...'

They were joined by one of the prettiest women Belle had ever seen, holding a curly-haired four-year-old boy tightly by the hand. She was, to someone of Belle's experienced eye, wearing a gown that allowed for her state of pregnancy, and Belle saw how Freddy's face lit up at her approach. 'My wife,' he said to Belle, with all the love and pride in the world.

Caught unawares, some emotion—some old pain, long-buried—smote Belle with such intensity that she shook. *No children for her.*

The lovely, charming Louisa took Belle's hand with her own free one. 'How delightful to meet you, Mrs Marchmain.'

'It's extremely kind of you,' Belle said steadily, 'to include me in your party.'

'Why on earth shouldn't we, my dear?' Louisa smiled. 'You are, after all, very special to dear Adam… Josh darling, what is it now?'

'It's my *birthday*!' Josh announced importantly to Belle, having pressed his way between his mother and her. 'My birthday, and I'm *eight*, you know.'

With much chattering and laughter, Freddy and Louisa got their lively family to their seats in the huge tiered amphitheatre. The show wasn't due to start for twenty minutes, but the excited audience had packed the place early and kept the vendors who moved around selling sweetmeats more than busy.

Belle saw how the boys fought to sit next to their uncle Adam. He'd bought them each toffee apples and Belle found herself wincing for him as they clambered all over his pristine clothes with their sticky fingers, but he seemed completely unconcerned, laughing with them and telling them about the spectacle they were shortly to witness. *A family. He should have a family of his own...*

'Mrs Marchmain?'

It was Louisa's voice. For a while, in the merry exchange of seats that seemed to be an essential part of the family outing, Adam's sister-in-law was next to her. 'Mrs Marchmain,' Louisa went on rather breathlessly, 'I so envy you your life in London! And your clothes are so beautiful.'

Belle smiled. 'I'm afraid some consider my clothes a little outrageous.'

Louisa stopped her by putting her hand over hers. 'Adam clearly doesn't,' she whispered. 'Adam is completely smitten. You've made quite a conquest, my dear; Freddy and I thought it would never happen. We are so glad for you.'

With that Louisa turned back to her little boys; just as well, because Belle couldn't have spoken a word. *She shouldn't have come here.* She'd made herself stupidly vulnerable by coming here.

The noise around them was rising as the lights were dimmed for the opening ceremony. The blood had rushed to her cheeks at Louisa's words;

she fumbled in her reticule for her folded fan and realised Adam was leaning close, his dark face shadowed.

'Are you all right, Belle?' he asked quietly.

A simple question, but after Louisa's comments it floored her. *Adam is completely smitten.* No, he wasn't. No, she was *not* all right, she was a stupid fool and this false betrothal was tearing her in two.

'Oh, absolutely!' she answered with a merry smile and wafted her fan in the air. 'I'm so excited, I must declare. And as for you, Adam—you've kept all *this* quiet. You have a family that dotes on you! Do you secretly dream of a place in the country, where you can rusticate, as your brother does?'

He gave her an answering grin. 'Oh, I leave that sort of thing to Freddy. He's good at it.'

'Adam.' She heaved air into her tight lungs and her smile vanished. 'Adam, I hate these lies. I hate these deceptions.'

His face was suddenly devoid of good humour. 'Then let's take a look at these *deceptions*, as you call them. For example—have you even told Edward yet that you know about his gambling debts? Have you told him what you've *done* for him?'

He saw a pulse flicker in the slender column

of her throat. She breathed, 'I—I didn't want to trouble him.'

'Trouble him!' His voice was rich with scorn.

'Not until his wife is recovered—at least a little—from her grief.'

'Your brother surely hasn't imagined his debt of five thousand guineas would vanish into thin air?' He sounded incredulous. 'You realise I could enforce that debt at any time?'

Belle breathed, 'You can't seriously think you need to remind me? Isn't my being here proof enough of the hateful power you hold over us *both*?'

Some latecomers were pushing their way in front of them, causing loud protests. After that Belle had an excuse to turn from him because Louisa was asking her something about her gown.

Adam watched her talk to Louisa, his eyes narrowed. She looked as vulnerable as he'd ever seen her, despite her defiant words. He felt something twist in his gut as he realised how pale, how forlorn she looked in her gaudy finery.

Suddenly it was as though Jarvis was at his shoulder. Jarvis, saying to him, *Devil take it, you've not even introduced her to your family yet. I want to see her broken if you're to get your damned land, understand?*

Adam gritted his teeth. Jarvis would only be satisfied if he ended the betrothal in public, indicating to the whole world that he no longer considered her a suitable match. Usually it was the woman's privilege to curtail a betrothal; for the man to break it was a fate reserved for females who'd shown themselves to be liars, libertines or worse.

Adam reminded himself grimly that the livelihoods of hundreds of men and their families depended on him. He was doing the right—the only—thing, wasn't he? She would survive it, as she'd survived so much else, and, God's teeth, she'd insulted him to kingdom come that day on Sawle Down.

But as he watched her, looking calm and steadfast but guessing very well that wasn't how she felt—as he watched her, Adam wasn't so sure.

He wasn't sure at all.

When the show began at last the boys were clearly thrilled beyond words by what they saw. They shrieked with delight as the tumbling acrobats made way for a troop of gorgeously apparelled horses, whose riders—clad in Saracen robes—galloped around the ring in breathtaking feats of horsemanship.

The noise from the applauding crowd, seated in tier upon tier around the covered amphitheatre, rose to deafening levels as a troop of gallant Crusaders suddenly rode out to a fanfare of trumpets and put the Saracens to flight. But that was only after much sword-fighting, during which Freddy's youngest, four-year-old Oliver, crept on to Belle's lap for a better view, his eyes round with awe. A parade of all the horses and their riders was followed by the return of the acrobats, who to the wild applause of the audience crowned their act by leaping on one another's shoulders until they'd formed a huge human pyramid.

The boys were still quite breathless with excitement as they left the arena and emerged with the crowds into the afternoon sunshine.

'That was *wonderful*,' gasped Josh, awed. Adam had gone ahead to find the carriages, so Freddy shepherded the remainder of the party to an agreed rendezvous while the boys chattered away. 'I'm going to ride a horse like that when I'm bigger.'

'You couldn't, silly!' That was six-year-old Tom. 'You have to be a—a Crusader! Don't you, Papa? Tell him!'

Freddy said tactfully, 'You could join the cavalry, Josh. When you're a bit older, of course.'

'The cavalry!' Josh's eyes widened. 'Yes, Papa, can I join the cavalry?'

'Me, too!' cried Tom. 'I'm joining, too! Where's Uncle Adam? I'm going to tell him!'

'He'll be back soon, darling,' said Louisa, laughing. 'Oh, here, Oliver, let me wipe your sticky face! Watch Tom a moment, will you, Belle?'

But somehow—*somehow*, though Belle was sure she'd got little Tom's hand tightly in hers—Tom got away. Within moments—that was all it took—he was quite lost, amidst all the people still pouring out of the amphitheatre.

'Belle?' Louisa's voice, sharp with panic. 'Belle, where's Tom?'

'He was here. I had him here...' Belle could barely speak for the panic thudding in her chest.

Louisa had gone quite white. She was already rushing towards her husband. 'Freddy. Tom's gone.'

Freddy, taller than they, was urgently scouring the crowds. 'Josh—Ollie—hold your mother's hands, *understand*? Look—Tom's over there, I can see him. He's spotted Adam!'

It was true, Belle realised. Tom had somehow

through the throng seen Adam returning and had run off to meet him, quite oblivious of the busy thoroughfare he would have to cross. Belle was the first to fly after him, panic and dread weighting her every step with lead.

For a second the little boy stood frozen amidst the horses and carriages. Belle ran on, knowing sickeningly that she'd be too late. Then—Adam was there. Adam was scooping Tom up and out of the way in his strong arms, just before the wheels of a heavy town coach rumbled over the very place where the child had stood.

Tom was unharmed. He cried a little in his fright, and once Adam handed him to his mother Louisa hugged him to her, kissing him over and over again. Freddy gathered his precious brood together and told them sternly that they must stay close, at all times.

Belle could barely breathe. *She* had been in charge of Tom; *she* had let him slip away from her grasp.

'Belle. Are you all right?' Adam's voice; he was at her side.

She whispered, 'Please will you take me home?'

Adam had lifted her hand; she was shaking. 'No one blames you, Belle.'

He saw how her lips were quite white; her

hands trembled as she shook her head. 'Everyone thought I was holding him safely. If it wasn't
for you—oh, Adam, if you hadn't got there in
time, he'd have been terribly hurt...'

'But I *did* get there in time. And Belle, he
slipped away from you—boys will be boys, you
know that!'

'I know that it was my fault,' she breathed, her
eyes dark with distress. 'Please, Adam. Take me
home.'

An hour later Belle was alone in her bedroom
in Bruton Street when there were strong footsteps
on the stairs, a familiar knock at her door. She
jumped to her feet as the door opened.

Adam, of course. He'd left her here—at her
insistence—then gone on home to act as host to
his brother and his wife, who were dining with
him that evening.

He came inside, his face unreadable in the
shadows. He said, 'You've not even lit any candles. I'll send for a maid—'

'*No.*'

'Belle, Lennox told me you've had nothing
to eat and nothing to drink. You're sitting here
in the dark. You should have come with me to
Clarges Street.'

'I—I cannot face your brother and his wife. I cannot.'

'I told you. Nobody blames you.'

But she blamed herself, more than he or anyone could ever know. She sat on the bed again with her head bowed, her arms folded tightly across her breasts. Adam sighed and went to light two candles above the fireplace. Then he seated himself on the big bed beside her, took hold of one of her hands and turned her gently to face him. 'Accidents happen,' he said. 'It wasn't your fault that Tom did something he knew very well was wrong. And he is *all right*.'

'Only thanks to you!'

'Perhaps, but even so you will not hide up here, as if you've done the child a grave injury—do you hear me?'

She was still trembling. 'Perhaps not *this* time. But I did, years ago…'

'You did what?' His arm was round her now, holding her. 'What, Belle?'

'My brother,' she whispered. 'Adam, my brother nearly died. Because of me.'

And so it all came pouring out. 'He was only six, Adam. The same age as Tom. I was almost eight and—and we were in the house my father once owned, in Bath. Our maid was meant to be looking after us, but I heard a troop of cavalry coming up the street and so I led Edward outside to watch them…' Her hand went to her throat.

'Take your time,' Adam said. 'I'm listening.'

Somehow, she told him the rest. How Edward, escaping from her hold, had run excitedly towards the trotting horses. How the one nearest to him, taking fright, had reared up and Edward had been knocked over by those plunging hooves.

'My little brother was badly injured,' she went on, her voice scarcely audible. 'His arm and wrist were broken, and his face—oh, Adam, a hoof caught his forehead. He was in terrible pain and was an invalid for a long, long time. I often think it's why he's—not as strong in other ways as he should be. He almost died and I shall never forgive myself.'

She was shivering, but she refused to cry. Adam kept his arm round her and felt raw emotion punch him in the gut. If she'd cried—damn it, yes, if she'd *cried*, as most women would have done—he'd have offered a few terse words of comfort then backed off as quickly as he could.

But she was the one backing off. Pulling away from him, hastily brushing her dark curls back from her face and saying in a fractured voice,

'There. You know it all now. You should go back, to your brother and his lovely family. I will be *quite all right.*'

But Adam wasn't all right. Adam was finding that all his safe and sure convictions—that he was a tough man, that the weakness of indulging in sympathy for others was not for him—were falling apart around him.

He said in a voice that was almost harsh, 'Belle. I understand that was a terrible thing to happen. But for you to let it tear at you like this, to let it scar your whole life, cannot be right. Are you really saying that the accident to Edward is why you sacrifice yourself for him? Do you think that *helps* him, for God's sake?'

She'd got up to walk distractedly up and down the room, still in that cherry-pink dress in which she'd looked so radiant when he'd picked her up to take her to Astley's. She was always beautiful, damn it; even more so now, because she looked so damned vulnerable.

She turned to him, her green eyes wide and translucent in the whiteness of her face. 'Whatever I do for Edward,' she breathed, 'can never be enough. *Ever.*'

Her low self-worth—her *despair*—tore at his

gut. He stood up to grasp her hand and make her sit again, next to him on the edge of the bed. 'By God,' he said, 'it's more than enough. Listen, Belle. You should *not* spend your whole life feeling guilty for your brother. You were only a child yourself. Surely your parents—your mother at least—realised your grief, your remorse? Surely the maid who was supposed to be watching you was as much to blame—if we are apportioning blame—as you?' Adam saw one silent tear trailing freshly down her cheek and yearned to kiss it tenderly away.

She dashed that tear aside with her own hand and said flatly, 'My mother died when I was two. My father never forgave me for Edward's accident.'

Adam sighed. He was holding both her hands in his; they felt small and cold. 'Oh, Belle. None of us are blessed with everything we want in our lives, but you deserve so much more than you have. Than you *allow* yourself to have.'

Her face flew up to his, her expression one of surprise and almost fear. 'No! You are just saying this, because of the accident to poor little Tom. I am really quite happy with my life and my shop...'

His arm was round her shoulder, warming her.

He affected her—oh, that touch!—in a way she would not have believed possible. And it simply would not *do*, because she knew that in Adam Davenant's life everyone and everything had a purpose—including her. He was using her to keep the husband-hunters at bay and was making her pay sorely for her brother's debts and her own insults.

He despised her, of course. Yet as his long, lean fingers fondled her shoulders through the thin fabric of her gown, she could scarcely breathe for the pleasure of it.

He was murmuring, 'So stubborn. So *determined* to exclude yourself from the kind of life most women long for. Yet you were wonderful with those children today. Belle, why didn't you have children of your own?'

She paused, gathering her thoughts. 'I was told I could not have them. I did hope to become a doting aunt to my brother's children, but Charlotte—she…' Her throat was suddenly too tight to speak.

'Charlotte's baby has just died,' he put in quietly. 'Belle. Tell me. Why didn't you marry again? You surely must have had suitors…'

He saw her stricken expression and stopped.

He went on, even more softly, 'Did you love your husband so very much?'

'There has been no one else,' she whispered. *'No one.'* Until now...

Then she rose to her feet and smoothed down her skirts, making a desperate attempt to pull herself together. 'To exist on one's own,' she declared, 'is perfectly feasible, as you so often declare, Adam. Families tend to be over-rated, don't you think? Though *yours*—gracious me, your brother and his family are quite delightful, as one might expect!' Another tear was rolling down her cheek; again she dashed it away. 'You'll forgive me for my slight exasperation, I hope, you—you wretchedly perfect man! Does *nothing* ever go wrong for you?' She was fumbling for a handkerchief; more tears were brimming over her dark eyelashes.

Suddenly Adam was on his feet, too. He strode across to her and was holding her. She lifted her hand in some half-hearted gesture of resistance, but that was actually worse than useless, because he caught her fingers and pressed a kiss to the delicate skin of her inner wrist that sent shivers pulsing through her. Gathering her remorselessly into his powerfully muscled arms, he lowered his head to hers and kissed her.

The sweetness of his tongue slipping between her parted lips, silkily tasting and touching, made her feel quite faint with desire. She was aware of his arousal now, throbbing darkly against her abdomen; her hands had instinctively twined around his powerful shoulders.

A physical reaction, her pleasure-besieged brain told her. Nothing more. Nothing at all more. That was why she didn't stop him when his strong hand moved to gently caress her breast. That was why, at the juncture of her thighs, she felt an ache of sheer, sweet longing that was almost a pain...

Yes, it was wrong, all wrong. But, oh God, she *wanted* this man. So badly.

Adam's emotions, too, were in roiling tumult. He was taking advantage of her and he hadn't damn well meant to. As his lips possessed hers, as his tongue explored the satin recesses of her exquisite mouth, he fought to stop a great surge of desire pushing reason out of the window.

Lowell had been right, he'd been wrong. For all these years she'd been faithfully grieving her lost husband. He'd exploited that grief. He'd also exploited, just now, her remembrance of childhood horrors for which she unfairly blamed herself.

He knew he ought to take his hands off her,

now. But he wanted her. He wanted her with an urgency he couldn't ever remember feeling in his entire life, and that big bed was too damned close...

He forced himself away. 'Tell me to stop, for God's sake,' he gritted. 'Damn it, Belle, tell me to stop now, for I swear if we carry on much longer, I will not be able to do so.'

'You mean—this is real?' she breathed. 'You actually find me desirable?'

What in hell was she talking about? He gave a harsh, incredulous laugh. 'Can't you tell?' He was brushing his lips along her cheek and throat, his arousal nudging hard at his breeches.

'Adam—we'd agreed there would be no intimacy!'

There was an edge of panic to her voice that made him freeze. Cupping her face with his hands, he gazed down at her. His blood was pounding, his loins thudding just from her being near, this beautiful woman whose full, tremulous lips he longed to kiss again.

'Belle,' he said quietly. 'You loved your husband very much, I realise that—'

He broke off, feeling her tremble in his arms. 'But it's five years since he died,' he went on, 'and I want to kiss you, Belle. I want to do more than kiss you—I think you want it, too. And if you don't want me to take this further, then say so, now. Say, *Adam, I want you to leave.*'

A soft sound—a moan, a plea—escaped from her throat. Once more she was lifting her sweet face to his, her full lips parted with desire. Adam found that his strong hands were shaking more than a little as he slid the shoulders of her cherry-pink gown almost reverently down her slender arms, then bent his head to trail kisses from her throat down to the sweet curve of her breasts. She wrapped her hands round his waist, gasping as he cupped one creamy globe with his hand and took its peak very gently into his mouth.

Belle shuddered as his warm lips enclosed her coral nipple, his strong tongue sweeping to and fro across its taut crest. Her body was hot and alive, throbbing to his touch, and the most sensitive part of her was aching for more. His mouth had gone to her other breast, then he kissed her again. That bed beckoned. Adam stepped backwards to swing her up in his arms and carry her towards it...

'Damn!' The back of his head had encountered something hard and unyielding.

'Adam?' Her lips were swollen from his kiss, her voice hazy.

Still holding her, he moved away from the wall. 'It's all right. That blasted Egyptian thing—I knocked my head against it.'

She gave a hiccup of laughter and tightened her arms around him, glancing quickly at the black Egyptian throne she'd insisted on buying, with its overhanging wooden canopy. 'I hate it, too,' she breathed.

'Good God. You mean...'

'I loathe it. I—I only said I wanted it, to annoy you.'

'You hussy,' he murmured. 'You wicked, delightful hussy.' And to Belle's joy, he strode on towards the bed, where he laid her down.

Belle was blind to everything except this man's ardent caresses and her own desperate need. All she wanted was for him to join with her, fulfil her. Adam lifted one hand to carefully sweep her hair back so he could lean forwards and kiss the sensitive skin below her ear. She was breathing rapidly, scarcely able to bear the glorious sensations he was creating as he ran his cool palm along her thigh, stroking up it towards the most sensitive part of her being, seeking the throbbing core of her arousal, until...

'Adam.' His name burst from her lips as his fingers caressed her pulsing centre, the pleasure

tearing through her. She reared against him, her own clothes in an impossible tangle, her emotions haywire as his faintly stubbled jaw brushed her breast while he tongued her taut nipples. Her whole body tingled with the impossibly delicious sensations shooting out from where he stroked her.

For a moment he went perfectly still, taking his weight on his strong arms, gazing down at her with dark hunger gleaming in his hooded eyes. Then he made his move, all masculine power and grace. He'd slid his breeches down; she could see the flatness of his taut belly, the dark silken line of hair leading down to his pulsing manhood; she felt her lips part in an involuntary cry at the sight of that silken, steely shaft, but he stopped her cry with his kiss, his tongue thrusting deep. She clung to him, her body shaking.

'Belle,' he murmured thickly, lifting his mouth from hers. 'My beautiful Belle.'

The endearment rocked her. Her hands were clutching at his muscled back beneath his shirt, her slender thighs falling helplessly apart to welcome his intimate possession. Needing his possession, as she'd needed nothing before.

She cried his name again in soft joy as he slid his lean hips forwards and she felt his hard shaft sliding smoothly inside her. A wave of rapture engulfed her and she clutched his shoulders, then lifted her hips urgently, welcoming him deeper still. He paused a moment, leaving her taut with anguish, then he began to move again, steadily, strongly driving his length deep into her. She clung to him, clasping him with her thighs, flying higher and higher, while her own breathing came in shallow, moaning gasps. His hand had slid downwards again to touch her there, to urge on her pleasure, and suddenly her back arched, her inner muscles clutched tight round his hardness and her world exploded into a rapturous vortex of sensation.

Moments later, she heard Adam's harsh breathing as he stormed his way towards his own climax and spilled his seed deep within her. Joy pulsed again in splintering ripples at the core of her being as he enfolded her in his arms and she lay with her head against his broad, warm shoulder.

She thought she could hear his steady heartbeat. His eyes were closed; she tried to move a little, but his arm tightened round her. A disturbing surge of exhilaration swept through her from her toes to her fingertips as she gazed silently at his perfectly sculpted features.

It was swiftly followed by anguish. This was *wrong.* She wasn't supposed to feel like this— safe, and warm, and vibrantly alive. As if the most wonderful man in the world had just made incredibly powerful, incredibly tender love to her...

Love?

The cynical words he had spoken long ago echoed through her reeling mind. *It's rumoured, Mrs Marchmain, that I don't possess a heart.*

She'd been an utter fool to let this happen. How could she have allowed her already vulnerable defences slip so badly?

Adam didn't want to move. He wanted to hold her and remember the cries of ecstasy rippling from her throat; to relive the exquisite sensuality of her sweet body as she enfolded him... What was he thinking?

Conscious of her starting to draw away from him, he pulled her back into his arms. No doubt she could feel him hardening anew, for she gave a little gasp as he eased his aroused body against hers. Hell, he wanted her again, badly. His hand was sliding down gently to touch her hip; her flesh there was smooth, delicately rounded...

He'd sworn not to do this. He'd vowed that

whatever else his agreement with Jarvis led him into, he would *not* seduce her. *I will expect nothing of you that you're not prepared to give, Mrs Marchmain.*

Had she offered herself to him? The point was debatable, the result beyond doubt. He had damned well broken his word and he was furious with himself.

Sighing he raised himself on one arm and gently brushed a lock of hair back from her cheek. 'Belle. This doesn't really make things between us so very different, though we have to talk, to get everything clear...'

Belle froze. Not different? To have shared such rapture with him, such intimacy—and he was saying—*nothing had changed*?

She lay very still in the crook of his muscular arm. The afterglow of her orgasm was still glimmering inside her, spreading a wondrous sense of fulfilment through every fibre of her being. His lean, muscled body still warmed her; her slender legs were still twined with his...

Not different? She sat up and smiled brightly at him. What a silly fool he would think her, were she to try to play the love-struck innocent. Her, a widow, twenty-seven years old. 'Goodness me,

Adam,' she said. 'We're mature people, both of us. And the world assumes we're lovers anyway.'

He looked at her. 'So are you suggesting that we continue to enjoy intimacy—as we just have done—for the duration of our betrothal?' He'd leaned back against the pillows again, his muscled torso gloriously bare, and was reaching to pull her back into his arms, with an expression of pure desire that simply scorched her.

Belle felt something stop in her throat. She had to survive this. Had to be strong, even though she was melting already at his nearness, at his husky voice. 'Gracious,' she said lightly. 'Why not? It was a pleasurable experience, no denying.'

'Then let's repeat it,' he said calmly.

And to that Belle could give no reply. With his indomitable strength he pulled her down beside him, his hands already roving her breasts, his lips brushing her cheek. He made love to her again, darkly, passionately, absorbing her husky cries as she shattered into a thousand pieces in his arms.

Afterwards he settled her head against his shoulder, drifting his fingers along her ribs, soothing her until her breathing returned to normal. He knew the moment she fell asleep. But Adam didn't sleep.

Jarvis had expressed doubt as to whether Adam

had actually bedded her. Well, he'd done it. And damn it, he could still hear the cries of ecstasy that had rippled from her slender throat. He still reeled from the sheer sensuality of her sweet body as she shook with pleasure in his arms.

But his bargain with Jarvis wasn't completed yet. Next, he had to break with her. Publicly, Jarvis had said, with maximum humiliation. And then, by God, Belle Marchmain could feel free to hate him for the rest of her life.

Chapter Thirteen

A week later Adam called for her in the evening at seven. They'd been invited to a charity ball at Lord Horwich's grand house in Eaton Square; Adam wore a coat of dark-blue superfine that was designed and cut by Weston of Old Bond Street and bore all the quiet perfection that was the prestigious tailor's hallmark.

But Belle, now—she took great pleasure in defying convention. With a half-smile curving his strong mouth, Adam watched her coming down the stairs of the house in Bruton Street.

Her ballgown was some frothy concoction in shimmering yellow and blue. But he wasn't really seeing her clothes. He was seeing—Belle. *The way she moved*, he was marvelling. So innately graceful, yet somehow so sensual. Everything about her made his pulse kick in sudden warning. Made his physical desire for her throb into life. *Careful*.

Yes, indeed. Careful. Or he would be gathering her in his arms, sweeping her up to her bedroom and making delicious love to her, as he had every night for the past week. Her passion amazed him; aroused him anew time and time again, as if both of them were storing this up, for when...

For when it was over.

Adam's mistresses had always been sophisticated women who could arouse and satisfy him. But he'd never before been with someone who caused sheer desire to surge through his veins every time he damned well saw her. *Learn to cope with it, you fool*. Yet the way she was gazing at him now made something tighten warningly in his chest because she looked vulnerable and almost afraid.

Afraid of *him*, if she'd any sense.

She treated their relationship lightly in public, just touching his arm now and then, teasing him or bestowing a mischievous smile. But it was as if she was two people, for in bed at night she was tender, giving and wildly passionate. Sometimes at moments like that he felt as if he saw her soul laid bare.

Now he must have frightened her with just his

look, because that natural joy had fled from her eyes and her usual sweet smile was uncertain as she declared, 'Gracious, Mr D., how you stare! Is my gown too much for you tonight?' She was coming towards him, hips swaying enchantingly beneath her full skirts.

He shook himself mentally. 'It's dazzling enough to frighten my horses…. No. I'm jesting,' he teased her gently. 'It's absolutely perfect. As always, Belle.'

He was always stunned by just how ravishing she was, with her curling black hair and tip-tilted nose and full, rosy mouth. Was amazed as ever by her startling raiment—this time a jonquil-yellow ballgown tiered with layers of gauze and trimmed with turquoise-blue satin. It made him blink, step back then think: *Yes. I've never seen such an outfit before—but she has got it perfectly right.*

'Are you sure it's suitable?' she asked hesitantly. 'I don't want to look stupid or showy. I don't want the *ton* to laugh at me, Adam.'

He drew her into his arms and kissed the tip of her perfect nose. 'They won't laugh,' he said steadily. 'Firstly, because you'll be with me. And secondly, because your taste is unusual but faultless. Everyone's aware that your shop also caters for those with quieter tastes—but what disap-

pointment there would be if Mrs Belle Marchmain *didn't* wear something spectacular to a
grand ball!' He pressed his finger to her soft lips.
'Don't be nervous. You look beautiful.'

Her smile wavered a fraction. 'You are always
so calm at these society affairs. They all look up
to you.'

'Money talks amongst these people.' There was
a trace of harshness around his mobile mouth
now. 'But just remember you're as worthy as any
of them, Belle. You are, after all, the—'

'Great-niece to a duke,' they chorused together
and laughed. He fought the urge to put his arm
round her—fought the demands of his body, and
the overwhelming impulse not to go out *anywhere*, but lead her upstairs and take off her
clothes piece by piece, and...

'My carriage is waiting outside,' he said softly.
'Will you accompany me to the ball, Mrs Marchmain?'

She made him an elegant curtsy. 'With the
greatest of pleasure, Mr Davenant.'

As his carriage took them the short distance
to Eaton Square, a shadow of premonition was
stealing through Belle's veins. *Careful. Guard
yourself.*

Because soon it would be over.

Sultry July had ushered in the closing days of the London Season. Lord Horwich's ball was one of the final events. And any time now Adam would come to her and tell her she'd paid off her brother's dues. He would cancel Edward's gambling debt, inform her she'd kept him safe from the husband-hunters for long enough and tell her their betrothal was at an end.

He'd always reassured her that he was fully committed to the shop as a business venture; she did not doubt that he would retain his stake in it, for trade there was flourishing. But more and more she'd noticed that Adam was using his secretary Bernard Lowell to deal with the financial side and this surely was the shape of things to come.

Belle guessed with sudden bleakness that he'd found it more amusing than he'd thought, perhaps, to parade her round town as his intended. Besides, the cries of rapture he'd extracted from her night after night in his skilled arms must surely have obliterated for ever those insults she'd hurled at him on Sawle Down.

She'd always known she was merely a pawn in this powerful man's finely calculated day-to-day activities, in his balancing of enjoyment, his consolidation of his position amongst the *ton* and the all-important business of making money.

Yes, she was a mere pawn; so what a fool she was to let her pulse race so every time he came near. To feel her heart jolt each time he paid her some light, meaningless compliment. She shook a little inside every time his fingers so much as brushed hers. And as for the dark, ravishing pleasure she experienced in his arms at night...

She was a stupid fool, because all this was for him simply a matter of extracting sensual enjoyment from a situation he'd initially designed as revenge against her family.

Pleasure and convenience combined.

'If it weren't for Adam Davenant,' she scolded herself fiercely as they entered the grand house of Lord Horwich, 'your brother would be a bankrupt and you would be struggling to make *any* sort of living from a stall in the Soho Bazaar!'

She lifted her head. She was Belle Marchmain, proprietress of one of the most fashionable shops in town, and at her side was one of the wealthiest, most eligible men in London. Yes, soon it would be over. But until then—she was going to enjoy herself.

* * *

There were hundreds of candles in each of the main reception rooms, reflected everywhere in the silver plate and gilt mirrors. Liveried footmen hovered with fine wines; a group of musicians were already playing in the ballroom and all the guests were wonderfully dressed. Everyone seemed to know everyone else...

Belle found herself clinging a little tighter to Adam's strong arm.

He smiled down at her. 'Lift your head up. You look superb.'

She needed the compliment. Because soon they were surrounded—*he* was surrounded— by beautiful women trying to catch Adam's eye; by beady-eyed matrons still hungry for gossip about Davenant's unexpected betrothal and by the many male friends of Adam's who seized yet again the chance to eye up Davenant's prize.

Belle shrank instinctively back. But then the crowds parted because someone whom everyone knew, Lady Jersey, doyenne of Almack's, was making her stately way towards them.

'My dear Davenant!' she exclaimed. 'Here you are, you heart-breaker, looking, as usual, too wickedly handsome for words!'

Adam bowed over Lady Jersey's hand with a

smile; she looked at Belle. 'So this is the beauty who's at last broken your resolve never to marry, Davenant. Mrs Marchmain, is it not?' Everyone watched and waited in breathless suspense—a mere comment from this woman could make or break her.

At last Lady Jersey clicked her pearl-encrusted fan and gave a little sigh. 'I hate to admit it, but you've done yourself proud, Davenant. Not only a beauty, but a superb *modiste*, I hear.' She turned back to Belle. 'I am wary of new sensations in the fashion world—but you are building up such a reputation! And your gown—a truly unusual colour—is it made of silk?'

'It's actually made of *faille*, my lady—just a little softer, as you'll see, than grosgrain.'

'I do see. Wonderful! And the lace?'

'Nottingham lace, my lady. I use English-made goods whenever I can.'

'Excellent. I must call in at your shop—in Piccadilly, isn't it?' She gave something that was almost a wink. 'They've been talking about you, you know, all the gossips, and not a single one told me how beautiful you are. But women being women, they wouldn't, would they?'

Lady Jersey tapped Adam's chest with her fan. 'I'm holding a rout next week, Davenant. A last flourish, before I escape to the country for the rest of the summer. I'll send you and your delightful fiancée an invitation.'

Adam bowed low again, a smile lurking at the corners of his mouth. 'I'm sure we'll accept it with pleasure, Lady Jersey.'

A cluster of eager women immediately surrounded Belle, anxious not to miss out on this latest sensation who had won the approval of Lady Jersey herself. But what meant most of all to Belle was the sight of Adam looking outwardly as calm as ever, yet in his sleepy grey eyes she thought she saw a flash of—pride.

And desire. Oh, God, *desire*.

She thought she was strong, but the sudden bolt of emotion that shot through her made her gasp for breath.

She ought to resist him. She should never, ever have submitted to him.

Because now she could not imagine life without him.

The dancing came next and Belle was overwhelmed with offers, though it was the cotillion she danced with Adam that she enjoyed most of all. Then came supper—but on their way Belle heard a piercing female voice just a few yards away.

'Adam, darling. How *are* you?'

Adam had turned swiftly. 'Lady Farnsworth. This is my fiancée, Mrs Marchmain.'

Belle froze inwardly at the sight of the beautiful Lady Farnsworth, who had once been Adam's mistress. 'Lady Farnsworth,' she said coolly. 'How do you do?'

'Oh, *I*'m well enough,' said the blonde beauty. 'But I hear things. I hear, for example, Mrs Marchmain, that your brother is too fond of the card tables—but that you, my dear, have found a novel way to pay off his debts!'

Belle felt her pulse hammering. She moistened her lips to reply; Adam was there first.

'You always were one for idle mischief-making, Lady Farnsworth,' he said coolly. 'But you're rather scraping the barrel this time—even for you.'

Lady Farnsworth coloured, shot a look that held daggers in it at Belle and marched off.

Belle felt cold. She'd just been accused of selling herself to Adam for money—and wasn't it true? The magic had suddenly gone out of the evening. She whirled on Adam. 'If *that woman* knows about Edward's debts, there'll be more who will.'

'And so?' Something in Adam's face frightened her. He guided her into a corner and said, 'Listen. The last thing you do is run away from this, do you hear me? Someone's been talking, yes, but you must face the gossips out with boldness. You're not a whore, but she is.'

'But she was your mistress!'

'Believe me,' said Adam grimly, 'I got out of her clutches very quickly. Wait here—there's someone I need to speak to, and meanwhile you can have a few moments of peace. You're doing marvellously, Belle. I'm proud of you.'

He was gone for a long time. The minutes ticked slowly by; Lady Jersey and some of her friends came to talk to her, but all Belle wanted was to find Adam again. Seeing his tall figure on the far side of the crowded room, she started to make her way towards him.

Only to pull to an abrupt halt a few feet away when she saw he was deep in intense conversation with—Lord Jarvis. Jarvis looked furious and was gesticulating wildly. Adam appeared rigid with anger. Cold fingers of fear were for some reason travelling up and down Belle's spine.

'Getting rather too fond of the little widow, aren't you, Davenant?' she could hear Jarvis snarling.

Adam spoke more quietly than Jarvis; Belle couldn't hear him. But whatever he said made Jarvis clench his fists in utter rage.

'Everything's at stake—do you understand?' she heard Jarvis hiss. 'Yes, you've seduced the Marchmain widow, you've coaxed her into a public betrothal, but you're damned well not playing by our rules. And until I see you doing so you can't expect me to keep my side of the bargain!'

Bargain? Rules? Belle's world was spinning dizzyingly around her. She couldn't hear anything else. She didn't need to.

'Why did you leave the ball without me, Belle? God damn it, I was worried sick...'

Belle had left Lord Horwich's house immediately, asking a footman to summon a hackney. By the time Adam reached Bruton Street twenty minutes after her, Belle was in her bedroom and had packed half her clothes. He'd pounded up the stairs and flung the door open without knocking, only to look at the piles of clothes in disbelief.

'You were *worried*?' she breathed, turning her face to him. 'Yes, I suppose you *must* have been anxious that Lord Jarvis might withdraw from the bargain you made with him. What was it—a wager?'

He'd run his hand through his hair. His white neckcloth was rumpled and he looked utterly, heartbreakingly handsome. 'How much did you hear?'

She dragged air into her aching lungs. 'Enough to know that he'd offered you something—no, I don't want to know what!—to parade me as your fiancée.' *Dear Lord, she'd opened to his embraces as hungrily as a whore.* 'Would you mind leaving me on my own, Adam?'

Adam's shoulders were rigid. 'You didn't hear anything else?'

Oh, God. This was bad. This had to be just about the worst moment of her life. 'I'm heartily glad I didn't,' she answered. 'I dread to think what else you had planned for me.'

'Belle…'

She turned back to the pile of clothes on the bed, throwing them into the valises set out there; now she whirled to face him. 'Do you really think I want to hear any more, Adam?' Her voice was etched with pain. 'Haven't you put me through *enough*?'

He was silent a moment. Then, 'What are you doing, Belle?' he said softly.

Just his voice tormented her in a way she hadn't believed possible. 'I'm packing some things, so that I can go and live above the shop.' Once more she faced him. 'I know that these clothes and the shop are partly yours, but, my God, Adam, I'll buy you out just as soon as I can. If I fail to raise the money, I'll sell up and move out of London. *Anything*, believe me, rather than live under the falsehood of this *arrangement* any longer!'

He went very still. 'Not everything was a falsehood, Belle,' he said.

The blood rushed to her cheeks. She couldn't answer. *The incredible sweetness of his kisses. The tender power of his lovemaking, night after night.* All an act. Oh, God...

'Listen,' he went on, gripping her arms and forcing her to face him. 'Let me explain. I wanted some of Jarvis's land. *Needed* it, for a railway I'm building in Somerset. He wouldn't be bought with money. The railway means jobs and prosperity for my men.'

She was quite white. She breathed, 'And Jarvis said he'd let you have that land, if—if you seduced me?'

'What you heard at Lord Horwich's tonight was only a part of it. Things changed between you and me. You know how very much they changed, Belle.'

'Stop,' she cried. '*Stop*. You mean you were to

display me as your infatuated fiancée as part of a *business* agreement...' Her voice suddenly faltered. 'Those complaints,' she whispered. 'My landlord, suddenly doubling the rent...'

'Not me, but Jarvis.' His voice was tight; she saw he was clenching and unclenching his fists.

Her hands flew to her cheeks. 'Then why didn't you tell me? I think you're lying again. I think you've lied to me from the day we met. Oh, there's no need at all for you to suggest we end our betrothal—I'll save you the trouble. I'm going to take myself completely out of your life.'

'No, you won't,' he said. He'd started picking out the clothing she'd put in her valises.

'What the hell are you doing?' she cried.

'You can't take these clothes. As you observed, I've paid for most of them. And I have to inform you it's essential that you stay on here—at least for the time being.'

Her green eyes flashed with defiance. 'No. Oh, no. That is impossible.'

'I'm afraid you must make it possible. I will not force my company on you, but it's essential for your own safety that you reside here under my protection for at least the next few weeks.'

'*Protection?*' She was almost laughing at the savage irony of this. 'Protection, when as far as

I can see the only person I'm in danger from is yourself? Anyway, how can you *make* me, without keeping me under lock and key…?'

Suddenly Belle needed to sit down, because her legs felt as though they wouldn't hold her any more. 'My brother. My brother still owes you all that money. And you will use his debt to force me to stay on, in this hateful situation.' She gazed up at him steadily. 'You've seduced me. You've humiliated me. You've used my brother's debts—all for a railway. A damned railway. Get out. I know this is your house, but please get out of here. Yes, I will stay. But—you cannot make me endure your company!'

His firm jaw was clenched. 'There's just one more thing.'

She wasn't sure how much longer she could control her shaking limbs. 'More orders?' she queried caustically.

'I'm afraid so. I've already told you not to go anywhere around town alone—but I've reason to believe you've been disobeying me.'

She said bitterly, 'My God, your spies have certainly been busy.'

'Call them that if you must. Nevertheless you will oblige me by not going anywhere, unless one of my men attends you.'

She closed her eyes briefly. 'For how long....?' But he'd already left her.

Belle sat on her bed and stared into blackness. Oh, God. So cleverly, so subtly he'd entrapped her. She'd tried her damnedest to resist. But Adam had worked his dark magic on her until she had been desperate for him. She'd abandoned herself completely in his arms to his powerful yet tender lovemaking.

And all he wanted was—land for his damned railway.

The tears began to fall at last and this time she let them, though she told herself it was the very last time she would allow herself to cry for Adam Davenant.

Adam returned to his big house in Clarges Street. He went to his study and paced the floor. If only the night could be relived. If only Belle Marchmain had trusted him. Then he might have been able to make her listen to the truth.

For tonight, Adam had told Lord Jarvis to keep his damned land, because their bargain was off.

Adam had heard several days ago that Jarvis had taken up with Lady Farnsworth. So, when she'd come up to them at Lord Horwich's house, Adam knew it signalled trouble. Indeed it did, for she'd blurted out what Jarvis, the fool, must have told her about Edward's debts. Adam had cuttingly silenced her, then had gone in search of Jarvis.

'We had an agreement,' Adam had challenged him bluntly. 'But I *don't* remember an agreement giving you permission to give details of our private deal to your latest mistress.'

'Getting rather too fond of the little Marchmain widow, are you?' Jarvis had growled. And had proceeded to utter the warnings, the threats that Belle, God damn it, must have overheard. 'You're damned well not playing by our rules.'

'That's because I've changed my mind, Jarvis.'

'You've…'

'I've decided I'll manage without your land for my railway. Understand? I'm not going to make a public spectacle of Belle Marchmain just for you.'

Jarvis's mouth had worked furiously. 'Then I will!' he got out at last.

And Jarvis, in a fury of rage and more than slightly drunk, had proceeded to issue specific threats against Mrs Marchmain. Spat out obscenities as to how Adam could damn well whistle for his railway land, and that he, Jarvis, would take Belle for himself—by force, if necessary—

then turn her over to his grooms once he'd finished with her.

Jarvis only stopped when Adam seized him by his lapels, thudded him up against the nearest wall and warned the man that he would take pleasure in pummelling him to kingdom come if he so much as harmed one hair of Belle Marchmain's head.

Now Adam paced his study. Belle's pale, vulnerable face as she accused him of nothing but the truth—*You've seduced me. You've humiliated me. You've used my brother's debts—all for a railway!*—would haunt him for the rest of his life.

He sat in the chair beside his desk, its surface scattered with maps and quarry plans. His efforts to remedy the damage done had come far too late. He should have warned Belle much earlier that it was Jarvis who'd endeavoured to ruin her Strand shop, but now that his treacherous bargain with Jarvis had been exposed she trusted Adam about as much as she'd trust a venomous snake.

She'd made up her mind that Adam was the villain in all this and who could blame her? He *had* agreed to Jarvis's initial, vile proposition and there was no getting round that fact. He remembered her face just now. Pale, defiant, proud. But underneath, he guessed, so hurt. So desperately hurt.

For five years, she appeared to have kept herself away from men in honour of the memory of her dead husband—but Adam had broken through her defences. Quite possibly he'd broken *her*.

He cursed Jarvis, cursed that damned agreement, and most of all cursed himself.

Adam went to only one social engagement that week and wished he hadn't. He missed Belle at his side. Missed her outrageous clothes, her humour, her mixture of defiance and vulnerability. He cancelled all invitations for the next fortnight—there were mercifully few anyway since the Season was all but over—and spent his days in meetings with bankers and businessmen, discussing the Sawle Down quarry's prospects, negotiating contracts for this new and valuable supply of Bath stone.

Already he'd sent orders to George Shipley, his chief engineer in Somerset, to hire men and begin excavations for the railway through his and his friend Bartlett's estates. But Jarvis's land still barred the way to the canal, and two weeks after the momentous ball at Lord Horwich's house Shipley arrived from Somerset at Adam's home one sultry night in late July with the ominous news that threats were being made against the neighbouring estate owners who'd offered to support Adam's railway.

'There's damage been done to fences and crops by night, Mr Davenant,' warned Shipley, who was tired from his two-day journey. 'Threats against tenants and families by anonymous bully-boys who ride into the local villages, then ride off again, setting up the kind of fear that sticks. And at the actual site, around the excavations your lads have begun digging, there's been accidents that look more like sabotage.'

Adam handed him a glass of wine. 'You look like you need this. Is it Jarvis?'

'He would seem the obvious culprit, sir, and I reckon he's got quite a few of the Somerset magistrates in his pay. What can you do?'

'A considerable amount, I think,' said Adam grimly, 'if I travel to Somerset myself.'

Shipley appeared heartened. But something else worried Adam. Could it be Jarvis's intention that Adam be lured away from his rigorous watch over Belle? Only this morning Lennox had told Adam he'd seen suspicious characters lurking around the Bruton Street house at dusk.

A warning had hammered in Adam's chest. 'You're ensuring she's never alone, Lennox?'

'The maid Simmons keeps an eye on Mrs Marchmain in the house, sir, and of course I send a groom with her whenever she sets off for her shop.'

'She still goes there?'

'Every day, without fail—she insists on it. I send a man to bring her home as well. Though I wouldn't put it past her to give one of them the slip some day soon, sir.'

Adam wouldn't either. He *had* to keep her under his protection, but he also had to go to Somerset. There was only one answer and Belle would absolutely hate it.

She would have to come with him.

Chapter Fourteen

It was true; Belle went into her shop every morning and worked till late, because work offered the only respite from the pain that engulfed her whenever she thought of Adam's betrayal.

Gabby and the others asked no questions, but just once Gabby had found Belle sitting alone in the workroom, with a single garment spread out before her on the sewing table. It was the crimson carriage gown she'd worn during that drive in the park with Adam. A customer had asked for one in a similar style and Belle had brought it in here to measure out the fabric, but the memories it evoked savaged her already raw emotions.

'*Madame?*' Gabby's whisper was full of concern. 'Are you all right, *madame*?'

Belle jerked her head up. 'Perfectly, thank you, Gabby!'

'*Madame*, I do not like to pry. But Monsieur Davenant—he cares for you, I am sure of it.'

Belle stood up, smiling brightly. '*So* much work to do, Gabby—now, I need a length of red lutestring and some gold braid...'

Gabby sighed and proceeded to help her.

After Lord Horwich's ball Belle had spent night after sleepless night agonising over her dire situation. What if Adam had meant what he'd said— that, yes, he'd made his agreement with Lord Jarvis, but things had changed? *You know how very much they changed, Belle.*

She was a fool to search for any kind of hope. He was a ruthless businessman. How could she ever forget that he'd used her brother's debts to force her into that betrothal? He'd bartered her, in effect, for the railway land he was so desperate for.

Adam never visited her now in the Bruton Street house, but sometimes she heard the servants talking about him. One morning Joseph, Adam's coachman, was speaking with Lennox in the hallway when she was about to descend the stairs.

'I've come to pick up the master's travelling clothes,' Joseph informed Lennox.

Belle froze. Adam had got into the habit of

leaving items of clothing here—some coats and changes of indoor garments—because of the nights he used to spend there so often with her. *Oh, those nights. Those magical nights.* After their lovemaking he would stay in her bed all night long, holding her in his arms as he slept...

'Going away, is he?' Lennox asked Joseph.

'Aye, to Somerset. To see about that railway of his...'

Belle stole back to her room, feeling shaky. So he was going away. She, too, should get away. From this place and from him—but his absence changed nothing. Edward's debts still kept her his prisoner.

After that she'd gone into the shop escorted by one of Lennox's men as usual, but that particular morning it was quiet—not only because the fashionable elite had left for the country, but also because of the rain that had been falling since dawn. Belle was so busy arranging some new rolls of silk on a back shelf that she didn't hear Gabby coming up behind her.

'*Madame.*' Gabby was tapping her on the shoulder. 'Someone is here for you.'

Something in her voice made Belle's pulse rate

hitch. She turned from her silks, and saw that Adam was there.

Two weeks since she'd seen him and something surged in her veins. Shock, and more. Sudden heat, instead of cold. A shameful racing of her blood, just at his presence. *Breathe, Belle, you fool.* Somehow she dragged air painfully into her lungs and felt her heart jolt back into action.

He was a tall, almost threatening figure. She'd forgotten in just this short space of time how big he was. His magnetic presence somehow filled the shop. His exquisitely cut coat of grey broadcloth glistened with the soft rain that fell outside; his dark hair gleamed with beads of water. She'd hoped she could hate him, but oh, God, fresh pain lanced her just at the sight of him.

Gabby emptied the shop still further by shooing out the assistants. 'You naughty creatures, *mon dieu*, what do you think you are playing at? We have four gowns to complete by tomorrow and you stand around doing *nothing*?' She followed them out after one swift, anxious glance at Belle.

'Mr Davenant,' Belle managed to say at last.

He bowed his head a fraction. 'Mrs Marchmain. I have business in Somerset that requires my immediate attention and I've come to ask you to accompany me there.'

That was it. As simple as that. Oh, Lord. She'd hoped she was prepared for him—this meeting had to come sooner or later—but she wasn't.

There was no hint of remembered pleasure in his flat remark. Her pulse was thudding as she reminded herself that this man had calmly used her as a pawn against Jarvis. Squandered her dignity, her reputation, in exchange for some *land* he wanted for his moneymaking. And it wasn't over yet.

He said he had business in Somerset. Could it be with—Jarvis?

She said, with a brilliant smile, 'Gracious me, Mr Davenant, what an invitation! And so charmingly expressed!' She let her smile drop. 'My answer is no.' And she turned back to the rolls of silk she was arranging.

'You'll have to pack. It's almost ten and I want to leave by eleven,' he said imperturbably.

She swung round. *'No!* How many times do I have to say it?'

'It doesn't matter how many times you repeat yourself; I'm not leaving you here.'

'Why?'

'Because I think you might be in danger.'

'Danger.' She put her head on one side, pretending to think. 'Now, what kind of danger might

present itself? I know—someone might decide to use me as a *commodity* in one of his devious business deals. Yes, I must by all means be protected from such a heinous villain! Oh, and Mr Davenant, *please* don't let me delay you in your urgent journey.'

Her silks once more engaged her attention. *Damn*, thought Adam. He knew her well enough to realise that beneath that usual calm exterior she was trembling with emotion. With distress. What the hell had he expected?

'I'm not actually giving you an option,' he said flatly. 'You are coming with me. Perhaps, on the way, we might be able to come to a better understanding of our present situation.'

'Oh, now, that *is* impossible,' Belle broke in airily.

His dark eyes were ominous. 'I have an important meeting in Bath in two days' time. I need to be on the road before noon and you're coming, too.'

This time the colour had left her face. 'I take it that if I were foolish enough to argue, you would refer yet again to my brother's debts?'

'If it will stop this pointless argument, then, yes, I will. Joseph is outside; he'll take you in the coach back to Bruton Street, where you can pack your things accordingly. I expect to be in Somerset for a week or so; you could use the opportunity to visit your brother and his wife. I'm sure Gabby and your assistants can look after your shop admirably for a while. I'll collect you from Bruton Street shortly.'

With that, he left.

It should be easy to hate him now. But Belle felt every fibre of her body hurting in a way she wouldn't have believed possible. Oh, this was bad. She hadn't realised that the cruellest of emotions—hope—still lurked somewhere in the recesses of her heart. Until now.

After flinging on a cloak against the rain, Belle went outside to tell Joseph that she'd be with him shortly. And from him she found out some rather interesting details about Adam's planned journey.

They would arrive in Bath tomorrow evening. Joseph was driving the carriage as far as Chippenham, which they should reach tomorrow afternoon; but at Chippenham, Joseph told her, Mr Davenant kept a light curricle which he would drive himself to Bath while Joseph followed more slowly in the coach with the luggage.

Belle's mind raced. She went back inside to

speak to Gabby. 'I'm going away to Somerset, Gabby, just for a few days.'

'To visit your brother and his poor wife?'

'I may do so, yes. Actually, I'm travelling with Mr Davenant.'

Gabby's eyes lit up. 'Oh, *madame*, I'm so glad—'

'It's not a cause for celebration,' Belle cut in. *Though I intend to make the event just a little more eventful than Mr Davenant has bargained for.* 'Is Matt around?'

Matt was out in the yard now that the rain had stopped, sawing up wood to make some new shelves for her silks. Matt's talents knew no bounds. At least, Belle fervently hoped so. She gave him his orders swiftly, ignored his protests, then turned to go back into the shop, feeling as tight as a coiled spring at the thought of the ordeal to come.

Half an hour later there was nothing more that needed her attention in the shop. She'd gone over everything with Gabby at least three times. Now for Bruton Street, to await Adam Davenant's autocratic, hateful presence.

Gabby was ushering her to the door. 'Oh, *madame*, I will miss you!' They hugged one another. 'I'll miss Matt, too,' Gabby went on. 'He's told me he's going away on a most important errand for you.'

'And I'm really grateful to him, Gabby. You have—the extra item?'

'It is here.' Carefully Gabby picked up a large wicker basket with a strap to hold its lid in place. 'But I would never have guessed that Mr Davenant—'

'Oh, Mr Davenant is full of surprises,' cut in Belle lightly. 'As am I.'

The basket wriggled a little. From within came the faint sound of scuffling. Then—silence.

Gabby carefully handed it over and stood at the shop door to wave as Belle climbed into the waiting carriage, to be taken by Joseph to Bruton Street.

Belle hoped that Adam might waver over taking her with him when he saw how much luggage she had. Even the ever-obedient maid Simmons had blinked at her travelling outfit, a tight purple jacket over a pale blue gown sprigged with purple daisies.

Casting Adam a challenging stare, Belle clutched her big straw hat on her head and with her other hand the wicker basket. Joseph held the horses while Lennox and a footman struggled to squeeze her valises into the luggage space at the back.

'I hope that's all you're taking,' Adam said. 'You'd oblige me by getting in. I'd like to make Newbury by nightfall.'

She tilted her chin to meet his hard gaze. 'Perhaps I'd oblige you most by not getting in at all. May I remind you that you've hauled me away from my shop with hardly a moment's notice?'

He glanced pointedly at his watch. 'Mrs Marchmain, you've already delayed my journey by ten minutes and—'

'Oh, fie, Mr D. You and your timekeeping!' Ignoring his proffered hand, she climbed in, placing the wicker basket on the seat beside her.

'That could have gone on the back with your other luggage,' he said.

'No, it couldn't.'

He pressed his lips together and climbed in to sit opposite her, somehow finding space for his long, heavily muscled legs. He was dressed, she reluctantly noticed, as immaculately as ever for their journey in buckskins and top boots, with a light-coloured greatcoat that was exquisitely cut...

She jerked her head away to look quickly out of

the window, pretending utter absorption in London's streets as the chaise moved off.

'I think you'll be pleasantly surprised,' he said after a few moments, 'by how well your business manages to run without you.'

'I sincerely hope so,' she answered briskly, turning back to him with a steady gaze. 'Because soon, Mr Davenant, I intend to buy you out. After that, let me assure you that I will owe nothing to anyone.'

Adam said, 'It's a pity that your brother didn't learn the same lesson.'

Belle snapped open her latest edition of *La Belle Assemblée* and began to study the fashion plates without speaking another word.

The silence lasted hardly longer than five minutes. Adam was studying the basket at her side. Then he was saying, in that dangerously quiet voice of his, 'Unless I'm very much mistaken, that basket beside you is starting to move.'

'Why, yes,' she acknowledged coolly. She turned to start undoing the straps of the basket. 'Since I acquired him, I never travel anywhere without dear Florizel.'

His eyebrows shot up as she opened the lid, pulled out a squirming puppy and cuddled it in her lap. 'He's an absolute darling,' she chattered on. 'Let me show you...'

His eyes were fixed with steely grimness on the small, fluffy white creature with ribbons round its neck and a little bell that tinkled. 'Precisely *when* did you acquire—Florizel?'

'Oh, recently!' she answered. *Just after Adam's visit, to be precise, thanks to Gabby.* It was Gabby who'd told Belle of the pups which were up for sale and who had been only too delighted to go and get one for her.

'Strange,' he said tightly, 'that Lennox never told me...'

'Florry lives at the shop. And I'm so very relieved to have *some* secrets from you, Mr Davenant.' Belle soothed the tiny dog tenderly. 'Florry is such a little darling,' she went on, 'and you will soon grow to love him, just as I do.'

'You think so,' he breathed. 'What kind of name is that for a dog?'

'Florry? Short for Prince Florizel, Mr Davenant! Fie, have you never seen Shakespeare's *Winter's Tale*?' He gritted his teeth, as he always did at any supposed reference to his lack of culture. 'It is all the rage, you know,' Belle blurted on, 'to carry a little dog. With ribbons that match the colours of my gown—see? Purple and green today. Isn't he a sweet little thing? He will sleep in my room, of course, when we have to stop tonight...'

'He's most certainly not sleeping in mine,' Adam said. 'And you'll have to deal with his bodily functions yourself. Don't expect my coachman to. He'd most likely throttle the thing.'

'Mr Davenant—really!' She pouted with indignation, but she bent to fondle the little dog with a rare sensation of triumph and went back to reading her journal.

But it didn't take long for her temporary optimism to dissipate. Adam Davenant exuded self-control; she tried to match it, but every time he moved—every time he breathed, even—she remembered how he'd made love to her and her wretched heart turned over. To be in such close proximity to this man—trapped, in fact, for hours—was going to be torture.

That he was powerful and rich she already knew. But who else would have his own horses kept at every posting station on the road to Somerset? 'Mr Davenant makes the journey so often,' Joseph told her at their lunchtime stop, 'that it makes sense, it do, to keep his own teams. The

master don't want some hired nags that are fit
only for the knacker's yard.'

Belle reckoned Adam probably wished he could
consign *her* to the knacker's yard, because she
was deliberately making an absolute pest of herself. Every time they stopped and the ostlers came
running to change his horses, she would make
a great show of taking Florizel for a walk round
the inn yard using his ribbon-plaited lead. But
Florizel wasn't the problem, Adam was. Just the
touch of his lean hand, or the inadvertent brushing of his hard male body against hers, made her
senses throb and her breath catch in her throat.

Most of the time as they journeyed westwards,
she buried her nose in her journal or played with
Florizel in her lap, but her mind was miles away.
What was his meeting in Somerset about? Why
had he said he needed her with him? *Because
Jarvis would be there?*

During the journey Adam had intended to address the vital documents he'd brought with him
in preparation for his meeting. But all too often,
as Belle read her journal or petted that absurd
little dog, he would find his eyes drawn against
his will to the alluring curves of her bosom, to

the creamy softness of her cheeks and her full, rosy lips.

Damn. Even the faint lavender scent of her skin caused the familiar arousal to surge through him. He wanted to slip his hands inside that ridiculous little purple jacket, caress her luscious breasts, feel her melt in his arms again...

Ridiculous. Apart from the fact that the dog would snap his fingers off, he'd noticed that her hostility to him never wavered. She shrank away from him even when he was merely offering her his hand to help her down from the coach.

She despised him for making that bargain with Jarvis for his railway land—hell, he despised *himself.* He'd tried to tell her he'd cancelled the agreement, but she wouldn't even listen. He couldn't blame her and she clearly hated him even more for making her accompany him on this journey. But he'd been truly afraid at the thought of what Jarvis might try to do to her if Adam left her in London.

It would be interesting to know, he found himself wondering bleakly as the miles rolled by, which of the two men—himself or Jarvis—she hated more.

He felt as though during the past few weeks she had hurled his whole existence into a disturbing state of tumult—so much so that he was just beginning to wonder if his iron-hard heart wasn't as impervious to stripes and brightly coloured ribbons as it damned well ought to be.

And he had something else to worry about. He guessed they were being followed.

They dined that night in the private parlour of a Newbury inn; the yappy little dog had fallen asleep in its basket in the corner, thank God, but now Adam almost wished it would wake up and distract her because he'd quite forgotten that the dark-panelled walls in here were hung with old regimental prints and battle scenes.

Seeing her glance at them, then turn quickly away, he chose a chair for her that meant she wouldn't have to stare at them all through this damned meal. 'I'm sorry,' he said, after the deferential waiter had brought in the food, then departed. 'You must find reminders of the war painful.'

'Such a terrible waste of so many lives,' she answered quietly.

And that was it, though he thought he saw her hand tremble a little as she put down her fork. He'd already noted that Belle barely ate enough to keep a bird alive. As soon as the waiter had cleared their plates away she rose and went over to the basket where the dog lay. 'Come, Florry,' she trilled. 'It's time to go up to our room!'

But Adam asked her to stay with him, just for a few moments.

She sat down again on the edge of her chair, clutching the dog. 'Yes?'

'I've reason to believe, Belle, that we are being followed.'

'Followed…?'

'When I've looked back at the road behind us today,' Adam explained, 'I've sometimes seen a lone horseman come into view, only to disappear again. Have you noticed anything?'

She gazed at him blankly. The little dog yapped in her arms. 'Why would anyone wish to follow us? Hush, Florry, it's all right…'

'I've no idea. But will you make sure your bedroom door is locked and bolted tonight?'

'Most definitely,' she asserted, with the most spirit she'd shown all day.

No doubt she meant she would bolt it against *him*. Adam clenched his teeth and said, 'That's all. Goodnight, Belle.'

They set off early the next morning and Adam got out some business documents which clearly absorbed him. He didn't mention their follower again.

He's getting ready for his important meeting. Belle shivered. They stopped for an early lunch; by mid-afternoon, Joseph reminded her, they would reach Chippenham and would transfer to the curricle Adam kept there, which he would drive himself.

Belle was sitting as far as she could from him with her nose jammed in her fashion journal. But after a while she realised that he was leaning over to look at it.

'That violet day gown would look marvellous with your hair,' he pointed out.

Too close. Oh, Lord, he was too close, she could feel the warmth of his body. 'Violet is not considered fashionable at present, Mr Davenant!' she declared breezily. Florizel, in his basket at her feet, woke up and started yapping. Belle leant over and stroked his fluffy ears. 'Hush now, Florry, Mr Davenant is trying to be nice to me.'

She heard the hiss of his indrawn breath. 'It's a business suggestion. You should *make* violet fashionable,' he observed. 'Only the waist should be tighter. With your figure, it would look wonderful.'

How could he talk so lightly? When he planned…

Lord knew what he planned, but one way or another he seemed bent on destroying her. Florizel whimpered; she pulled the puppy up on to her lap and said, in as smooth a tone as she could manage, 'I thought, Mr Davenant, we were agreed on one thing at least—that nothing personal, of any kind, would pass between us ever again. Compliments, insults, or anything else for that matter.' She looked directly at him, her eyes burning. 'You could do me that kindness, at least.'

'Belle,' he said. His voice was different. Something in his eyes made her heart shake. 'I know you will find this difficult to believe. But I would give a great deal, if we could only start again from the beginning, you and I.'

Something broke inside her. He was her enemy, he had to be, just as Lord Jarvis was; Adam was using her, and she... Florizel chose that moment to start whining for attention; quickly she bent to fuss over the little dog. Adam went back to reading his damned papers and said no more.

For Belle the next few miles went by in an agony of apprehension. When they stopped at the busy Chippenham coaching inn just after two, Adam prepared to transfer the two of them and a single valise each to the light curricle he kept there, leaving Joseph to follow on with the coach and remaining luggage at a slower pace.

Belle walked with Florizel round and round the inn yard, desperately watching every traveller, every horseman, until Adam fetched her and made her get on board. 'We can leave the dog,' he said icily, 'but I'm not leaving you.'

She jutted her chin, but said nothing. Adam took the reins, so Belle was left to sit inside with just Florizel and *La Belle Assemblée* for company. But to be honest she hadn't read a thing for the past few miles. Suddenly, with a clattering of hooves, the horses swerved violently. She could hear Adam shouting a warning to her; her heart hammered. The horses neighed frantically as the curricle, with a dreadful creaking sound, lurched sideways and settled itself at a lopsided angle halfway over the right-hand ditch.

Belle stumbled outside. The horses reared and fretted in their traces. And Adam lay very still, on the road. Oh, *no*. She'd only meant to make him miss his meeting. Not this. Please, God, not this.

Chapter Fifteen

Feeling sick, Belle crouched at Adam's side in the mud to check beneath his coat for his heartbeat. He was still breathing, but his eyes were shut and there was a livid bruise on his forehead. Her own pulse was hammering. She had to get help. The two horses were terrified, pulling at their harness, tossing their heads, and no wonder; just ahead of them a sapling tree lay right across the road.

Hurriedly she went to tie Florizel's leash to the curricle's wheel and tried to soothe the horses. *Adam must have swerved to stop them crashing into that sapling.* But Matt had said…

She ran back to kneel at Adam's side; he still lay prone, helpless. The curricle needed righting and the horses might try to bolt any minute. Should she unharness them? Walk for help? But where? Her stomach lurched again. This had all gone so horribly, terribly *wrong*.

Just then the sound of a horse and rider coming up fast set her pulse thudding anew—especially when she realised that the rider galloping up was her brother.

She scrambled to her feet. 'Edward. Oh, God, Edward—what are you doing here?

Edward was jumping from his horse and staring at Davenant. His face was pale. 'I meant to make the arrogant bastard stop, that was all.'

Oh, no. 'You don't mean—oh, please, you're not saying... Was it *you* who caused his curricle to overturn?'

'Damn it, Belle, I didn't mean to hurt the man! But I couldn't think how else to make him listen to me. I just *had* to have this out with him when I heard he was on his way here with you!'

Belle was white-lipped. 'For God's sake, *what* did you have to have out with him, Edward?'

He was bracing his shoulders now, with that look half of fear, half of defiance in his eyes that she remembered so well. 'Why, I was defending your honour, Belle. I'd heard you were betrothed to him and I knew he must have somehow forced you into it!'

She found she was trembling with shock and distress. Yes, he had, but...

Belle cast another anguished look back at the unconscious man. Whatever he'd done, whatever his plans for her—she couldn't bear to see him hurt. 'For God's sake, Edward. We can't waste time talking. Tie up your own horse and see to Adam's pair. Calm them down, will you?'

She was down at Adam's side again. *Please don't be badly hurt. Please.* She called out to Edward, 'We passed an inn a mile or so back. If I can drive him there, they will surely know of a local doctor—'

She broke off at the sound of more hoofbeats coming along the road. A solitary rider was drawing near. Belle scrambled to her feet. It was Matt.

'Mrs Marchmain. And Mr Hathersleigh...' Matt jumped off his sturdy horse and took in Edward, the curricle and the frightened horses. Suddenly he saw Davenant's prone figure and looked horrified. 'What's happened here? I thought you wanted me to follow you, ma'am, and make Mr Davenant late for some meeting of his—'

Belle broke in sharply. 'I did, Matt, yes. But my brother's taken some action of his own, you'll observe, and he's been rather over-thorough... Please. *Both* of you. Help me!'

* * *

For Belle the next few minutes passed in a haze of anxiety. While she held the horses Edward and Matt together hauled the curricle upright— it was still roadworthy, thank goodness—and got Adam's prone body inside, laid awkwardly out along the seat. Belle put Florizel back in his basket and into the curricle while Matt climbed on to the driver's seat to take the reins.

Her brother still looked stunned. 'Honest to God, Belle, I didn't mean to actually harm him. But—I still don't understand why you let yourself be betrothed to him...'

'Edward. Mr Davenant bought up your gambling debts. Five thousand guineas, wasn't it? What else could I have done, when my getting betrothed to him was what Davenant required in return for keeping you out of prison?'

'Prison? He didn't say that, did he?'

For heaven's sake. 'Where else did you think your debts would lead you?'

'But—to *force* you...'

'Edward, I'm not wasting any more time discussing this. Whatever's happened in the past, you've only made things a thousand times worse. I must get him to a doctor.'

* * *

Matt drove the curricle back towards the little roadside inn while Belle sat beside Adam's body and tried to cushion his head against the jolting. Edward followed them on his own horse, also leading Matt's mount.

Adam had not opened his eyes. Belle watched his drawn white face and felt as wretched as she'd ever felt in her life. When the inn finally came into sight half a mile away, she called to Matt to stop and said to her brother, as he drew up alongside, 'It's best if you go now, Edward. We don't want *anyone* to know you had anything to do with this, least of all Mr Davenant. You, too, Matt.'

Matt looked stubborn. 'But, ma'am—'

Edward was running his hand through his hair; she saw the old childhood scar on his temple. 'Belle. You won't actually tell Davenant, will you, what I…?'

Her throat tightened with emotion. 'Heaven help me, Edward, I'll protect you as ever,' she'd said with bitter resignation. 'Now *go*. Both of you. I can drive the curricle at least as well as you, Matt. You, Edward, go home to your wife; Matt, go back to London. Oh, and Matt, will you take Florizel? You can strap the basket to the back of your saddle, can't you?'

Matt looked prepared to argue, but she said, rather desperately, *'Please.'*

Matt and Edward rode off together. Belle drove at a steady pace towards the little inn, but her mind was in utter turmoil.

She'd been terribly afraid that Adam might have been taking her to Somerset to use her to bargain with Jarvis over that land he so desperately wanted. So she'd ordered Matt to follow them and use his ingenuity to delay Adam once he was driving his own curricle—loosen a wheel, perhaps, or tamper with the harness a little. Just enough to make Adam miss his vital meeting and give herself the choice, perhaps, of making her own decision as to what to do next.

She'd never intended such harm to him. Whatever he'd done to deceive her, he didn't deserve *this*.

Within half an hour of their arrival at the inn a doctor had arrived and was giving Belle his verdict in the small parlour where she waited, tense with anxiety. 'He's got a bruised head from his fall, but no bones broken,' said the doctor in his calm voice. 'Your husband came round as I examined him and I gave him some powders to soothe him. He's sleeping calmly now. I would advise him to rest for the night before you travel onwards, of course, but there's really nothing to worry about, ma'am.'

From their arrival at the inn it had been assumed they were married; Belle nodded, outwardly calm, but the relief she felt at the doctor's words frightened her with its intensity. 'What else can I do, doctor?'

'You should go to him now,' he encouraged. 'He'll sleep a while, but he'll be relieved when he wakes to see you at his side, ma'am.'

Oh, wrong there. If Adam knew everything—about Edward, about Matt—he would not be relieved in the slightest. But she nodded. 'Thank you. I will go up to him.'

She thought she had her emotions under tight control. But she stopped with a low cry when she entered the room. *The doctor had said he was all right.*

Well, he wasn't. Any fool could see that. He just—wasn't. His eyes were closed and the dark stubble on his jaw emphasised the pallor of his face. His shirt had been ripped apart—to allow the doctor to examine him, presumably—and Belle could see that his muscular chest was gleaming with perspiration. To witness this strong man so helpless clawed at her insides like some almost unbearable torment.

If he caught a fever, had a relapse... Oh, she should have asked the doctor for more advice before he left!

Seeing a jug of cold water on the wash stand, she quickly dampened a clean towel and sat on a chair beside the bed to carefully bathe his face. She could see the bruise on his temple, already darkening.

His breathing had become easier, but Belle felt helpless and wretched. She sat there at his side, her mind in turbulence, until as the sun started to sink over the Somerset hills the innkeeper's wife knocked and came in with a tray of soup and bread rolls.

'Oh, is he still asleep? So shocking, your accident. But Dr Molloy said your husband'll be all right, don't you fret now, ma'am.'

Belle let the soup go cold. Instead she tried to smooth his pillow and stroked the damp towel once more over his temples and hard cheekbones. *Oh, my.* How very sensual his mouth was; how well-shaped those firm lips that had kissed her to distraction, and more...

He stirred. His slate-grey eyes opened, but they

were burning now with dark-gold flecks as he gazed at her. 'Belle. What…?'

Her chest tightened. 'You were hurt,' she whispered. 'In an accident.'

His intent gaze never wavered. 'Don't go,' he said quietly.

'Of course I won't go.' Her voice sounded ridiculously calm and normal. They were—supposedly—man and wife, so she'd have rather a lot of explaining to do to the innkeeper if she *did*. She pulled herself away from him. 'You need to rest, Adam. I'll take a pillow and a blanket—there's a sofa there that I can sleep on…'

'No,' he said sharply. 'I'm afraid someone is after us.' His hand closed around hers. 'You must stay next to me, so I know you're safe. There's a pistol under my coat, on this chair just here. If I can't get to it, you must use it.'

'But Adam—' *Now was the time to tell him. Now.* But she couldn't, because his powerful, heavy arm had curled tightly around her.

'Use it,' he repeated.

His eyes had closed and his grip relaxed a little. She undressed over in the corner—she could not sleep in her shoes or in her stays, for that matter, and God knew she had to have her sleep tonight; she'd need all her wits around her to deal with tomorrow.

The innkeeper had brought her valise up here; she delved in it for a huge white nightgown. If Adam had any lingering intentions towards her whatsoever, the garment would extinguish his ardour.

So *that* was all right. Except—why was her pulse starting to beat so hard when she scrambled into the bed, at the very far side from him? *You're completely safe—he's scarcely able to move.* And whether or not he'd meant what he said in the carriage about wishing they could start again from the beginning, she was surely justified in hating him for making that loathsome bargain with Jarvis?

But she *couldn't* hate him. Just the opposite.

She lay in utter despair, listening to his breathing, slow and deep. Then she slept, too, at the far side of the bed, bone-tired from the events of the day. Yet she woke up in the dead of night. Not because of any intruders, but because she'd become aware that she was curled snugly in his arms, her back against his broad chest.

Her white shroud of a nightgown wasn't much protection *here*. His breath was falling warm on her neck, his body was hard and solid against hers and a honeyed warmth made all her flesh languorous. Dear Lord, how long had she been lying like this in his arms? There was just one answer to that—*too* long.

Adam wakened in time to see Belle jump out of the bed and grab her shawl, her dark curls tumbling round her shoulders. Hell, he thought. What was she doing in his bed, dressed in that white shroud? Come to that, where in damnation was he?

Gradually the memories crowded in, prompted by his aching head. The curricle. The tree in the road followed by blackness, until he'd come round to the sound of the doctor's calm voice in this unknown room. Then Belle had joined him. Willingly? Damn it, no—he'd practically forced her to sleep in his bed, to keep her safe. And here he was, he thought bitterly, practically preparing to ravish her luscious body in his dreams...

Good work, Davenant, he reprimanded himself.

He tried to force down his painful arousal. But it wasn't easy with her standing so near, her dark curls framing the perfect oval of her face and her delicate lavender fragrance haunting his senses.

Damn it, she even made that old-fashioned high-necked nightgown somehow sweetly enchanting.

'I'm sorry,' he grated. He'd raised himself on one arm. 'For a while I couldn't even work out where I was. But now I remember. I had to swerve to avoid something in the road and was flung off, wasn't I? And the doctor told me this is a roadside inn.'

He saw Belle shivering as she stood facing him. 'That's right. There was an accident…'

He swung his legs abruptly off the bed to sit on its edge facing her. He was still wearing his breeches; that was something to be grateful for. He only prayed that in a few minutes he'd get his body—to be specific, his mighty erection—under control. He said, '*No*. It wasn't an accident, Belle.'

She went to sit on a chair by the empty fireplace. She looked—haunted. She whispered, 'Then what—?'

'I told you,' he said grimly, 'that I'd thought since we left London someone was after us. And I believe that sapling was laid deliberately across the road to make my curricle overturn.'

She took a deep breath. 'It could have been some highway thief, perhaps, who saw us coming.'

'I would be inclined to agree, if I didn't know

you already had an enemy.' He was on his feet now, going to find tinder and flint to light a candle.

'Enemy?' Belle said brightly. 'Gracious, how you do overdramatise, Mr D.'

He reached for his white shirt and eased it over his powerful shoulders. His eyes were deadly serious. 'Belle,' he said. 'Your enemy—and mine—is Lord Jarvis.'

The colour left her cheeks, but she still managed to tilt her chin in that defiant way of hers. 'Lord Jarvis? But Adam, he's your ally. Don't I know, only too well, how you would do anything to get his land for your railway?'

'I didn't get his land, Belle,' he interrupted quietly, 'because I didn't keep *my* side of the bargain.'

Her hand flew to her throat.

He was buttoning up his shirt with lean fingers, but his dark eyes never left her face. 'I *did* make a hateful bargain with Jarvis—something for which I shall never forgive myself. I said that I would persuade you into a betrothal, then end it, in return for the land I needed from him. But I found I couldn't carry on with the bargain…'

His words in the carriage drummed through

her head. *I would give a great deal, if we could only start again from the beginning, you and I...*

Belle whispered, 'You—ended it?'

'Yes. I tried to tell you that night after Lord Horwich's ball, but you wouldn't listen and how could I blame you?'

He *had* tried to tell her. Oh, Lord, she remembered it now. *What you heard at Lord Horwich's was only a part of it, Belle. Things changed...*

'I told Jarvis it was over and he was angry,' Adam went on. 'He made threats against you.'

She swallowed. 'What kind of threats?'

Adam remembered Jarvis's brutal warnings—how he'd sworn he would bed Belle himself, with force if necessary, then turn her over to his grooms if Adam didn't give up his entire railway project. 'Believe me, you're better not knowing. But I told him in no uncertain terms that you would *not* be leaving my protection.'

She could barely speak as understanding poured through her. 'You ordered me to stay at Bruton Street. You told me I must not go anywhere without one of your men to accompany me...'

'Exactly. Then I realised I had to go to Somerset to deal with some problems for which I believed Jarvis was responsible. But...'

'You couldn't leave me,' she breathed.

'I couldn't leave you, because Lord Jarvis is still in London.'

She sat down, her legs suddenly weak.

'I knew, of course,' he went on, 'that my men in London would be keeping you under close guard. But the thought of Jarvis getting anywhere near you was intolerable.'

And something in his eyes burned so fiercely that Belle felt her ribs aching with the need for air.

She didn't know what to say. She felt shattered with emotion and bleak despair. He'd told her, after Lord Horwich's ball: *It's essential for your own safety that you remain under my protection.* She'd not believed him. She'd flung his words back in his face. Now she put her palms to her temples.

He'd wanted that land—*needed* that land, because he cared for his workers. But he'd lost it now. He'd lost it, because he wasn't prepared to sacrifice *her.* Yet on the road from Chippenham Edward could have killed him; she herself was almost as culpable, for hadn't she ordered Matt to follow them from London and tamper with his curricle, to delay him?

Matt—quite rightly—had been unhappy with

the whole affair. *Messing with those vehicles is a chancy business at best, Mrs Marchmain.*

How could she tell Adam all this now? Her fresh despair must have shown, because Adam sighed and started pulling on his boots. 'I'm going to find the landlord and ask him for a second room.'

'But—he thinks that we're...'

'I'll tell him you have a bad headache after the shock of the accident,' he said abruptly. 'Or something. Anything. We both need our sleep. In the morning—which isn't far off now—we'll try to sort out this mess.'

She nodded, feeling sick inside. 'Very well. But I've been so foolish, Adam. Dear God, you just don't know how foolish.'

She turned away from him suddenly. He saw her trembling.

Adam was capable of immense self-control, but just at this moment his emotions were in tumult. She thought that hideous nightdress protected her. Well, it didn't, because all the time they were talking he could see it softly outlining the surprising fullness of her breasts, the long, slim length of her shapely legs. He was aroused—more than aroused. He was also full of anger at Jarvis and anger at *himself*, for thinking he could get away with accepting Jarvis's blasted proposal without hurting anyone.

'Damn it,' he said aloud. He strode across the room to her. She still had her back to him and was doing something with her long dark hair to tidy it, as women did. He put his hands on her shoulders and turned her round abruptly.

Her face was very pale, her eyes huge and vulnerable; one tear slid like a diamond from beneath her dark lashes. All Adam's anger melted away. He felt, instead, something gripping his insides. Something he couldn't identify, but it burned hotly in his veins.

'Belle,' he said softly. 'Sweetheart. Please forgive me.'

He thought he heard a sob escape her. Quickly he pulled her into his arms, her cheek against his chest, against his heart. He eased his grip just a little and wordlessly she lifted her face to his.

'Adam,' she whispered. 'There's something I have to tell you.'

'What?' His whole body had tensed.

'You seem to think that you were guilty of seducing me.'

Dear God. 'And wasn't I?'

Instead of answering straight away she lifted

her face to his, her expression full of anguish. 'Adam. Do you remember our first kiss?'

His fingertips caressed her silken cheek. 'When you came to my house—into the lion's den?' He smiled. 'How could I *forget* our first kiss? But you detested me.'

'No. No, I didn't. In fact, ever since that kiss, Adam, I longed, so much, for—'

'For what, Belle?' Tenderly he cupped her face with his hands.

'For you to make love to me,' she whispered. 'I want you to know that and not to reproach yourself, because...'

'Hush, sweetheart. Hush. Why talk of blame?'

Why talk of anything at all? He was already kissing her. She let out a low moan; her eyes were closed, but her soft, full lips opened so deliciously for him that desire almost got the better of him. He was ready to pull her on to the bed, and...

Slowly. Be sure, this time.

'Adam. Please...'

Was it a protest? An endearment? He couldn't be sure, but he kissed her again and her tongue, like a flame, was mingling with his, drawing him deep. With a groan he lifted her, featherlight, in his strong arms and carried her to the bed. He kissed her again, then started pulling away his own clothes; she was already lifting her night-gown and her breasts fitted his waiting hands so very perfectly.

He bent to kiss them, sucked each nipple in turn, heard her soft sigh as his own arousal throbbed thickly, darkly; he saw how her skin was flushed, her lips swollen with desire.

He'd missed her in his arms. It frightened him how much he'd missed her. He ran one palm slowly over her breasts and down across her ab-domen—she quivered with need, moaned his name—and then his fingers were lower, rubbing back and forth at her tender core.

Her dark lashes flew open to reveal the bril-liant green of her shimmering eyes. He leaned down to kiss her mouth.

She suddenly shivered. *'Adam.'*

'What, sweetheart?'

She moistened her lips. 'You were hurt. You shouldn't...'

'Ah, but I've made a miraculous recovery,' he breathed. His lips touched her breasts again. Then Belle gasped because he was moving *down-wards*. Easing her slender thighs apart. Letting his skilled fingers trail again in the honeyed heat, the silken folds of her most intimate place, stroking her, tantalising her.

She trembled with desire. She shook, at the sensations pulsing through her. Then—dear God, he bowed his dark head and his tongue was there, caressing her furls of flesh, pleasuring her. Bolts of rapture shot through her again and again at the sensual onslaught. She cried out his name; she lifted her hips for him, offering herself. She gloried in the spasms of delight that shook her. 'Adam. Please...'

He was moving up her body to kiss her mouth again, his eyes dark with desire. Taking his body's weight on his bent arms, he eased his hips between her parted thighs so that the head of his erection was poised at her core.

He was kissing her lips again, tasting her, licking her, his tongue lazily thrusting. She clutched his strong shoulders almost helplessly, her body trembling with acute need. He cradled her bottom as his mouth moved down to one breast, suckling it gently at first, then harder until she began to cry out, and his heavy shaft was nudging its way between her slick folds. Finding her, sliding into her, as she opened to him, calling out his name.

'Belle. My beautiful Belle,' Adam was murmuring.

She clenched her legs round him, opening even more to his sweet caresses, finding his rhythm in fresh astonishment and delight. When he withdrew just a little she whimpered with loss, reaching to clutch him to her again; he smiled darkly and kissed her fevered cheek.

He buried his free hand in her raven curls. He drove himself into her again, slowly, deeply, filling her. She had never felt anything so shatteringly beautiful. She was crying out now with his every incredible move, frantically running her hands over his muscled back, needing more.

'Come with me, Belle,' he was murmuring, his lips warm at her throat, his fingers caressing that most sensitive part of her. 'Come with me, sweetheart.'

Wave after wave of ecstasy was building inside her. Her lungs were at the point of bursting. Every part of her strained with need and just when she felt she could bear it no more, the pleasure engulfed her; her world exploded and she soared. And still he was holding her, kissing her, as he drove himself to his own powerful release.

She lay sated in his arms, her heart thundering. Every part of her was stupidly hoping this beautiful dream would last for ever—but like all dreams it was surely made to be shattered.

She could feel him holding her tightly until gradually his breathing became deep and steady. When he was asleep at last, she eased herself away from him and curled herself in the big chair near the embers of the fire so she could just watch him. Remember him.

Pain squeezed her chest. This could never last—but he'd shown her how very beautiful love between a man and a woman could be. She twisted the ring on her finger. The *hateful* ring. Adam thought Belle had loved her husband. He was wrong.

They'd told Belle she'd looked like a fairytale bride on the day of her wedding and indeed that night Belle had felt like a princess, waiting in the bedchamber for her handsome young officer husband to come to her. She'd been so shy. So—anxious.

Because since their betrothal, her doubts had assailed her thick and fast. Oh, Harry Marchmain was witty and charming, but he'd been so very angry when he'd realised how small her dowry was.

Belle, only eighteen years old and an innocent, had no one to talk to, no one to confide in, about her secret worries that Harry was disappointed with her wedding portion and also spent a little too much time drinking with his friends. He was a recruiting officer and unlikely, he'd told her, to see service abroad; she'd been glad, of course, that he wouldn't be caught up in the terrible battles of the Peninsula, but she didn't like the way he and his friends spoke scornfully of the men being sent off to war. She'd even seen him flirting with other women, but she told herself everything would be different, everything would be perfect once they were married.

Disillusionment set in swiftly. On their wedding night, in fact.

Harry had come staggering into the bridal chamber at, oh, it must have been one in the morning. He'd been downstairs with friends and as he pulled her into his arms he smelled of brandy. He'd mauled her with his hands and thrust his tongue into her mouth. Then he'd pushed her away with a snarl.

'Come on, girl, show some eagerness. What in hell's name are you wearing? Looks like a goddamned shroud...'

After unbuttoning his breeches he'd rucked up her nightdress, pulled her legs apart and roughly forced himself into her. She'd tried to tell Harry he was hurting her, but he wasn't listening. She'd felt nothing but pain for a few moments, the fierce pain of male possession. One harsh deep thrust as he spent himself—and it was over. He'd gone to sleep instantly.

He'd tried to take her again the next morning, but she'd been frightened at the thought of more pain and flinched from him. Harry never forgave her after that. 'God, woman,' he'd exclaimed, 'I knew you weren't going to make me rich, but I thought at least I'd get some bed sport out of you!'

Her fault, Belle had thought. She'd learnt to tolerate his lovemaking—but that was all. Other women sighed with pleasure over the mysterious prowess of their husbands, so it must be that she was simply unable to please a man in that way.

Adam had revealed to her the intensity of her own sensuality and she had misjudged him sorely. He had been trying, in this journey to Somerset, to protect her, not harm her; fresh agony seared her as she lay in his sleeping arms, filled with the sweet warmth of his lovemaking, yet totally full of dread.

As it happened, Harry Marchmain's plans had gone wrong. He'd been sent to join Wellington's army in 1814 and during the fighting at Toulouse he'd met his death. God help her, she'd tried to miss him, she'd tried to mourn him, but her marriage had been a disaster.

Now she'd found someone who really cared; someone she loved. But all through the long hours of the night her thoughts were turbulent with despair. *Tell him, you fool. Tell him everything. About your husband, and about Edward and the awful accident to the curricle...* But then she would have to tell Adam about Matt and her own plans to delay him, which had been so stupidly reckless.

Adam drew her to him in his half-sleep and murmured, 'Tell me. Whatever happened to that damned dog?'

Her pulse jolted. 'Oh,' she said lightly, 'he was taken up by some kind passers-by who promised to take him on to Bath for me. I knew that his barking would annoy you, Adam, and I feared you were very badly injured.'

And so the lies begin again. She started to ease herself away from him. 'It's almost seven. I really should get up now.'

'Clock-watching, Belle?' he teased. He was reaching for her sleepily. 'Mmm. How I love the scent of your hair. I can't say I'm sorry about the foolish creature...'

She was already on her feet.

He was fully awake now, raising himself swiftly on one elbow, grey eyes alert.

'You're regretting it already,' he said quietly. 'What happened between us last night.'

She nodded, closing her eyes so she wouldn't have to see his expression.

He, too, was on his feet, pulling on his clothes. He said in a set voice, 'Rest assured, this is the last time you'll be able to claim I made you act against your wishes.'

Oh, God.

'I'll go downstairs,' he said tersely, 'and order breakfast while you finish getting ready. I've still got my meeting to think of.' He looked at her sharply. 'What do you want to do next, Belle? Clearly you want to be rid of me as soon as possible. Shall I take you to your brother's house?'

'No!' Her denial was so emphatic that he raised his dark brows.

'That is,' she went on, flustered, 'I will call on Edward and Charlotte, of course, but I—I have no desire to put them to any inconvenience. If you could take me into Bath, perhaps, to some small hotel, I would be very much obliged.'

He was standing by the door, ready to leave. She felt quite sick with shame and loss. 'I still fear,' he said, 'that Jarvis might seek some kind of revenge on you.'

She met his dark eyes steadily. 'Not if I'm no longer in London. He'll lose interest in me very quickly, I imagine, if I'm living over a hundred miles away.'

'You're considering leaving London permanently? But what about your shop?'

She drew a deep breath. 'I have been thinking,' she blurted out, 'that I have had enough of London and London society. You will be anxious about your investment in the shop, Adam, I know, but Gabby can run it all. She is just as talented a seamstress as me and the clients love her. I will open a small dress shop in Bath, perhaps—after all, it is my home. And then I think it would be perfectly clear to Lord Jarvis that I am no longer under your protection. That, in fact, you have done exactly as he wished and so—and so you might even get your land from him—'

She broke off. She'd suddenly noticed the bruise on his temple and it smote her. Edward had done that. Her own brother. But it might just as well have been her.

His hand was on the door again. His eyes were like narrowed chips of flint. 'Whether you wish it or not,' he said, 'I'll make it clear to Lord

Jarvis that you're under my protection wherever you are.'

Then he was gone. Belle felt as if every part of her—every fibre, every nerve ending—was hurting with the kind of pain she hadn't known existed. She sank into a chair by the window and put her head in her hands.

She wanted to lie on the bed where she'd slept in his arms and remember the warmth of those arms. She so desperately wanted to confess to him about Edward stupidly causing his accident and how she'd told Matt to delay his coach. But it was too late. She'd lied too much for him ever to forgive her now.

Adam paced the parlour downstairs. The landlord had served coffee, which was bitter and scalded his throat but also brought a measure of sense back to his tumultuous thoughts. Ensuring the safety of those who worked for him was Adam's first priority now. There'd been sabotage on the railway excavations and his neighbours had been threatened; he should have been there already.

Belle Marchmain wanted nothing more to do with him, that was plain. Every time they made love, she must feel she was betraying her beloved husband all over again. As for the bargain that Adam had made with Jarvis—Belle was right, it was unforgivable, whatever he'd tried to do to make up for it afterwards.

Time, for God's sake, to stop thinking about her. Time to prepare for the last stage of this journey. But at that moment he heard a chaise rattling into the front courtyard, then the voice of a young man talking in some agitation to the landlord outside. There were hurried footsteps and the door burst open. It was Edward Hathersleigh.

Chapter Sixteen

'Mr Davenant,' Belle's brother began. 'I've come to make a confession. I'm very sorry, sir, but it was me who caused your accident yesterday.' Edward's hand was nervously pushing back his dark hair and Adam found his eyes fastened on the puckered childhood scar at his temple.

'I only wanted to stop you,' Edward blurted on, 'because I thought that you were making off with my sister. At first I felt it best to keep quiet about—the accident on the road. But I can't do it, you see, because what I did just wasn't right, though I didn't mean to actually knock you senseless!'

Adam listened to him in stupefaction. Then he heard light footsteps on the staircase. *Belle.* She stood there frozen. Her brother, with his back to the stairs, had not seen her.

'I've come to say I'm sorry I misjudged you so,

sir,' Edward went on. 'Thinking that you were after Belle and so forth. She told me yesterday— after the accident, I mean—that you've actually been more than good to her, setting her up in a fine shop in London, with no evil intentions to her whatsoever. And she told me I was quite wrong to stop you as if I was one of the High Toby; in fact, she tore a strip off me, I've never seen her so upset...'

Adam said, 'Your sister's behind you, Hathersleigh.'

And indeed, Belle stood there, looking as though her world was falling apart around her.

Edward let out a gasp of dismay. 'Belle. Belle, I just *had* to tell him...'

Adam said softly to Belle, 'So you knew all along that it was your brother who overturned my curricle.'

Her face was chalk-white. 'Yes.'

Edward stepped forwards again. 'I know I was wrong, sir. But I was only trying to protect my sister's honour!'

'A pity,' said Adam, 'that you didn't consider your sister's honour when you made her prey to every man in town thanks to your gambling debts.' He turned from Edward to Belle. 'We need to talk, you and I. We need to get a few things straight...'

But Belle was already hurrying upstairs. Adam looked at his watch. Damn it. Damn it, he had to get to his meeting today...

Edward was still protesting his apologies. 'Hathersleigh,' Adam said, 'do me a favour and stow it, will you, while I go and sort things with your sister?'

'But sir, my debts! Belle told me that you bought them up. Why haven't you called them in?'

Adam cast him a withering glance. 'If I've shown any clemency at all, Hathersleigh, it's been for your sister's sake, not yours. She's far, far better than you damned well deserve.'

And Adam turned, to take the stairs two at a time.

Edward went dejectedly out to his chaise, his head bowed so it took him a moment or two to realise that Belle was sitting inside it, with her valise.

'Belle!' he cried. 'How did you get here? What the...?'

'Take me to Bath, Edward. *Please.*'

'But what about Davenant?'

'I think it best,' she said in a voice that was taut

with strain, 'if I never see him again. Oh, he's done me no harm, Edward, far from it. And as for *you*—he could enforce that debt and ruin you, any time. He could put you in prison for waylaying his carriage. Do you realise that?'

Edward was white-faced. 'Do you think he will?'

'I rather think that he's more honourable than either of us deserve.' Her voice shook a little. 'Take me to Bath.' *Away, from him.*

If hearts could break, hers was well and truly shattered.

Adam discovered too late that there was a back staircase. By the time he'd got downstairs again he'd realised she'd evaded him and gone off with her blasted brother. Should he go after her? He was pretty damned certain she wouldn't want him to, but he was furious and worried: furious with her, and furious with himself for driving her away from the shelter of his protection, when that protection was the one thing he could offer her now.

He hoped she would be safe at her brother's house, but her brother had the common sense of a flea.

The meeting at the Sawle Down quarry later

that day didn't improve Adam's spirits. Shipley had ordered his workmen to press on with the excavations and none could have worked harder, but the weather had turned against them and, since mid-morning, it had been raining steadily.

Adam, on site again at dawn the next morning, found the excavations had been turned overnight into a quagmire. At least the attacks on the neighbouring villages had stopped, thanks to the night guards Adam had ordered Shipley to hire.

But there had been another accident—sabotage, his men suspected. One of the timber supports had given way and a man's leg had been broken in two places. It looked as if Jarvis was seeking other ways to destroy the railway.

Grimly, in spite of the rain that poured down, Adam threw himself into helping his men to clear away rock and soil from the site with an energy and strength that awed all of them. Now that a compromise with Jarvis looked impossible, Adam knew he would soon have to tell his men they would need to take the long and difficult diversion around Jarvis's land.

But then George Shipley came up to him with the news that Lord Jarvis had arrived in Bath that morning.

'His lordship's been heard muttering something

about getting even, sir,' said Shipley worriedly. 'You, me and all of us had best be on our guard.'

Swiftly Adam dragged on his coat and flung himself astride his horse, apprehension tightening every sinew. 'I'll be back later, George,' he called. 'There's something—*someone*—I've got to see.'

For too long now he'd been trying to hide from himself the fact that Belle Marchmain had somehow found a place in the heart he'd believed to be cold as ice. Dear heaven, he missed her more every hour that went by. She'd become a vital part of his life, with her clothes and her teasing. He couldn't forget the passionate hours they'd spent in bed together. He couldn't even bear a grudge for the trickery over his journey here—who could blame her for thinking he really might be about to throw her into Jarvis's ugly hands?

She loved her dead husband, he knew; she could never love *him*, especially after the bargain he'd made with Jarvis. But damn it, he had still sworn to protect her. She'd gone with Edward and Adam had assumed she would be safe—but things had changed.

Did Jarvis know that Belle was nearby? And that her foolish brother was now her only protector?

* * *

A butler had opened the big door to Hathersleigh Manor two miles outside Bath, but almost
immediately Edward himself was there.

'Mr Davenant!' Edward turned to his butler.
'Thank you, Turner, that will be all.' He turned
nervously back to Adam once they were alone.
'What can I do for you, sir?'

'I came for your sister,' Adam began, 'not
you...'

Just then another door into the hallway opened
and a soft voice said, 'Edward?'

Adam saw a wraith—a young woman with pale
hair and pale eyes—who whispered, 'Edward. Is
it the doctor?'

She went to her husband and clung to his arm,
her black gown hanging shapelessly from her
thin frame. 'Has he come to tell us our baby is
well again? Edward, has he?'

'No, Charlotte.' Adam saw Edward clutch his
wife's hands to his in a kind of fierce despair.
'It's not the doctor. It's a man I need to see about
some business, my love.'

'My baby,' whispered Charlotte. 'My...'

'Yes, I know, dearest—you'll excuse me a moment, Mr Davenant?' Gently Edward led his wife
to another room, leaving Adam dripping water

into the hallway. Adam remembered from his last visit how the place wore all the signs of genteel poverty. Everything—the floor tiles, the oak stairway, the plasterwork—had seen far better days. On the wall hung an old map showing the Hathersleigh estate as it had been fifty years ago; Adam turned from it as Edward came back into the hallway.

'I'm sorry,' Edward said. There was utter despair in his eyes 'My wife has not been well since our baby died. Will you come into my study, Mr Davenant?'

Adam indicated his soaking clothes and boots.

'No matter.' Edward opened a door quickly and ushered him into his study, where the desk was strewn with files and sheets of paper.

A mess. The whole estate, a mess. But all Adam wanted was to know that Belle was safe. To tell her—God, what *could* he tell her?—that he was here if she needed him.

Edward was looking at him squarely. 'Have you come to tell me that you're going to prosecute me for causing the accident to your curricle?'

What? 'Good God, no, I just came to… Has your wife had good medical care, Hathersleigh?'

Edward ran his hand through his hair. 'As soon as we realised she was pregnant again we hired an expensive doctor, who promised her that this child would live. She was desperate, Mr Davenant. I—I didn't have enough money to pay him, so I tried the gaming tables and at first it went well...' He gazed at Adam in despair. 'Those debts at White's that you bought up—you'll no doubt want me to repay you.'

'I'll give you time,' said Adam.

Edward looked overcome. 'This is good of you, Mr Davenant; in fact, more than I deserve.'

'I'm not doing this for you, Hathersleigh. I'm thinking of your sister.'

Edward drew a deep breath. 'Yes. Belle told me how you helped her so much with her shop.' He braced his shoulders. 'You'll have to forgive me for saying this, sir. But it's occurred to me that if anyone at all deserves my sister, *you* do.'

Those words of praise tore at Adam's gut. He shook his head bitterly. 'You must know as well as I, Hathersleigh, that she adored her husband and would never look at anyone else.' *Devil take it, a man would have to practically force her into his bed. Just as he, Adam, had done.* 'I've come because I'd actually like to speak to your sister about something rather urgent.'

'But Belle's not here!'

Adam felt the ground shift under his feet. 'Not here?'

'No! She absolutely insisted that I took her to Bath, that day we left you at the inn. She's staying at a small hotel in Trinity Street.'

In Bath. Where Jarvis was heading. Adam started to the door, but stopped because Edward was blocking his way.

'One last thing, Mr Davenant,' Edward said resolutely. 'Something you said just now. Do you really imagine that my sister *loved* that husband of hers?'

Emotion roiled in Adam's gut. 'Didn't she?'

'No, sir. No, she damned well did not!'

And Edward Hathersleigh began to tell Adam— everything.

Once in Bath, Belle had lost no time in looking for a suitable shop for rent and on the fourth day she found one, in a cobbled lane near the river. In anguish she forced herself to stop thinking about Adam and the wrecking of all her impossible dreams.

She would recover, she told herself, as the rain poured down and turned Bath's elegant streets into streams of mud. She might even stop some day imagining every moment that she could hear the husky voice of the man she loved. Might stop imagining that if she turned she would see his impossibly handsome face smiling down at her, in the way that he used to.

She would sell her share of the Piccadilly shop to Adam and Adam would keep Gabby and the rest of the staff on, if he had any sense. Then she would move here quietly and alone. Raw pain clawed at her heart. Yes—*alone.* Adam would be glad to forget her, after the tangled mess she'd made of everything.

The shop she'd found was a quaint little building with bow windows between a confectioner's and a hat shop—empty and a trifle dusty, but it took Belle's quick mind no time at all to mentally furnish it with shelves full of delicious fabric and knots of ribbons. *'Bath is full of old maids and dowds,'* Adam had once said dismissively.

Well, she was weary of thinking about Adam. Of remembering his kisses and his tender yet powerful lovemaking. *He doesn't care, you fool.* In fact, far from caring, Adam would be sick to the back teeth of her and Edward. Bad enough that he'd found out she'd covered up for Edward's stupid trick with the curricle, but if he discovered that she, too, had laid her plans for Matt to stop him reaching his vital meeting, he would despise her with all his being.

Best, by far, that she simply remove herself from Adam's life. But her heart seemed to split in two every time she faced up to the fact that she would never see him again.

One morning when a watery sun was trying to dry up the puddles, Belle walked briskly from her small hotel to the office of the lawyer who'd agreed to handle her purchase of the shop's lease. She thought she had just enough money of her own for the deposit and the lawyer had assured her that he would be able to deal with the sale of her share in her London business.

'You mean,' she'd said, 'that I won't even have to *meet* Mr Davenant?'

'Not at all, Mrs Marchmain,' Mr Cherritt, the lawyer, had told her breezily. 'There will be correspondence, of course—a document or two to sign—but I can handle it all, I assure you.'

So far, so good—but this morning, on her way once more to Mr Cherritt's office in Monmouth Street, something made her stop.

Bath was busy with traffic and pedestrians as usual. But she thought she'd seen a hateful face she knew amongst the crowds. Her heart began to thump rather sickeningly.

She'd started to feel strange sensations these past few days. A little dizziness, if she got up from a chair too swiftly, an unwillingness to eat. It was simply fatigue, she told herself; just as her belief that she'd seen Lord Jarvis staring after her a moment ago simply must be a product of her tired imagination...

She turned this way and that, trying to find him again. But the familiar-looking figure had disappeared into the throng.

Impossible. Jarvis must still be in London. But she still felt afraid. She'd got so used to *not* being afraid, when Adam was with her. No good thinking of Adam. No good letting the pain of losing him claw at her stomach as it was now. Swallowing down the sudden tightness in her throat, she pressed on and entered her lawyer's office. But Mr Cherritt, normally so friendly, did not look pleased to see her.

'Mrs Marchmain,' he began, 'I regret to say the landlord of the shop you are after has been given some adverse reports about your business history.'

What on earth...? 'I run a successful shop in London's Piccadilly!'

'Maybe. But the landlord understands your previous business failed, due to your inability to pay the rent. He's also been told that custom had dropped away badly after a number of complaints.'

'How? How could anyone know all this?' Belle's voice trailed away as she remembered Adam's warning that Jarvis had been determined to ruin her shop in the Strand. *That hurrying figure she'd seen just now...* Her heart raced then slowed. She said, 'Do you—or this landlord—happen to know Lord Jarvis?'

The lawyer flushed a little. 'That is neither here nor there. Mrs Marchmain, I regret the landlord has decided against letting you have the premises in Bridge Street. And now, if you'll excuse me, I have other clients waiting.'

Cherritt had got up from his desk and was holding the door open. Belle didn't move. 'Lord Jarvis is in Bath, isn't he?' she said steadily. 'Tell me. Tell me where he is staying.'

'My dear madam, how should I know that?'

She wanted to hit him. Then it struck her. *Jarvis would, of course, choose none other than the most expensive hotel in Bath.* 'Is he at the York House Hotel?'

Cherritt said nothing. Belle whirled from the room, banging the door hard behind her.

It was raining heavily now. Unfolding her umbrella, she hurried to the York House Hotel in George Street and entered the spacious reception area where a liveried footman approached her. 'Can I be of assistance, ma'am?'

'Yes,' she began hurriedly, 'I want to know if...'

There was no need to say any more.

'Well, Mrs Marchmain. This is a pleasant surprise.' It was Lord Jarvis, strolling up behind her. Waving the footman away, Jarvis drew close—hatefully close—and was murmuring with a smile, 'Looking for me, were you? Of course, when you and I first met two years ago, I didn't offer you enough—I realise that now. How much did Davenant pay for your services? A generous amount, I guess, together, of course, with that elegant Bruton Street house. But I can do better, you know!'

Shivers ran up and down her spine, but she stood very straight. 'You tried to ruin me, Lord Jarvis,' she breathed. 'And are still trying. But you will not succeed.'

'I think you are a little late—I *have* succeeded. Poor Mrs Marchmain. Such weak judgement. Offering yourself to Davenant, of all people—he is a low-class upstart. But he's rich, isn't he?' Jarvis's face was twisted with malice. 'And money, even dirty money like his, buys power. Buys *women*.'

'Your money is the kind that strikes me as dirty, Lord Jarvis,' Belle said steadily.

A flush appeared slowly in his cheeks as he glanced around the crowded foyer. 'You and I have some talking to do. Come upstairs to my room.'

'I will never—'

'Come upstairs,' he repeated softly, 'or your precious Mr Davenant will be in an even worse mess than he is now.'

She froze. He pointed the way to the big staircase. 'After you. Oh, and I've sent for your things, from that shabby place where you were staying.'

'I will not stay here!'

'You're right, because you're coming with me to London. But first we must talk. In my room. And if I were you I wouldn't worry too much about your reputation. I told that footman I was expecting a whore.'

'You bastard,' Belle said quietly.

He bowed. 'After you, my dear Mrs Marchmain.'

* * *

All day Adam had searched desperately for Belle. After finding she'd checked out of the small hotel that Edward had told him of, Adam had set his men to enquire at every other hotel and lodging house in Bath for her. But she was laying low. At least, he hoped she was. The alternative—that Jarvis had found her—did not bear thinking about. After giving up temporarily on his search for Belle, Adam had hunted Jarvis down to the York House Hotel, but was told that he'd set off for London an hour ago in a hired post-chaise.

Then one of Adam's men came to him with news. 'Seems Mrs Marchmain's been visiting a lawyer called Cherritt, Mr Davenant. She was interested in the lease of a shop by the river and asked his advice.'

Adam knew Cherritt. Knew he'd worked in the past for Jarvis, damn it.

It was pouring with rain again by the time Adam reached Cherritt's premises. A clerk in the reception area flinched at his rain-soaked, formidable figure, then blustered and said the lawyer was busy. Adam pushed past him and went straight into Cherritt's office.

The little lawyer jumped to his feet like a nervous rabbit when he saw who it was. Adam wasted no time.

'I believe you've recently had business with a lady from London. Mrs Marchmain.'

Cherritt shook his head. 'I can't say I recognise the name *at all*, Mr Davenant, sir...'

Adam drew nearer. 'I think you're lying to me, Cherritt.' Then he saw it. A document lying on a sheaf of other papers. Cherritt was already grasping for it, but Adam was quicker by far.

It had Belle's name on it and an address in Bridge Street.

'Sit down again,' said Adam. 'And tell me what exactly's been happening.' He was already glancing quickly through the document. 'This refers to the lease of a shop. Is Mrs Marchmain going ahead with this transaction?'

'No!'

'Why not?' Adam was still on his feet, hands resting on the edge of Cherritt's desk so his formidable figure leaned menacingly over the little lawyer. Outside, the rain drummed steadily on the windows and the very candles in the room seemed to shake with the force of Adam's scarcely controlled emotions. 'Tell me,' Adam breathed. 'Tell me everything you know about Jarvis and Mrs Marchmain, or I can make life very unpleasant for you—understand? I know damn well you've been acting for Jarvis. I know damn well—as I'm sure you do—that Jarvis has been breaking the law by sabotaging my land and workers. I can break you, Cherritt.'

'That particular shop is no longer available, sir,' Cherritt stuttered, 'at least not to Mrs Marchmain—because Lord Jarvis gave the landlord some information that made him halt the transaction.'

'Do you have any idea where Mrs Marchmain is now?'

'She—she's gone to London, sir! With Lord Jarvis...'

This time Cherritt cowered from Adam's formidable figure, from his clenched fists. 'You *knew* about this?' grated Adam. 'By God, he's as good as abducted her and you stood by?'

'Sir. Sir.' Cherritt was trembling. 'She went with him quite willingly, sir. It will soon be a matter of common knowledge, I believe, that—that she has agreed to be Lord Jarvis's mistress!'

The blood pounded in Adam's temples.

'Money will buy any woman, sir,' said Cherritt, anxiously trying to appease him. 'And she is, after all, only a dressmaker—'

Adam was round the desk and on him, his big

hands round Cherritt's throat. 'You shouldn't have said that, Cherritt,' he said softly. 'You most definitely should *not* have said that.'

Cherritt quaked. 'Sir. Mrs Marchmain anticipated that you might call on me,' he stuttered. 'And I have a letter for you.'

He was already bringing it out from a drawer in his desk. Adam broke the seal and read it in dawning disbelief.

Mr Davenant.
I cannot repeat strongly enough that I want nothing more to do with you. The money my brother owes you will soon be repaid. My share in the London shop is yours also. Now that I am under Lord Jarvis's kind protection, I have better things to do with my days and nights than to sew clothes. Mrs Belle March-main.

No. *No.* Adam could not believe it. It might be Belle's writing, but...

He put the letter down, breathing hard. Cherritt's small eyes were flickering nervously between the letter and Adam's face.

'Cherritt,' said Adam, 'it strikes me that you

know rather a lot about Lord Jarvis's business affairs, don't you?'

'H-his lordship is simply one of my many clients—' The stuttering little lawyer broke off as Adam gave him a warning look.

'Lock the door, so we're not interrupted. Then sit down again. Do you have Jarvis's private papers here—his deeds and everything else?'

'Yes!' Cherritt positively quivered with fear. 'Yes, but...'

'Shut up. Where the hell are they?'

'I—in there.' Cherritt pointed with shaking fingers to a door at the back of his office. 'They're locked in a safe.'

'Then damn well get them out,' said Adam, settling himself in a chair on the other side of Cherritt's desk. 'All of them. Or you're finished. In every way possible.'

Chapter Seventeen

On her journey to London with Jarvis Belle had been sick, literally sick, and that was what had saved her. Nausea had racked her as she was shaken in Jarvis's rough carriage and during their one overnight stop at an inn he'd made no attempt to force his attentions on her.

But she wouldn't be sick for ever. And she could not forget the agreement Jarvis had wrung from her in Bath. In the private sitting room of the York House Hotel he'd paced to and fro, his pale eyes never leaving her, while she stood defiant, refusing the chair he'd offered.

'I will not rest until Davenant is humiliated,' he told her softly. 'Suddenly that's become even more important to me than stopping his damned railway. Oh, I can carry on hindering his workers. Accidents, landfalls, faulty supplies—it can all drag on and on—and no one will trace it back to me. But he's as stubborn as me—he'll kill himself sooner than give up on his railway.'

'That is because he *cares*,' declared Belle. 'About his workers and their families.'

'Then he's a damned idiot,' said Jarvis curtly. 'As I said—building a railway's a dangerous business. And Davenant's in the thick of it—did you realise? He's out there day after day with his men, trying to get those rails laid before the autumn rains really set in.'

Belle struggled to stay calm. 'Why are you telling me all this?'

He suddenly pointed a finger at her. 'Because it's up to you now,' said Jarvis softly. 'Davenant's been fool enough to fall for you, hasn't he?'

'No!' Her cry was from the heart. 'Absolutely not, I assure you—nothing could be further from the truth...' She was fighting the sudden, overwhelming tightness that had clenched her lungs.

'Good try,' he sneered. 'But all of London knows that stone-hearted Davenant has fallen for a little dressmaker... No, don't try lying and protesting, my pretty, you're too clever for that. Now, as I said, I'm getting a bit tired of Davenant's obstinate ways. And I might have to take drastic action against him very soon, in the form of a convenient accident.'

No. Dear God, no.

'But there *is*,' went on Jarvis, 'an alternative.' He paused, letting his eyes run over her in a way that made her feel cold to her stomach. 'I'll let him proceed with his railway without any further interference. I might even sell him that damned land, so he doesn't have to make an expensive detour around my boundaries. But only if you, my dear, will consent to be my mistress.'

What could she have done, other than say *yes*? During the journey to London she'd kept Jarvis at bay with her travel sickness; she hadn't needed to feign it either.

He'd threatened Adam's life and Belle could not bear it. She knew everything was over between herself and Adam, knew he could never forgive her for her stupidity in so many ways. But she knew also she would always love him.

He was proud and honourable. He'd been a wonderful, tender lover and proved himself to be a man who cared, really cared for all the workers who depended on him.

That Jarvis would carry out his threat to injure or even kill Adam by means of a so-called accident she didn't doubt. She'd heard Adam mention the mishaps that were already occurring as his men struggled to lay the new railway across difficult terrain. She also knew how Jarvis was accustomed to paying to get the law on his side.

No hope, no hope, the noise of Jarvis's carriage wheels taunted her as they retraced the journey she'd made with Adam. She would never see Adam again and perhaps it was as well, for he would think her beneath contempt once he'd read that letter she'd written.

In London Jarvis installed her in a drab little house somewhere in Whitechapel. They'd arrived there as darkness was falling, and though she strove to recognise some detail of the dirty, cobbled lane where his coach stopped, he'd gripped her arm and led her into the house so quickly that she had no chance to find out any more.

Adam would never find her here, she thought desperately. Then remembered—why would he *want* to? He would know she was Jarvis's from her letter. He wouldn't ever understand why. He would think himself well rid of her indeed.

For the first day she didn't move from her bedchamber and barely spoke to the two servants she saw, a surly maid called Tibbs and a man called Harris who had foul breath and a face that was as battered as an ex-boxer's. There was no bolt on her bedroom door so she had to suffer their frequent intrusions as they brought her food and other necessities. Most of the time she just sat by the window to gaze at the narrow but busy lane below—it was somewhere off Botolph Street, she guessed—and watched the people and horses go by.

Early in the evening she tiptoed downstairs to the front door, only to find it locked. And burly Harris was there almost instantly, wiping his nose with his sleeve.

'Now, I do hope you're not thinkin' of leaving us, my pretty,' he'd leered.

She'd hurried back upstairs and slammed her door. *You fool, Belle.* And how could she even think of escaping after the threats Jarvis had made against Adam?

The worst—the very worst of it was that Adam would never know that she'd done all this for him.

Two days after bringing her here Jarvis came up the narrow little staircase to see her. 'How are you feeling, Mrs Marchmain?' he asked, removing his hat and gloves.

'Sick at the sight of you,' she said.

He laughed. 'Indeed, you're looking pale. And

your clothes—dear me, is this the Belle Marchmain who used to dazzle society with her daring attire?'

The maid Tibbs had shown her a wardrobe full
of new gowns; Belle had deliberately chosen the
drabbest of them and covered her shoulders with
a grey shawl. She looked up at him steadily. 'My
former life is over, Lord Jarvis. You must realise
that.'

'It's by no means over,' he answered softly.
'You see, you're going to attend a party I'm giving in a week's time, and I intend to present you
as my mistress. Yes, London's quiet now the Season's over, but any event of mine will muster up
quite enough prestigious guests to serve my purpose. And I can't think of a better way for the
news of our happy union to reach Davenant in
Somerset.'

Something in her expression must have altered when he spoke Adam's name because
Jarvis leaned forwards to touch her cheek and
laughed. 'Yes, your hero's still far away. Perhaps
you hoped he might come running here looking
for you? I'm afraid not.'

He reached out to touch her again, but she
jumped back and spat out, *'Don't.'*

His mouth thinned. 'Oh, by the way,' he said.

'There was a nasty rock fall the other day above the valley where your former lover's labourers are digging and some stones missed Davenant himself by inches. Accidents, these accidents.'

'You said you'd *stop* this. You said you'd let him have the land he needs!'

'Oh, indeed. Once you're mine—once you're clearly, openly mine—I'll let him have his land at a price. Change your mind and he's dead.'

When he'd gone she sat down again because her legs were shaking. Jarvis hadn't tried anything more than touching her yet, but surely it couldn't be long. She pressed her hands to her cheeks.

For how many nights, how many weeks, would she have to endure—oh, God—Jarvis's possession? Not long, she suspected, her heart squeezing painfully against her ribs. Not long at all—once she told Jarvis she was pregnant.

It was true. After relinquishing all hope of pregnancy during her brief years of marriage, the miracle had happened. And Adam, her baby's father, would be convinced after reading her letter that she'd surrendered herself to Jarvis.

She would survive this, she *must*, for her baby's sake. But sometimes despair all but overwhelmed her. Jarvis called daily at the house in Whitechapel. If Belle tried to protest at her captivity or complain about the watch Tibbs and Harris kept on her, he would raise his eyebrows and say, 'I'd imagine Davenant will be working on one of the most dangerous sections of his railway excavations today. Gunpowder, rock falls—so very many risks, so many mishaps that might befall him.'

She guessed that Jarvis's forthcoming party— her first appearance in society with him—would mark a new stage of their horrifying relationship. He'd already told her that she must appear happy and relaxed at his side. After that, she feared very much that he would feel entitled to do whatever he wished with her.

The sullen maid Tibbs had clearly been ordered to make Belle appear more presentable, but because Belle had lost weight and was pale with inactivity, every item of clothing Jarvis had provided for her looked lifeless and dull. Jarvis, exasperated, told her he was ordering a *modiste* to attend on her. He wouldn't let Belle leave the house, so Madame Monique Tournier arrived to see her three days before the party with lengths of fabric and various fashion illustrations.

She was dark, French and saturnine. Jarvis

seemed impatient as he led her into Belle's sitting room.

'Let her brighten you up, for God's sake,' he said to Belle. 'Or you know what will happen to a mutual acquaintance of ours.'

Belle couldn't help herself. 'Is he still...?'

Jarvis snapped to Madame Tournier to wait outside, then said, 'He's still working on his damned railway, yes. Coming up to the most dangerous stage now, when they have to lower the rails into place. And, by the way, he's still not given a second thought to your disappearance from Bath. But I really do want him to read in the news sheets about you looking radiant and happy—with me.'

Belle whispered, 'For how long do I have to endure this hateful captivity?'

Jarvis's lip curled. 'We'll discuss all that after the ball.'

She gazed at him. 'If you let anything happen to him,' she said steadily, 'I'll kill you. I mean it.'

He laughed. 'So you'd hang for him? I think not.' He stormed from the room.

Belle sat down, her trembling hands folded across her still-flat stomach.

Madame Tournier came bustling back in and Belle allowed herself to be measured and consulted over the fabric samples simply because it was easier than resisting. Just as the dressmaker was leaving she said to Belle in her expressionless way, 'You will have to come to my shop, *madame*, for the ballgown to be completed. I can make it up from these measurements, yes—but there are certain adjustments for which a final fitting on my premises is essential.'

'But Lord Jarvis won't allow—'

'You have to come on the afternoon of the ball in three days' time,' repeated Madame Tournier flatly. 'I will speak to milord.'

Just for a moment Belle's thoughts whirled. *A chance for escape?* But she was a hostage; the life of the man she loved was at stake, and the cruellest thing of all was that Adam would never know it.

The next day when Jarvis visited her as usual a little after midday he said, 'I gather you made some progress with the dressmaker. She says she needs you to go to her shop on the day of my ball for a final fitting.'

'And you'll let me out of here?' said Belle scornfully. 'Aren't you afraid that I'll tell Madame Tournier I'm your prisoner?'

Jarvis's pale eyes slid over her. 'She's in my

pay and asks no questions,' he said. 'Anyway, you know what will happen to Davenant if you do anything stupid. Besides, I'll send Harris with you. He won't let you out of his damned sight.'

That was true; Harris followed her everywhere, his eyes mentally undressing her. Belle said bitterly, 'I can believe that.'

'As long as you behave during your outing, I'll tell Harris to restrain himself.' Jarvis's lip curled. 'If not—well, I think you know what the consequences will be.'

Belle braced herself against the sickness that shook her as she remembered Jarvis's long-ago words—*As a young widow you must be quite desperate for male companionship. I'll enjoy watching. I promise you won't be bored...*

Jarvis was already leaving. 'By the way—' he turned back '—I've ordered Madame Tournier to prepare a gown for you that's as flamboyant as anything you used to wear for Davenant. Only this time—' his voice was a lethal purr '—you'll be at *my* side. And I want news of your devotion to me to spread around town and further.'

On the day of the party Jarvis's carriage arrived for her at midday and the foul-breathed Harris bundled her aboard.

She heard him speak to the driver, expressing surly surprise. 'Who the hell are you? I don't know you, do I?'

'I'm new.' The coachman's voice was equally gruff. 'Usual man's ill.'

Harris curtly gave him directions, then sat opposite Belle and didn't take his lecherous eyes off her.

And for once, Belle didn't give a damn about Harris, because her mind was racing. Harris hadn't known the driver. But she thought, oh, she'd thought just for one wild moment that she recognised that voice...

Her heart wouldn't stop thumping. At Covent Garden the traffic was at a standstill because two carriages had collided—she could see it from her window—and coachmen and bystanders were getting embroiled in a noisy argument. Harris, cursing, called out to their driver to find some other way. The driver retorted, 'I'm doing my best. Drive the thing yourself if you think you can do better.'

Wild, surging hope riveted Belle. *Matt's voice.* It was Matt, just as she'd dared to hope.

Harris, swearing loudly, was already getting out. 'I'll give that damned fellow a piece of my mind as well as the feel of my fist.' He turned back to Belle. 'If you move from there you're finished—understand?'

Harris had thrust his way into the crowd of pedestrians and was elbowing his way to the driver. Belle, gazing tensely out of the window, heard him give an exclamation of angry surprise—and realised Harris was in the grasp of two burly constables.

'Make way, ladies and gents!' the constables were calling to the crowd. 'Just caught a pickpocket here—make way, while we take him to gaol where he belongs!'

Then the door on the other side of the carriage swung open just as it started to move and someone leaped in. 'It's all right, Belle,' a husky male voice said. 'It's all right.'

Adam. It was *Adam*. Her heart was suddenly full of joy—joy she thought she would never feel again. 'Adam—how...?'

'Those two constables are my men.' He smiled, settling on the seat beside her. 'And Matt is driving the carriage.'

'I knew it!' She was in his arms. 'I recognised his voice. But Adam, how did you...?'

'Find you? We've been searching for days. Jarvis was clever; he went to all sorts of lengths to conceal his visits to you, but he made a mistake.

You see, Madame Tournier knows Gabby and she told her about you. But first things first.' He was holding her tightly; his eyes were full of fierce tenderness. 'Has Jarvis hurt you? Have any of his men hurt you?'

Oh, God, he looked divine. Her heart was thudding wildly at the sight of him. He wore a rough grey coat over breeches and riding boots; his neckcloth was rumpled, his thick dark hair just a little untidy and an unshaven beard darkened his jawline. No more the suave man about town. But—the look in his eyes. The raw *emotion* in his voice.

'I'm all right,' she said quickly. 'For some reason he's not touched me yet, Adam.'

'Good.' His voice was grim. 'I think he knew I'd kill him if he so much as harmed a hair on your head. I guessed he held you prisoner, but he denied it, and I couldn't damn well prove anything until Madame Tournier appeared. I've got him now. But Belle, why did you leave Bath with him?'

'He said—' she tried to keep her voice steady '—he said he'd arrange an accident on your railway. He threatened you'd be badly hurt. He made me write that letter—'

'I guessed as much.'

'And he said he would let you have that land you need so badly if I stayed with him.'

'You would do that, for me and my railway?' he asked wonderingly.

'For you and your workers, Adam. And I've been so stupid. I've got to tell you what I did...'

He was still holding her. Now his fingers touched her cheek. 'Tell me if you must.'

'I got Matt to follow us to Bath. I'd told him, on the second day, to try to delay your journey.'

He put one finger to her lips. 'I know,' he said quietly. 'Edward told me.'

'Edward?'

'Edward told me a good deal. I'd been hateful to you, Belle—and I damned well deserved your plotting.'

'No. No,' she cried distractedly. 'I've been such a fool.'

He held her face between his big, warm hands and gazed down into her eyes. There was something in his expression Belle had never seen before and it fractured her heart. But she mustn't hope. Hope was cruel.

'You were going to give yourself to Jarvis. For me,' he said quietly.

'I think he would have tired of me very quickly.'

She was beginning to shake, try though she might to hold herself steady, to be strong.

'Belle,' he said. His arms were around her again. 'You're not going back to him ever, believe me.'

'But—'

He touched her lips with his finger. 'Listen. I have one last favour to ask you. Do you feel strong enough to come to Lord Jarvis's party to-night—with *me*?'

'To Jarvis's party?' she breathed. Her eyes were dark with emotion in her pale face. 'But how…?'

'He sent me an invitation. I imagine he hoped to see my face when I saw you standing at his side. Belle, will you do it?'

Slowly—incredibly—she began to smile. He'd always thought her beautiful, but *now*…

She looked radiant. 'Mr Davenant and guest,' she breathed. Her eyes sparkled suddenly. 'Adam, I don't see how I can refuse!'

He held her tightly and kissed her forehead. 'My brave, brave Belle. I promise you—everything is going to be all right.'

Despair engulfed her once more. All right? No—it could never be all right. She clamped down on the tight pain in her chest.

She ought to tell him. She ought to tell him

right now, but she couldn't, not when he was holding her in his arms and his face was so full of caring. What would he say? How could she explain her own stupidity this time?

She had told him quite plainly that she was unable to bear children. And oh, what an old, tedious female trick that was, to entrap the man you wanted. If Adam had desired a family, he'd have married a suitable bride years ago. But he didn't, and how his beautiful eyes would narrow with cynicism—disgust, even—when she told him she was pregnant.

If she told him.

The carriage was swinging round towards Piccadilly; she turned to him, questioning. 'Adam, where…?'

'We're going to your shop, for a ballgown for tonight,' he told her. 'Madame Tournier's been paid for her efforts, but we don't want her gown. We don't want anything Jarvis has had a hand in. Meanwhile—Gabby's been busy, sweetheart.'

Adam saw her into her shop, then told her he was going with Matt to return Jarvis's carriage and horses. 'I'm not having him accusing me of theft,' Adam said. 'But finding his carriage outside his house with no driver, no Harris and no *you* will give Jarvis plenty to think about.' He hesitated. 'Belle, we've got so much to discuss. And that's what we'll do—after tonight.'

He took her hand and kissed it in the old, familiar way that tore at her already overburdened heart. Then he was gone and Gabby was there, hugging her; they laughed and exclaimed together.

'Oh, *madame*! Monsieur Davenant came here days ago looking for you! He's had his men searching all over London—he was so very anxious! We are overjoyed that you're together again!'

Something clutched at Belle's throat. 'I don't think it's for long, Gabby.' She wondered how much to tell her. 'I've been so foolish.'

'You *still* think he does not care for you?' Gabby looked astonished. 'Then—wait here, *madame*!'

A few moments later Gabby came out of the back room, carrying a frothy, gorgeous ball dress. 'For you,' she breathed, touching it tenderly. 'Yesterday Mr Davenant told us to put all else aside, so *this* was ready.'

'*Oh.*' Belle once more felt that lump in her throat. 'It's so beautiful.' The puff-sleeved gown was of ivory silk, its full skirt adorned with tiers of Vandyke lace trimmed with tiny turquoise satin roses and pearls.

'There is more, *madame.*'

Indeed, there were small roses made of ivory satin to wear in her hair, long kid gloves, ivory satin pumps and an exquisite pearl necklace. Gabby laid them all out for her joyously—then suddenly realised there were tears in Belle's eyes.

'There, there, he loves you, I'm sure!' Gabby was offering her a handkerchief and Belle scrubbed fiercely at her eyes.

Love her? No. He'd rescued her from Jarvis, yes—but he was still using her, by taking her to the party tonight. And why not? She'd stupidly destroyed anything he might have felt for her. He was thinking of far more important things than her: his quarry, his vital railway, his hundreds of workers and their families. Whereas she'd mistrusted him and insulted him, never realising how honourable, how brave he was, until it was too late.

After tonight—what would happen then?

She wouldn't let him kiss her. She must not even let him touch her again. Instead she would ask him if he would help her open a small shop in Bath and she wouldn't tell him her secret, ever. She simply could not expect him to provide for a child he had not wanted; a child he would feel he had been deceived into fathering.

She would never see him again. The thought was intolerable, but bear it she must.

Joseph and two more of Adam's men had come with a carriage to take Belle to Bruton Street and Gabby accompanied her, to dress her. Being back at that lovely house simply tore at Belle's heart, because everything reminded her of those weeks with Adam and their wonderful, passionate lovemaking. The sphinxes and the gilded Egyptian tables were still there—oh, Lord, how had Adam tolerated her wilfulness?—and Lennox and the servants were warm in their welcome. Belle felt that she did not deserve any of their kindness.

'We are delighted to see you here once more, ma'am,' said Lennox with a grave bow.

Even though she'd threatened to dress the poor man in purple. Belle smiled, but there was a stupid lump in her throat. 'Thank you, Lennox.' *But I doubt I'll be here for very long.*

Gabby must have spent almost two hours adjusting Belle's gown, arranging the satin roses in her dark curls and chattering nineteen to the dozen—which was as well, because Belle's emotions were in such tumult she could hardly speak.

Gabby had only been silent once, and that was when she was starting to lace up Belle's stays. Almost instinctively, Belle had put out her hand. *'No.'*

Gabby stopped, frowning.

'Not too tight, Gabby.'

Gabby's brown eyes widened. *'Madame.* Oh, *madame*, you are...'

'Yes, Gabby, I am,' breathed Belle. 'But—I do not want Mr Davenant to know. Do you understand?'

'You are going to tell him later? As a surprise?'

Belle put her hands on her friend's arms. 'Gabby. I beg you to say *nothing*. Leave it to me. Please.'

Gabby gave a Gallic shrug. 'I promise.'

Adam called for her at eight, looking sensational. He wore black and his snow-white cravat emphasised the perfection of his hard cheekbones, his chiselled jaw. He looked—he *was*, quite simply—the man of her dreams. She remembered first seeing him on his big horse on Sawle Down that sunny March day, and her heart turned over with such pain that she had to catch her breath. If only she'd known what kind of a man Adam Davenant really was. If only...

As he handed her into the carriage, his dark eyes were full of something that made her insides melt. 'You look beautiful,' he said quietly as he helped her to arrange her full skirts. 'Are you ready?'

She nodded, with a smile. 'Fie, Mr Davenant, this is just like old times!'

'Almost,' he agreed, tenderly tucking her gossamer shawl round her shoulders.

Yes, she was ready for Lord Jarvis's ball. She felt she could face anything with this man at her side. But afterwards? Oh, it was going to take all her courage to face *afterwards*. When she would have to tell him she was leaving him.

Chapter Eighteen

Belle would always remember that party as a kaleidoscope of vivid pictures, a shimmering sequence of scenes darkly threaded with danger, because it took place at the home of her enemy Lord Jarvis.

As at any social event, she was aware of the music and dancing and loud chatter; aware, too, of the myriad wax candles and the scents of over-rich food and wine filling room after room in Jarvis's ornate mansion in Grosvenor Square. A mirage of opulent splendour in which—for her—the only reality, the only safety, was Adam's presence at her side.

Their arrival together caused a sensation. Adam ordered the footman to announce both their names, at which the great entrance hall, busy though it was, fell absolutely silent. As Lord Jarvis came towards them people moved back to watch. He'd fixed a thin smile to his face, but his voice was etched with vitriol and Belle drew instinctively closer to Adam.

'Davenant,' Jarvis said. 'You've been busy, I believe, one way and another. And—Mrs Marchmain.' He made a low bow, then turned back to Adam. 'You and I, Davenant, have a few matters of business to discuss.'

'Indeed we do,' said Adam smoothly. 'Here? Now? I'm all yours.'

Something in Jarvis's eyes flickered and he looked almost afraid as he glanced round his crowded hall. 'You shall *never* get my land for your damned railway,' he hissed in a low voice. 'Not now this woman here has broken our agreement.' But because people were still gathered around them, staring and whispering, he said, 'Perhaps later, Davenant, don't you think? Business can be so tedious.' He bowed his head tightly. 'I'm so very glad you could both avail yourselves of my hospitality.'

Adam and Belle were the sensation of the evening. The gossip had been rife, clearly about their departure to Bath, and now the tongues were wagging furiously. Enviously.

'Mr Davenant—so handsome! And he's with his widow again, Mrs Marchmain—my dears, did you ever see anything like her gown? It's incredibly pretty, and clearly she still has Mr Davenant tightly in her clutches...' The gossiping dowagers fluttered their fans; the younger women looked on enviously because Belle was easily the most beautiful woman there.

She knew, because Adam had told her so. It was he who made her beautiful, he whose presence kept her strong in their enemy's house. The two of them danced—oh, he was such a wonderful dancer, his hand at her waist making her want to melt into the lean length of him. Afterwards, as they circulated, Belle drew strength from him just being at her side. But all the time—all the time she felt the tension building in the room; saw how Jarvis kept glancing at them, like a serpent ready to spring for its prey.

The crisis, when it came, was sudden. Adam was surrounded by a group of bankers and London businessmen who were eager to know about the progress of his railway; Jarvis kept casting him poisonous looks, but Adam ignored him.

At last Jarvis barged into the men gathered round Adam. 'Gentlemen,' he said, 'I'm going into supper. Coming with me?' He tried a sickly smile. 'I fancy that in this corner of the room the smell of quarry dust taints the air.'

There was a shocked silence. Belle felt herself freeze; then Adam's hand touched her gloved arm lightly, reassuringly. Keeping her by him.

'Jarvis,' he said smoothly, 'I've got something here that may interest you.'

'If it's a matter of business,' sneered Jarvis, 'save it for your quarry workers and country rustics.' But he looked afraid and his skin was sweaty beneath the flush of alcohol.

Adam said coolly, 'What I've got is quite fascinating. So fascinating I think I'll explain it to everybody. It's a document showing that the land I've been after for my railway never belonged to you at all.'

'*What?* You...' Jarvis had lunged towards him, but the cluster of men who'd gathered round Adam held him back, saying, 'Steady, Jarvis. Let Davenant have his say.'

Adam spoke quietly and calmly, but every single word filled the stark silence that had fallen.

'You and your lawyer Cherritt,' said Adam to Jarvis, reaching in his pocket, 'swindled the Hathersleigh estate out of that piece of land I need for my railway, many years ago. I have here the original map showing it belongs to Edward Hathersleigh. When Edward's father died, your lawyer Cherritt substituted a forged plan in the deeds and Edward—who was only a child when he was orphaned—had no idea where the exact boundaries of his estate truly lay.'

'No!' Jarvis had lunged forwards; several of Adam's colleagues held him back.

Adam gave Jarvis a look of narrow-eyed contempt, then coolly began to unfold the document. People gathered round to look.

'Edward Hathersleigh,' Adam went on, 'has agreed to sell the land to me. Care to face prosecution for your part in this fraud, Jarvis?'

Jarvis was shaking off the arms of those who held him, but he looked white and afraid. 'Your little widow's put you up to this,' he said loudly. 'She sold herself to you, Davenant. She's a whore and you've made all this up because you can't stand the way polite society has always looked down on you and your low-class family—'

'If you're an example of polite society, Jarvis,' interrupted Adam, 'you can keep it.'

And with one bunched fist he knocked Jarvis flying across the floor.

People applauded. People gathered round and cheered. Adam took Belle's hand and drew her very close. He gave an elegant bow to the delighted crowd. 'Ladies, gentlemen,' he announced, 'your sentiments are much appreciated, both by me and by my fiancée—the extremely beautiful Belle Marchmain, whom I hope to make my wife in the very near future!'

He kissed her full on the lips and the room was filled with happy sighs and murmurs of approval. He kissed her so thoroughly that her mind was in a daze, her insides melting at the honeyed warmth of his lips, the heat of his strong body.

Time enough. Time enough for her to shatter this beautiful dream and face reality. It would be over as soon as he realised the full extent of her unwitting deception.

The next few moments were filled with the kind of happiness she knew could never last. Amidst a storm of congratulations from well-wishers, Adam held her tight round her waist with one hand while with the other he seized a bottle of champagne and a glass from a nearby waiter. Then, his dark eyes still dancing, he led her outside and down the steps to where his coach was waiting, with Joseph up on the driver's seat.

'To us,' he said softly once he'd swept her inside the carriage. He pulled out the cork and poured the foaming liquid into the glass.

'Not for me,' she said quickly as he offered it to her. She forced a smile. 'Not just yet. Adam, tell me. Tell me how you came to learn about the land.'

He drank some champagne himself and told her, in a voice of taut triumph, how he'd seen an old map at Edward's house.

'You went there?' she broke in.

'I did,' he said softly. 'Looking for you, Belle. And I learned a good deal.'

'Edward's poor wife...' Something in his gaze was making her feel shaky.

'Yes. I met Edward's wife, and that wasn't all.' Adam's eyes were steadily on hers as the coach rattled along. 'Your brother told me about your marriage, Belle.'

'He shouldn't have. He had no *right*!' She was distressed now.

'I'm most glad he did,' Adam said gravely. 'We'll talk about your husband later. To finish my answer to your question—I tackled Cherritt about you in Bath, and I realised he was in Jarvis's pay. So I—*persuaded* him to show me Jarvis's deeds...'

And that was how he knew, marvelled Belle. As Adam's fine carriage swung down the street she listened to him with wonder and relief and genuine joy, because Edward had been able to help him. Edward had given him the land gladly, Adam told her, in return for the cancellation of his gambling debts, and now the Somerset railway line was forging ahead—indeed, would reach the canal within days.

She loved hearing him talk about it all; loved seeing his animated face, noting every detail of those dearly familiar features which she'd once thought so hard, so cynical. *He'd* not changed at all, but she had. She'd finally seen him for the man he truly was—honest and brave and in every way noble.

She'd refused champagne, but she grew heady drinking in everything about him as he talked to her in the coach: the thickness of his dark hair, which he'd rumpled with one careless hand; the beginnings of the stubble darkening his chiselled jawbone; the beauty of his strongly made body, accentuated rather than hidden by his formal attire.

Too late, she thought wildly, pain clawing at her insides. She'd misjudged him and insulted him from the fateful day she'd met him, on Sawle Down.

They'd arrived in Bruton Street. He got out first and was helping her down. Desire and despair burned her up in equal measure.

'Will you allow me to come in with you?' he asked, his eyes searching hers.

Her heart shook. She wanted to throw herself into his arms, and tell him everything. 'I noticed earlier that the rooms are still full of sphinxes and sarcophagi.' She smiled. 'You enter at your own peril!'

He grinned—a gorgeous, wide, white smile— and went with her laughing up the steps. Lennox let them in, but very swiftly made himself scarce.

Belle took off her shawl and fiddled with her gloves. She felt sick again. He'd told everyone at Lord Jarvis's that he was going to make her his wife. Even if he meant it, he'd soon change his mind when he learned everything.

She had her back to him as she laid her mantle across one of the hideous sphinxes.

He came up behind her, his hands resting warmly on her shoulders, and said, huskily in her ear, 'Belle. May I stay with you tonight?'

She stood very still in her gorgeous ballgown, her heart thumping painfully against her ribs. 'Adam,' she said quietly. 'What you said earlier, about marrying me. I know you never wanted marriage, at any cost, and believe me, I quite *understand...*'

He lifted her hand and kissed it, his eyes burning into her. 'Don't you want to marry me, Belle?'

Oh, dear God. His lips sent blood pounding to her heart. *More than anything. Oh, Adam, my love.* 'It's not a question of that,' she said desperately. 'It's that I know you never wanted to be tied down, ever.'

'That was because I'd never met anyone like you.' He was still holding her hand, still fingering her sensitive palm.

'But...' she was floundering now '...you didn't want commitment. Children. You told me so.'

'Children?' He looked at her, his eyebrows slightly gathered. 'Belle. My dear, practical Belle— why this sudden interrogation?'

She drew a deep, agonised breath. 'Adam... I'm pregnant.'

The hand that still enclosed hers had gone very still.

'It's true,' she went on in a low but desperate voice. 'I'm quite sure. And it's my fault, because I told you I could never have children. I truly believed it—in fact, the doctor told me so when I'd been married a year—but it seems he was wrong—*I* was wrong, so I've deceived you, yet again...'

He was frowning.

'So I've made my plans,' she went on steadily. 'I shall go to live in Bath and set up a shop there. Bath is such a lovely place to bring up a child, close to the countryside and—'

He gathered her in his arms, holding her close. 'My God. Don't *I* get any say in all this?'

She gazed up at him. 'But I didn't think you...'

'Our child,' he said steadily. '*Our* child, Belle.'

For the first time in his life, Adam was almost overwhelmed by the surge of emotions that pounded through his blood. After what he'd seen of his own parents' marriage, he'd dismissed all thoughts of fatherhood and a family. Had never thought he would say those words, *Our child.*

But with this woman, his life had opened up to new and wonderful horizons. He and Belle— surely they would be better parents than his own? If only because of the love, the hope, the honesty they shared...

He kissed Belle's pale forehead tenderly. 'All this means,' he said with hope in his voice, 'is that we have to alter our plans accordingly.'

She could hardly breathe.

'We have to get married all the sooner!' he said joyfully. And pulling her closely to him, Adam kissed Belle, with a slow, sensual kiss of ravishing intimacy.

* * *

Later, when they'd got upstairs and he'd removed her beautiful gown with such tenderness that she thought she'd die of it, he made love to her with a passion that reached new heights for both of them.

'It's all right, isn't it?' he'd asked tenderly, kissing her bare shoulders as her gown slithered to the floor. 'With the baby?'

'Oh, yes,' she breathed softly. Besides, she couldn't have said no to this wonderful man if she'd wanted to. Everything he did was amazing that night. His every touch melted her as he crushed her slender body to his, compressed her soft breasts against his hard chest and inflamed her with his kisses. Was it because she'd thought she'd lost him? Or was it because they'd finally found each other?

A combination of both, she decided deliriously as Adam, who seemed to know exactly what her yearning body and her ardent heart craved, aroused her to fresh heights of longing—teasing her and tormenting her until she cried out aloud, desperate for the silken strength of him inside her, completing her. Afterwards he cherished her, holding her steadily in his arms and kissing her flushed face as the aftermath of her pleasure rippled through her again and again, leaving her breathless, speechless, melting with joy.

He talked to her then, as the single candle burned steadily over the fireplace. He told her in his husky voice how he'd never thought he would meet anyone who could mean what she did to him.

'It was my stupid pride, Belle,' he told her, stroking her cheek. 'I was so tired of being told I should marry and I'd seen what marriage did to my parents.'

'Your brother, Freddy, is happy,' she reminded him, stroking his deliciously stubbled jaw as the shadows fluttered around them.

'Freddy is *very* happy, yes, and Louisa is wonderful. Freddy wasn't as scarred by our upbringing as I was.'

'Because you protected him.' She laid her face against his chest.

'I tried to make sure he didn't hear what I heard. I hoped he didn't realise just how much our mother despised our father.' He drew a deep breath. 'Then, of course, I always felt the weight of the family inheritance on my shoulders. People assumed that all I cared about was money and I did—I still do. But in many ways I see wealth as a way in which someone like me can change people's lives for the better.'

'Like your railway,' she murmured, nestling into his strong arms.

'Like my railway. If you could hear, Belle, how people like Jarvis speak with such contempt of their workers. God knows I'm no saint, but I do have some desire to make their lives a little easier. I am driven, yes; I'll always be ambitious. Apart from early on vowing never to endure a repeat of my father's unhappiness, I never thought I'd have time for marriage and a family—until I met you. And then...' he cupped her face tenderly in one hand '...then I was smitten, not just by your beauty, but by your pride, your spirit. But I thought that you loved your husband.'

'No,' she breathed. 'No. He hurt me so much that I never wanted to be with another man. He told me I was—*undesirable*.'

'Do you believe that now?' He was holding her closer and pressing his lips to her cheek. 'Do you?'

'No, Adam.' Her eyes shone. 'With you, I feel the most beautiful woman in the world.'

'Which you are,' he chided softly, drawing one tender finger down her cheek to her lips. 'But I thought I'd lost you, Belle. That bargain I'd made with Jarvis was unforgivable. Believe me, it wasn't long before I began to regret it bitterly. I told Jarvis so at Lord Horwich's ball.'

'Though even when you tried to explain I wouldn't listen,' she breathed. 'I was foolish and proud.'

'No more so than me. And I paid for it. I almost lost the one thing that mattered most of all—your love.'

The pad of his thumb brushed across her trembling lips, and she was pierced by the raw emotion in his eyes. She caught his hand and kissed it. 'I've made mistakes, too, Adam. In so many ways.'

'You've been brave, my love,' he whispered. 'Brave and selfless. You were willing to give up so much for your brother, and then you would have sacrificed yourself for me. My God, I nearly lost my mind when I realised Jarvis had taken you from Bath.'

'You never believed—' her voice was racked with anxiety now '—that I would have gone with him *willingly*?'

'Never,' he assured her. 'But I didn't realise you were prepared to go so far, for my sake. We will work everything out now, sweetheart.' His voice was husky, his breath warm against her cheek as he whispered, 'I love you. Never leave me again, Belle. Promise me.'

'I promise. Oh, Adam, I love you, too, so very much!'

'We must get married very soon. If our baby's a girl I'll love her and spoil her terribly, to make up for all the love that you didn't have as a child.'

'If it's a boy?' she teased, stroking back his hair.

He was silent a moment, then, 'If we have a son, I'll teach him never to lose sight of all the things in life that really matter.' He caught her hand and kissed it. 'There's an exciting new world ahead of us, Belle. Steam railways are only the beginning. Our sons—and daughters—will see it all.'

Belle smiled mischievously. 'It sounds as if you're planning on a whole brood.'

Adam grinned back. 'I don't see why we shouldn't have a try at outnumbering Freddy's family. But...' and he paused, a mischievous glint in his eyes '...no lapdogs.'

'And no Egyptian furniture.' She spoke emphatically.

Adam held her very tightly. 'Hussy,' he said. 'Shameless, wilful hussy. To force me into buying that hideous stuff—how am I going to extract payment from you for *that* little trick?'

Already the familiar surge of heated desire was flaring inside her as her fingertips drifted across his hair-roughened chest. She nibbled at his ear with her lips and murmured, 'I can think of *several* ways you might like to be paid. Only it will be instalments, Adam my love. Night—after night—after night...'

He held her close, his eyes burning darkly. 'This is really for ever, sweetheart.'

Just a day ago, she faced despair. Now, she was the happiest woman alive. 'For ever, Adam my love,' she breathed.

Epilogue

June, ten months later

Speedily Adam climbed the wide staircase of the Clarges Street mansion and strode into the light, airy sitting room that was now a nursery. Settling himself on the sofa beside Belle, he gazed down at the sleeping baby in his wife's arms.

'How is she?' he breathed.

'Exactly the same as she was two hours ago, when you went out,' Belle teased. 'Well fed and happy. Adam, how was your meeting?'

'Absolutely fine,' he told her, putting his arm round her shoulders and drawing her close. 'The shareholders of the Sawle Down quarry want to invest in more equipment and there's interest in our stone from builders and architects all over the country.'

'Which means more jobs, more prosperity for

Somerset. I'm so glad.' Belle hesitated. 'Adam, I had a letter from Charlotte this morning. She and Edward want to come and stay with us next week for a few days. I think she has some news.'

'Really?'

'I don't think she's pregnant,' Belle said quickly. 'I don't think she ever will be, sadly. But you know, don't you, that she's been helping at the church orphanage in Bath? And she and Edward—they may be able to adopt.' Her face softened. 'There's a baby girl called Sophie—I think they've fallen completely in love with her. You don't mind, do you, if they visit us? You'll remember how entranced Charlotte was with Clara when she first saw her. And I'd be really happy if she had a baby of her own.'

Adam leaned over to kiss her cheek gently. 'I'll be glad to see them.'

'It was so good of you to make Edward a shareholder in the Sawle Down quarry, Adam.'

'Not at all. Your brother's proved himself an asset in promoting our Bath stone and I'll be able to discuss some new contracts with him when he arrives in London. Meanwhile—on to more important things.'

Belle looked anxious as he reached in his coat pocket to pull out a news sheet. 'Here you are,' he said, his eyes dancing. 'Forget your brother, and Bath stone and railways; now for the *real* news of the week. Remember Lady Causton's ball last Friday? Well, here's a piece about it.' He unfolded the paper and started to read aloud. *'Mrs Adam Davenant looked sublime in a ballgown of violet sarcenet adorned with rouleaus of cream silk. A headdress of pale pink gauze and feathers completed an outfit that took the fashionable world by storm...'*

'Oh, no!' Belle laughed and pretended to hide her face blushingly against her husband's shoulder. 'Adam, you know very well that Gabby and I practically threw that outfit together in about two hours when you told me I just *had* to leave Clara with the nursemaid for the evening and come with you to that ball!'

'And baby Clara was none the worse for it,' said Adam softly, touching his daughter's tiny curled fist. As if recognising her father's touch, Clara opened her eyes—eyes of green—and her perfect little fingers fluttered against Adam's big palm.

Belle, on seeing his expression, felt her heart overflow with joy.

'There's more.' He picked up the news sheet again. 'Listen. *Mr Davenant's wife was once famous...'*

'*Once* famous!' she protested indignantly.

'*Was once famous for the avant-garde styles she created in her fashionable Piccadilly shop. She is believed to still have a hand in the designs sold in the shop, though it is now run by her former assistant, Mrs Gabrielle Bellamy.*'

'Oh,' breathed Belle, 'this means dear Gabby will be busier than ever. That shop means so much to her.' She paused a moment. 'As it did to me,' she added quietly.

His arm was tightly round her again. 'Do you miss it, sweetheart? Do you miss your independence?'

Belle gazed down at their baby sleeping again in her arms, then looked up at Adam, her eyes shimmering with happiness. 'Well,' she said carefully, 'I suppose I'll always want to stay in touch with Gabby and the latest fashions. After all, I would *hate* my husband to grow bored with me…'

'No danger of that,' Adam said very softly. 'No danger of that whatsoever.' He turned her face to his, his eyes searching hers. 'I owe you everything, Belle, from the day you rode into my life on Sawle Down.'

'You accused me of trespassing.' She laughed.

'Oh, you were so arrogant! And I was so unforgivably rude to you, Adam.'

'You were,' he agreed. 'But you were the most beautifully *rude* trespasser I'd ever seen. From that day to the day you agreed to marry me, you've thrown my life into a state of expenses, turmoil, unpredictability...'

She looked distressed. 'Adam, please don't remind me!'

'I haven't finished. And great, great happiness, my darling. Happiness I never expected and never deserved.'

'You deserve every happiness, Adam,' Belle breathed. 'Oh, my love, you deserve everything I can possibly give you.'

He touched her lips with his and the familiar pulse of heated desire flared inside her as she reached up to explore and cherish the lean contours of his face. Just then baby Clara gurgled softly and waved her tiny fists in the air.

'I love her so much,' Belle whispered as she cradled her baby close. 'But Clara and I—we have thrown your life into disarray, haven't we? You used to have everything running so smoothly, but now...'

'Don't worry,' he laughed. 'We simply have to adapt, you and I. Like we did this morning.'

'This morning? *Oh!*' Belle blushed suddenly, remembering how she'd woken in her husband's arms an hour before daylight, only to find Adam was awake, too, and...wanting her. Desiring her. As she desired him, would always desire him. Their lovemaking had been slow, delicious and achingly sensual, yet full of love. She smiled up at him as Adam's strong hand caressed his tiny daughter's cheek. 'Adam, shall we have an early night?' she whispered.

Adam's eyes were tender as he took their baby from her and revelled in the wonder of life and love that was theirs. 'As early as you like.'

Belle reached to kiss her husband's cheek. Sheer joy and contentment filled her heart. They had love to last a lifetime—and more.

* * * * *